THE
FLOATING LADY
MURDER

THE HARRY HOUDINI MYSTERIES

THE FLOATING LADY MURDER

DANIEL STASHOWER

TITAN BOOKS

THE HARRY HOUDINI MYSTERIES: THE FLOATING LADY MURDER

PRINT EDITION ISBN: 9780857682925

E-BOOK ISBN: 9780857686206

Published by Titan Books
A division of Titan Publishing Group Ltd
144 Southwark St, London SE1 0UP

First edition: February 2012

2 4 6 8 10 9 7 5 3 1

Visit our website: www.titanbooks.com

A CIP catalogue record for this title is available from the British Library

Printed and bound in the USA.

What did you think of this book? We love to hear from our readers. Please email us at: readerfeedback@titanemail.com, or write to us at the above address.

To receive advance information, news, competitions, and exclusive offers online, please sign up for the Titan newsletter on our website: www.titanbooks.com

THE FLOATING LADY MURDER

1

OH, YOU WONDER!

AGAIN, THE DREAM.

A dark curtain lifted and he saw his brother, blue and lifeless, hanging upside down in the Chinese Water Torture Cell. Harry was bobbing gently in the grayish water, his hair pulsing like seaweed, his arms folded across his chest as though settled snugly into a coffin. He could see every detail. The dark mahogany and nickel-plated steel of the cabinet. The thick glass panels. The tiny clusters of air bubbles clinging to his brother's nose and lips. He could even hear the ominous strains of music rising from the orchestra pit. "Asleep in the Deep."

He would take a step closer, then, as the music started, and stretch out a hand as if to touch his brother's face. A terrible urgency would grip him as he knelt beside the front panel, peering through the clouded glass. Already he could hear the voices calling from behind, pulling him away.

A moment longer. That was all he required. In another moment, surely, his brother would open his eyes and give a sly wink. The blue-tinged lips would break into a smile as a stream of air escaped. Another moment. Just one more moment…

And then the ringing of the alarm. The dream always ended this way, leaving him confused and doleful. Perhaps next time, he thought.

The old man swung his legs over the side of the bed and

padded to a wash stand in the corner, trying to dispel the foggy residue of gloom. He chided himself as he made his way down the hall to bathe, and by the time he returned to his room to dress he began to feel better. Why did he let it trouble him so? He glanced at the calendar. That was it, he told himself. It seemed impossible, but another year had passed. He hoped that perhaps this year the anniversary might pass quietly. He sat down and began polishing his black wing-tips, just in case.

He had finished brushing his jacket and was considering a damp press for his collar when he heard the front door chime. He parted the curtains and peered down at the front stoop. A reporter. No mistaking it. The old man had known plenty of reporters in his time, and he recognized the type. Slouch hat, pencil behind the ear, well-thumbed note pad. In fact, it appeared to be the same man who had come out the previous year. What was his name? Matthews, was it? Yes, Matthews. Call me Jack. He'd brought another photographer with him, too.

He heard the chime again and listened for the sound of Mrs. Doggett's footsteps galumphing through from the kitchen. Mrs. Doggett kept a clean house and did not much care for this annual intrusion of cigarette-smoking newspapermen from the city. She would show Matthews and the photographer to the parlor with pursed lips and a furrowed brow. A moment later she would return with a tray of tea and Keepa cakes, clucking all the while.

The old man hurriedly fastened his collar and knotted his filetto silk tie, regarding himself in the hall mirror. He had selected his best coat, merino wool in a crow's foot pattern, but now he wondered if it might be showing a bit of wear. Were the pockets sagging? Were the shoulders riding a bit high? He ran a hand through his hair and centered his Windsor knot. He knew, at his age, that time spent preening was time wasted. Might as well go downstairs in his robe and slippers. Still, he had standards to maintain. In the old days, they called him "Dash."

The old man studied his reflection and wondered if there

would be time to go down the hall and splash on a bit of Lendell's toilet water. No, he thought, probably not. Already he could hear Mrs. Doggett coming to the foot of the stairs, calling up to him about the visitors in the parlor. He frowned over his cuffs and picked at a loose thread on his elbow. Ah, well. The show must go on.

They came every year, these reporters, on the anniversary of his brother's death. Just once he wished they might spare a question or two about his own career. *Say, Mr. Hardeen, you were quite a celebrated performer yourself in those days, weren't you? You had a record-breaking run at the London Palladium, isn't that right?* But no, it would be the same old shibboleth: *Tell us about your brother, Mr. Hardeen. Tell us about Houdini.*

The old man paused with his hand on the bannister and wondered what he would tell them this year. He had long since exhausted his supply of boyhood anecdotes, though "Enrich of the Air" was always good for half a column or so. *My brother would hang upside down from a makeshift trapeze in our yard, and he would pick up needles with his eyelashes!* That one was a complete fabrication, but the reporters seemed to like it. Or maybe he could trot out that perennial favorite about the Belle Island Bridge leap in Detroit. *The river had frozen over, but my brother refused to cancel the stunt. "But Harry!" I cried. "How are you going to do an underwater escape when the river is frozen over?" "That's simple," he replied, "we'll chop a hole in the ice..."*

No, not this year. That one was beginning to wear a bit thin. Wasn't true, in any case. Not a word of it. Harry started putting that one about in 1906. Funny how things catch on.

The Floating Lady, perhaps. That one might be good for a column or two. Incredible story, really, if he decided to tell all of it. Certainly they would be familiar with the illusion. Was there anyone left in the world who hadn't seen the Floating Lady by now? They call it different names—Asrah, Levitation, Lighter Than Air—but the effect is always the same. A female assistant is placed under "hypnosis" and then made to float in mid-air.

These days, of course, it's thought to be a bit old hat. Decades of endless repetition on the stage has robbed the effect of its power. They've even started to do it on television, where everything always looks like a cheap sideshow. But it was different back then, back when the Floating Lady was a prize worth having. That one effect in a magician's repertoire could guarantee years of work on the Orpheum or the Keith circuit. It could make a man's fortune.

See how she floats, as though on a gentle zephyr, borne aloft by the hypnotic force of animal magnetism. Please don't make a sound, ladies and gentlemen, for the slightest disturbance may break the spell...

The old man stopped outside the parlor door. But would he tell all of it? Would he tell them about Kellar? About the enchanting Francesca Moore? About Servais Le Roy and that astonishing hoop skirt? He hesitated, smoothing his lapels while he tried to arrange the details in his mind. Yes, he told himself, it could work. Besides, who would be harmed if he told the story now, after so many years? All he needed was a hook—a snappy curtain-raiser to catch their attention and hold it. He frowned over the loose thread at his elbow. Ah. Certainly. Very well, then.

You see, young man, Harry and I were present when that famous illusion was created. Oh, yes. No one has ever heard this story before, because it had a rather tragic outcome, I'm afraid. The first time it was performed—the first lady ever to float in mid-air—well, she died. The trick killed her. How? Well, that's a very strange thing.

And here the Great Hardeen would allow himself a dramatic pause. *You see, young man, she drowned.*

The old man smiled, squared his shoulders, and stepped forward to greet his interviewer.

I'm sorry, Mr. Matthews? Yes, that's what I said. She drowned. Yes. While doing the trick. While floating. Yes. In mid-air.

Pardon? You'd like to hear about it? Well, it's rather a long story, and you seemed so interested in that Belle Island Bridge leap, perhaps you'd prefer if we—no? Very well, but I must warn you that it's been many years since I've thought back on the Floating Lady, and it's possible that some of the details may have grown a bit muddled. Mr. Kellar made us both promise that we'd keep silent about the matter, out of respect for Miss Moore, so I've never had occasion to tell the story before. But it can hardly matter now, can it? They're all long gone. So far as I know, even Silent Felsden has never—pardon? My apologies. I suppose I'm getting a bit ahead of the story.

I seem to recall that the newspapers were in high dudgeon over the tragedy of the U.S.S. *Maine,* so it must have been January, or perhaps February, of 1898. Times had been pretty hard for Harry and myself. We'd had a brief burst of notoriety the previous year when we successfully escaped from Sing Sing prison, but it hadn't lasted long. Harry had yet to find regular work of any kind, and was a long way from achieving the worldwide fame he so desperately craved. My job in those days was to serve as Harry's advance man and booking agent. "You will sort through the various offers and opportunities as they present themselves," Harry had informed me, "and you will inspect each potential venue to determine whether it will be suitable for the Great Houdini." To be candid, there wasn't a whole lot of sorting and inspecting required. I don't recall that a single offer or opportunity ever "presented itself" in the manner that Harry imagined. I had to go out and beat the bushes. Much of my time was spent knocking on the doors of talent scouts, sitting in the waiting rooms of booking agents, and twisting the arms of theatrical managers. I can't say I was especially good at it. Every so often Harry pulled a week or so at one of the Dime Museums down around Union Square, and sometimes we'd do a month or two with the Welsh Brothers Circus, but on the whole we lived fairly close to the bone.

I was twenty-one years old at the time, and Harry was two years older. We were barely out of short pants in some respects, but when it came to show business, we felt like old hands.

Worse, we were beginning to feel washed up. Strange as it may seem, in his youth Harry did far better as a magician and circus performer than he did as an escape artist. The "self-liberation" act had yet to find its audience, and Harry had not yet cultivated his genius for self-promotion. Whatever bookings came our way usually owed something to the bright sparkle of Harry's wife, Bess. There wasn't a theatrical manager alive whose icy heart failed to melt at the mere sight of Bess. I suppose you couldn't have called her a beauty in the conventional sense, but there was something about her that just stopped you right in your tracks. Trust me on this.

One of my duties as Harry's manager was to keep an eye on the notice columns of the *New York Dramatic Mirror*. That's where I saw Kellar's posting, and I suppose that's how all the trouble began. I read the *Mirror* religiously each morning with my tea and toast, trolling for tips and opportunities, and I would remain a faithful reader for many years, long after I no longer had the need. It was a marvelous paper, filled with column after column of news bits, booking information and "situation wanted" notices. I especially loved the back pages, where the call and response of daily business was played out in tiny snippets. *Toupées manufactured, discretion assured. Stage gowns fitted, credit available. Voice culture lessons, the speaking voice thoroughly trained and developed. Stage dancing, positions secured.* Over time, one could track the waxing and waning of a career or touring company. *Edwin Thanhouser, Light Comedian, At Liberty. Grand Annual Tour of the Brilliant Comedienne Alma Chester, Supported by a Powerful Company of Recognized Artists in a Repertoire of Splendid Scenic Productions. Wanted by Mabel Paige: A Gentleman of Reputation to Work with her in a Sketch for Vaudeville.*

Truth be told, it was seldom that I came across a notice that held any promise for Harry or myself. On that particular morning, however, it appeared that our prospects had suddenly brightened. There, on page 28, beneath a booking call for Proctor's Leland Opera House, was a thick, blocky headline reading: "Oh, You

Wonder!" Beneath it were the words: "Opportunities with the Famous Magician Kellar." A photograph of the great man stared out at me, with the familiar egg-shaped bald head and clear, searching eyes.

I need hardly say that the name of Harry Kellar was as familiar to me as my own. Without question he was the most famous magician in America, and perhaps the entire world. Indeed, at that time there were many who ranked Kellar ahead of Bosco and Signor Blitz as the greatest conjuror of all history. His staging of an illusion entitled "The Witch, The Sailor, and The Enchanted Monkey" had been the sensation of the previous season, and the catch phrase "Oh, You Wonder!" had been on the lips of every member of his vast audiences.

My heart quickened as I read the small print beneath the photograph. "Staff required for '98–'99 Season," it read. "Apply Dudley McAdow, Mgr., 131 B'way." I folded the paper into thirds and reached for my coat and Trilby. Our troubles were over, I told myself. I felt certain Harry would be overjoyed by this news.

With my heart aglow at the prospect of steady employment, I hurried to my mother's flat on East 69th Street. In those days, Harry and Bess lodged with Mother as a matter of economy, while I kept a room at Mrs. Arthur's boarding house seven blocks away. Finances being what they were, it would probably have been better for all concerned if I had stayed at home as well, but I could not bring myself to do so. I felt that a man of twenty-one ought to be cutting the apron strings and making his own way in the world, though my brother held quite a different view. Also, I fancied myself as something of a dashing rake at the time, and I feared that living at home might place unwelcome restrictions on my social life. That particular concern, I regret to say, was unwarranted. Apart from the occasional night of theater with my friend Biggs, and a periodic hand of whist with fellow lodgers at Mrs. Arthur's, my social calendar was not overburdened. I spent a great deal of time at the library.

I arrived at East 69th Street to find my mother hovering over the stove as always, preparing the cabbages and carrots for a goulash. The air was heavy with paprika.

"My darling Theodore!" Mother called as I came through the kitchen door. "Sit! Sit! I will bring you a plate! You could use a little something on your stomach!"

It was a familiar greeting. In my carnival days I often had occasion to work with a 412-pound man named Hector Armadale. Hector was a delightful fellow and a wonderful storyteller, and it was always my hope that I would find an opportunity to bring him home to my mother, just to see if she would insist that this professional fat man could "use a little something on his stomach."

"Good morning, Mama," I said, setting my hat on the sideboard. "Thank you, but I won't take anything to eat just now. I have already had my breakfast." I nodded at my sister-in-law, who was stirring a pot of heavy porridge oats. "Good morning, Bess."

"Good morning, Dash," she said, giving me a peck on the cheek. "Why are you so bright and eager this morning?"

"I come bearing the promise of steady employment," I replied, brandishing the *Mirror.* "There might be something here for all three of us!"

"Thank heaven," she said, wiping her hands on her apron. "Mama and I have been taking in extra sewing, but—"

"I know, I know," I said. "But this could be the solution to all our worries, if only he can be made to see it that way. Where is the justly celebrated self-liberator, by the way?"

"You mean the all-eclipsing sensation of the stage? The man whom the *Milwaukee Sentinel* described as the 'most captivating entertainer in living memory'?"

"That's the one."

"He's still in the bath."

"He's running a bit late this morning," I said, pulling out a chair from the kitchen table. "Normally the smell of Mama's porridge is enough to—"

"Actually, Dash, you might want to go check on him."

"Pardon?"

"He—he's in training. He's been in there an awfully long time."

"Oh." I stood up again. "I'll just go and make sure he's still with us."

"Yes, run along, Theodore," Mother said. "Tell your brother his breakfast is getting cold."

"Among other things," Bess said.

I hurried down the center hall to the water closet and gave a quick rap on the door. Receiving no answer, I turned the knob and stepped inside.

As Bess had indicated, Harry was having a long bath, as one might have expected from one so fastidious in his personal grooming. What might have struck the casual observer as odd, however, was that my brother was entirely submerged beneath the waterline, and there were large chunks of ice floating on the surface.

I should perhaps explain that it was not unusual for my brother to bathe in ice water. He had recently hit upon the idea of leaping from bridges, fully tied and manacled, in order to win free publicity for himself. It was his hope that a regimen of cold immersions would inure him to the shock of the frigid river waters. At the same time, these long sessions in the family bathtub gave him an opportunity to build up his lung power.

I glanced at my Elgin pocket watch and waited as two minutes ticked past. How long would Harry stay down? How long had he been down before I arrived? I perched on the edge of the tub and stared down at my brother. His eyes were closed, his hands were clasped across his stomach and his expression was entirely peaceful. A tiny trickle of air bubbles escaped from the corner of his mouth. I looked again at my watch. Three minutes.

I took off my jacket and unfastened my shift cuff. Reaching down, I dipped my hand in the water and tapped my brother on the shoulder. Harry opened his eyes and let out a watery cry of delight, sending up a rush of air bubbles. "Dash!" he cried, breaking the surface abruptly. "Did you see me? I believe that may have been a new record!"

"Harry, you need to be a bit more careful," I said, noting the bluish tinge of his lips. "How long have you been in there?"

"Oh, not long," he said carelessly. "But that was certainly one of my better sessions. I believe I might have stayed down there another minute or two if you hadn't startled me. It's a question of mind control, really." He rose dripping from the tub and reached for a towel. "I've been reading the most fascinating little monograph about the fakirs of India. It seems that they can suppress their breathing altogether when the conditions are right. What did they call it? *Kakta? Kafta?* Never mind. I understood what they were driving at. It has to do with the power of the mind." He vigorously towelled himself dry and slipped on a robe. "It seems that if one can learn to focus the mind's energy upon a single—say, Dash, what are you doing in here, anyway?"

"I'm the only talent agent in New York who makes house calls," I said, thrusting the *Mirror* notice at him. "Cast your eyes on that!"

"A job?" Harry asked. "At last! I was beginning to think I'd never—" He snatched up the paper and scanned the item. "What?" he cried, his features darkening. "Impossible! It won't do at all!"

"But—why—?"

"I wouldn't even consider such a thing!" He tossed the paper aside. "The very idea is preposterous!"

"But Harry—?" I picked up the paper and looked again at the Kellar notice, wondering if there had been some mistake.

"Not at present, in any event. That sort of thing might do for you, Dash, but the Great Houdini must look elsewhere."

I followed him down the hall to his bedroom, where he persisted in giving voice to his ill opinion as he dressed in his familiar black suit, starched white shirt and red bow tie. The peroration continued as he led me back along the corridor to the kitchen. We arrived just as mother was serving up a steaming bowl of porridge oats, a dish I have never been able to tolerate. I noted with rising alarm that a place had now been set for me.

"Sit down, boys," Mother said, pouring out a fresh pot of tea. "It will be cold soon."

"Mama," I said weakly. "I told you that I'd already had breakfast at Mrs. Arthur's."

"And did Mrs. Arthur give you a nice cup of wheat grass tea?" Mother asked sweetly.

"No, but—"

"Was there a slice or two of brown toast?"

"No, but I—"

"And does Mrs. Arthur give you fresh cream with your porridge?"

"No, of course not, but—"

"Then you haven't had breakfast." Mama touched the back of my chair and beamed at me. It was a smile that would brook no resistance. "Sit, Theodore," she said.

With a sigh, I shrugged my shoulders and took my seat. Harry was already tucking a napkin under his chin. "Why do you fight it, Dash?" he asked, amused by my evident discomfort. "You can't possibly expect to do a full day of work without one of Mama's breakfasts."

"I've already done a day's work," I replied. "You're just too pig-headed to acknowledge it. You just aren't—" I broke off as Mother leaned in to fill my tea cup. "Thank you, Mama. You just aren't prepared to be reasonable, Harry."

"What's this all about, Dash?" asked Bess, who had now taken her place next to Harry. "You never did show me the notice."

I passed across the newspaper I had rescued from the floor. " 'Staff required,' " she read. "Why, that's wonderful! Harry, whatever is the matter with you? Mr. Kellar's magic show is the finest in the world! It's perfect for us! He travels for months at a time, often to exotic foreign countries! Australia! China! Russia! Can you imagine? There might be as much as a full year of steady work for us. Perhaps more!"

"That's what I've been trying to tell him," I said. "He won't hear of it."

"I just don't think it's quite the right opportunity for us," my brother said, staring down into his tea cup.

"Harry," I said with considerable heat, "you and I are only one step removed from taking up our old positions at the tie factory. It's the only steady work we've had in months. Is that what you want? Do you want to be a tie cutter for the rest of your life?"

"No, Dash, but neither can I throw myself at every job you find in your newspaper. You'll have me working as a carnival busker next. Besides, I think that Mr. Kellar's day has passed."

"Indeed?" Bess folded back the newspaper and began to read. " 'Mr. Kellar has been entertaining in Philadelphia, New York, and Chicago for the past three seasons. He perplexed the natives of Philadelphia for 323 consecutive performances at the Temple Theater; he amused New York for 179 consecutive performances at the Comedy Theater on Broadway; and at the Grand Opera House in Chicago he found it worth his while, last summer, to give 103 consecutive performances before bringing the run to a close over the strenuous objections of the management.' "

"Sounds like a career in trouble," I said with lifted eyebrows. "The poor man can probably barely keep body and soul together."

"Eat your porridge," said Harry.

" 'Mr. Kellar's fame is scarcely less luminous upon distant shores,' " Bess continued. " 'In recent years he has appeared before Queen Victoria at Balmoral Castle, Emperor Napoleon at the Palace of St. Cloud, the Czar of Russia at the Winter Palace of St. Petersburg, and Dom Pedro II of Brazil at the Imperial Palace of Rio de Janeiro.' "

"That's absurd!" cried Harry. "Napoleon has been dead for more than fifty years!"

"I believe it may have been a reference to Napoleon III," I said.

"Oh. Well, it's misleading, in any case."

" 'The principal appeal of Mr. Kellar's entertainment consists of the rare and startling phenomena to which his own original and collective brain has given existence,' " Bess resumed. " 'His work seemingly sets at naught all natural laws. It is replete with mysticisms and those occult deeds ordinarily ascribed to the redoubtable Prince of Darkness. Yet everything is simply done, and Mr. Kellar frankly disclaims any supernatural agencies. There is no entertainment similar to it in the country, nor is there any word in the English language which can properly describe it. It is entirely *sui generis*.' "

"What?" asked Harry.

"*Sui generis*," I said. "Means 'in a class by itself.' "

"Why doesn't he just say so!" Harry reached for a slice of toast. "*Sui generis*, indeed."

" 'Mr. Kellar is as entirely different from the work of the commonplace magician as the electric light outshines its coal-oil predecessors,' " Bess continued. " 'His phenomena are unique, amusing, and full of utter impossibilities developed from his own inner consciousness. The man himself is a marvel. He has traversed every part of the civilized as well as the uncivilized globe. He speaks with ease all the modern languages, and half a dozen besides of Asiatic and African dialects. He charms you by a grace of manner that is bewitching; he entrances by the subtle power which he so greatly possesses, and mystifies and bewilders you by the deftness and dexterity with which he executes his remarkable feats. He is simply a marvel beyond the comprehension of the ordinary mortal.' "

Bess neatly folded the newspaper and placed it beside her plate. "Mr. Kellar would seem to have a very spirited press agent," she said.

"Or perhaps an energetic younger brother," I suggested.

"His day has passed," Harry repeated. "The man is still performing the Enchanted Fishery! I ask you!"

"Harry," said Bess, placing her hands flat on the table. "Out with it. Opportunities like this one don't come along every day."

Harry picked up his teaspoon and polished it with his napkin. "Bess," he said to the spoon, "you must defer to my experience in these matters. My long years upon the boards have given me a certain amount of expertise when it comes to—"

"Harry," Bess said again. "Out with it."

My brother stirred his tea, carefully avoiding her eye.

Bess simply folded her arms and waited him out. It didn't take long. Harry stirred his tea for another minute or so, whistling a carefree tune and trying to appear unconcerned. Still avoiding Bess's eye, he began to hum and rap his fingers on the table. Then he gave a heavy sigh and his resolve crumpled. The truth was that my brother could withstand a long submersion in icy bathwater far better than his wife's disapprobation.

"You don't understand, Bess!" he cried in a sudden rush. "It isn't fitting! The Great Houdini is no mere stagehand! The Great Houdini is not a simple lackey to be ordered about at the whim of Mr. Harry Kellar! I am an artist! I am an original! I am the man whom the *Milwaukee Sentinel* called the 'most captivating entertainer in living memory'! I will not beg for scraps from the table of Mr. Harry Kellar!"

Bess looked over at me and nodded. At least now the cards were on the table. "Harry," she said in a much softer voice, "think of the experience. Think of the contacts. It could be the break you've been needing."

"It is impossible," he insisted. "Besides, he is a mere magician! I am an escape artist! I am the world's foremost self-liberator!"

"Harry," I said, pushing away my bowl of porridge. "So far as we know, you're the only self-liberator on the face of the earth. We've been over this before. No one knows quite what to make of your act. Sure, you've had some good notices, but it's hard to build a career on a few scattered successes. The Kellar show could give us all some seasoning."

"Seasoning!" he snorted. "Mama, do you hear that! Dash thinks I need seasoning!"

"Is that right, dear?" asked Mother, who had little time for idle chat when there was a goulash on the stove.

"Seasoning! As though I were a pepper roast!"

By way of a reply, Mother nudged my porridge bowl back in front of me. "Eat, Theodore," she commanded.

"Seasoning!" Harry said again. "Imagine!"

I lifted my tea cup and watched to see what my sister-in-law would do. She was a woman of many talents—an excellent singer, a graceful dancer, and perhaps the finest magician's assistant ever to carry a dove pan or clatter box. But of all her gifts, by far the greatest was her remarkable ability to manage my brother's various moods and tempers. I watched as she carefully assessed her husband's latest display of pique and considered her options. After a moment, she picked up a slice of brown toast from her plate and nibbled at a corner. "I suppose you're right, Harry," she said, dabbing at her lips with her napkin.

Harry lifted his eyebrows, clearly surprised. "Indeed I am," he said quietly.

"He is?" I asked.

"Certainly," Bess said. "After all, Harry has a certain reputation to consider. It wouldn't do for a man of his considerable renown to be seen as a mere assistant. What was it your father used to say? About a man and his reputation?"

"He said that a man's reputation is his greatest treasure," Harry declared.

"Indeed." Bess took a sip of tea. "Quite right. We won't discuss the matter any further."

I regarded her with some fascination.

"Best not to say another word on the matter." She gazed serenely into her tea cup. "And yet..." she added, as though a new thought had struck her, but then she thought better of it and let her voice trail off.

21

"What is it, Bess?" Harry asked.

"Oh, it's nothing. Let's not speak of it."

"No, tell me, Bess," Harry insisted. "We must have no secrets between us."

"Well," she said, with considerable reluctance, "it's just that I've read so much about Mr. Kellar, and I seem to recall—no, let's not speak of it. I'm sure you know best, Harry."

"Bess." Harry reached across and took her hands. "Please tell me what you are thinking. Although you lack a man's training and experience, I believe that you possess a certain—a certain naive wisdom that is always refreshing. Please, tell me what troubles you so."

My sister-in-law gave a demure sigh. She may have even fluttered her lashes. "Very well," she said. "When Mr. Kellar was a young man, he served as an assistant to a very well-known magician, did he not?"

"He did," Harry confirmed. "The Wizard of Kalliffa."

"But it wouldn't be quite accurate to describe their relationship as that of master and apprentice, would it? They were really more like father and son, were they not?"

"Yes, indeed," said Harry, warming to the subject. "The Wizard came to regard Kellar as his heir."

"I see," said Bess. "So in many ways, Mr. Kellar's career has served as the continuation of a great magical pedigree. A form of show business royalty, you could say."

"I suppose so," Harry allowed.

"Yes. A pedigree. I find myself wondering, could it be that Mr. Kellar has reached the stage of his own life where he finds himself ready to pass the mantle to some worthy newcomer? Is it possible that he is looking about for some eager and talented young man who shows himself willing to work hard and honor the great traditions of the craft?"

Harry put down his spoon and regarded Bess with narrowed eyes.

"And wouldn't it be a shame," she continued, "if Harry

Houdini, who is easily the brightest light of his generation, should miss this opportunity because he was too proud to answer a simple newspaper notice?"

"Bess—"

"Tell me, Harry, how did the young Harry Kellar first come to the attention of the Wizard of Kalliffa?"

Harry turned his head away from us, as though he had caught sight of something fascinating in the wallpaper. "He answered a notice in the newspaper," he said softly.

"'Staff required,'" said Bess. "That's all the notice says. It seems foolish that we should not even trouble to see what positions Mr. Kellar is looking to fill. We have no other engagements at present, and no other calls upon our attention. Wouldn't it be simple enough to present ourselves at the theater and see what opportunity awaits?"

Harry turned back toward us. "There may be something in what you say."

"A man must keep an open mind in this day and age, Harry. Wasn't that another of your father's lessons?"

"Yes," he agreed, gathering conviction. "Indeed it was."

"Well, then," said Bess. "It's decided."

As it happens, I can't recall my father ever having said anything about keeping an open mind, and it must be said that open mindedness was not his greatest strength. At that stage, however, as Harry became caught up in his wife's reasoning, she could just as easily have convinced him that our father had desired us to colonize the ocean floor.

"Dash, we shall call at the theater this afternoon!" Harry cried, springing to his feet. "We shall show him the substitution trunk! Mr. Kellar will be positively dazzled! Why, I shouldn't be surprised if he places us at the head of one of his touring companies! After all, a talent such as mine doesn't come along every day! Mr. Kellar would be wise to have me as a colleague, rather than a competitor! Come along, Dash, we must get the trunk out of the store room!"

Bess poured herself another cup of tea, then looked up to find me staring at her with frank admiration. "Dash," she said with a smile, "you've hardly touched your porridge."

She may have lacked a man's training and experience, but— as Harry had suggested—she possessed a certain naive wisdom that was always refreshing.

2

THE MAN FROM MESOPOTAMIA

"HARRY," I SAID, AS OUR HORSE-CART TURNED ONTO BROADWAY, "would you care to explain why you're rubbing beef fat onto your shoe?"

"Uh…" he gave me a sidelong glance. "For luck."

"For luck? You're slathering animal lard onto your shoe for luck?"

"An old show business custom."

We were riding in the back of the neighborhood milk cart, having bribed the delivery man, Bert, into hauling our magic trunk down to the theater district. Along the way Harry had insisted that we stop at a local butcher's shop, where he had darted inside in a state of high animation. Moments later he had emerged carrying a small brown parcel, which proved to be a strip of moist beef tallow. "Just the thing," he told us, as he energetically rubbed grease into the leather of his shoe.

"Harry," said Bess, with a note of exasperation in her voice, "there is no show business custom involving beef tallow. Would you please tell us why you're doing that?"

"Very well," said Harry, tossing the brown wrapping aside, "but you may think it a bit odd."

Bess peered up at him through the netting of her hat. "Odd? Do you suppose so?"

Harry wiped his hands on his handkerchief and settled

himself against a milk canister. "It has to do with Brownie."

"Brownie?"

Harry nodded vigorously. "The story goes that when Kellar was a boy, he ran away from home and worked a series of odd jobs—selling newspapers, sweeping offices, delivering parcels."

"Sounds familiar, Harry," I said.

"Yes," Harry said. "Mr. Kellar seems to have spent his boyhood working various jobs as an errand boy, just as you and I did. At one stage he was working as a farm hand in Buffalo when he saw a notice in the local paper announcing that the Wizard of Kalliffa needed a boy assistant. Young Harry was terrified that someone else might get the position, so he ran all the way to the wizard's home—two miles, as I recall."

"We know the story, Harry. What has that to do with beef tallow?"

"I'm just getting to that part. When young Harry arrived, a small terrier ran from the house and began wagging its tail. A moment later, the Wizard of Kalliffa himself stepped from the house and told young Kellar that the job was his. It seems that the wizard placed enormous faith in his dog's ability to judge character. The dog had barked and growled at each of the previous applicants. Only Kellar seemed to meet with the dog's approval."

Bess grasped for the railing as the milk cart clattered around a sharp corner. "Are you saying that Kellar had rubbed his shoes with animal fat? Is that why the dog appeared to like him so much?"

"No. Not as far as I'm aware. But I cannot afford to take any chances. If Mr. Kellar has a dog, and if he considers that dog to be a good judge of character, you may be sure that dog is going to be positively ecstatic when the Great Houdini enters the room."

"Harry," I asked, "do we even know that Mr. Kellar owns a dog?"

"Well, no," Harry allowed, "but it stands to reason, doesn't it? Kellar's big break came as the result of a dog's judgment. It only makes sense that he would choose his own successor in the same manner."

"Harry," Bess began, "all the newspaper notice said was 'Staff required.' We don't want to assume that Mr. Kellar is—"

"Who is Brownie?" I broke in.

"Brownie?"

"You said that the story had to do with someone named Brownie. You can't mean that Brownie was the name of the Wizard of Kalliffa's dog! How could you possibly know that?"

"Well," Harry said, burying his chin in the collar of his furry astrakhan cloak, "I don't know for certain. I just always imagined that the dog's name would be Brownie. It struck me as a good name for a wizard's dog."

Bess and I exchanged a look. "Harry," I said, "perhaps you'd better keep quiet about your, uh, your expectations of Mr. Kellar. We wouldn't want to—"

"Nonsense!" he cried. "Mr. Kellar is obviously seeking a successor to carry on his illustrious legacy, and I am clearly the only man who could shoulder this heavy burden. It makes perfect sense, does it not?"

"Harry," Bess began, "let's not—"

"Do not concern yourself, dear," he said, reaching over to pat her hand. "Our worries are at an end. We're nearly at the theater now."

I had already been down to the theater once that morning to set up an appointment with Mr. McAdow, the manager of the Kellar organization. From what little I had been able to gather, it was clear that Mr. McAdow wished nothing more than to "have a look" at his prospective employees, and I was assured that a formal audition would not be required. "Maybe a couple of card tricks," I was told. "McAdow likes card tricks." In spite of this, Harry decided that he would favor Mr. McAdow with a performance of his most elaborate effect—the Substitution Trunk Mystery.

"Harry," I said, glancing over my shoulder at the trunk as it bounced and rocked on the back of the cart, "are you sure you won't reconsider about the card tricks?"

"It is certainly true that my card manipulations are without equal," Harry replied, "but no demonstration of the Great Houdini's genius can be complete without his signature effect. As you well know, the Substitution Trunk Mystery has won rave reviews all across America. The *Toledo Evening Bee,* as I recall, felt the effect to be 'the most baffling mystery ever presented on the stages of our fair city.' High praise, indeed!"

"Uh, Harry—"

"And I seem to recall that the *Chicago Inter-Ocean* also had kind words for my performance. 'Mr. Houdini and his wife have elevated the conjuror's art to a new level of elegance.' Nothing more than the truth, I might add!"

"Uh, Harry—"

"The critic from the *Pittsburgh Post* was moved to write—"

"Harry, for God's sake!"

"What is it, Dash? I must say you are in a strange humor today."

"Don't you remember? I wrote those notices! I was the one who reviewed the act in Toledo! I was the one who reviewed the act in Pittsburgh and Chicago! That's what a publicity man does! Especially when he's your younger brother!"

Harry's eyebrows shot up. "You wrote those notices?"

"Harry, we've been over this a dozen times. I've been planting items in the press since you were fourteen years old. Remember the *Brooklyn Eagle*?"

Harry spent a moment or two watching the passing buildings. "Well, in any case, what you wrote was nothing more than the truth. And anyway," he added, as the cart drew up in front of the theater, "I'm sure that if you hadn't written in praise of the act, someone else would have done so in equally extravagant terms."

"No doubt, Harry." I said, as we hopped down off the cart. "Just remember what we discussed. Mr. McAdow is a theatrical professional. It would be best if you presented the trunk trick without the usual rhetorical flourishes."

"Yes," Bess agreed, perhaps a bit too eagerly, "we don't want to take up too much of the man's valuable time."

Harry shouldered the heavy trunk and gave her a wink. "I shall be captivating," he declared, "as always." With this, he gave a resounding knock on the stage door.

I should perhaps confess that the Belasco Theater has always held a special significance for me. Its high dome and stately columns had long been a fixture of the New York theater district, and season after season it managed to attract the finest actors and productions. As a boy, I once stuffed myself through the coal chute off the service alley in order to hear Mr. Edwin Booth give one of his final performances of *Hamlet*. I neither appreciated nor fully grasped the drama, but I understood the event to be of great significance in the theater world. I spent the entire first act and much of the second crouched below the rear stairs. I thrilled to the sudden and mysterious appearance of the ghost of Hamlet's father—who rose from the floor of the stage as though emerging from the sea—and I later described it breathlessly to my brother as the finest magic trick I had ever seen. It was my hope that the effect might be repeated, but during the third act I was roughly turned out by a ruddy-faced theater warden in a striped vest and bowler.

I felt a moment's unease when that same florid-cheeked gentleman answered our knock at the stage door, but I soon recovered myself, confident that he would not recognize me as the youthful Shakespeare enthusiast of the previous decade. The warden showed us through a maze of causeways and past a series of dressing chambers and property lockers while Harry and I maneuvered the ungainly substitution trunk around a number of tight corners. Finally we rounded a battery of curtain cleats and came onto the main stage itself.

"Mr. McAdow?" the warden called, peering out over the forward lip of the stage.

Down in the empty house, in the front row of seats, a pair of men were huddled over a sheaf of papers. One of them was tall, slender and fair-complexioned, with ginger hair swept straight back from a strong, heavily lined forehead. The other man was smaller and dark-haired, with a flowing moustache. "Yes, Connell?" the taller man said, looking up from his documents. "What is it?"

"These gentlemen and the lady to see you, sir."

McAdow gave a dismissive wave of the hand. "Yes, yes," he said. "Wait there. Be with you in a minute."

Connell gave a courtly little bow to Bess and withdrew, leaving us standing with the trunk at the center of the stage.

We were the only people in the entire theater who did not appear to be engaged in some furious activity. All around us the members of Mr. Kellar's company were busily going about their business, and the air was alive with the sounds and shouts of workers and their tools. Toward the rear, a team of carpenters could be seen lifting large scenery flats onto the braceworks. Overhead, a pair of wiry young men swarmed through the rigging high above the stage, pulling at the counterweights and sashes. In the orchestra pit, a handful of violinists and cellists bent over the pages of a musical score, sending up a few stray notes as they studied their parts. To our left, a matronly property mistress fussed over a bewildering array of wooden cups, houlettes and metal trays.

"This is astonishing!" said Bess, raising her voice to be heard. "Do all these people work for Mr. Kellar? I don't think I've ever seen such—"

Her remark was cut short by a startling sound—the roar of a fearsome jungle creature. We turned to see a crew of four men wheeling a large wooden cage forward on a flat dolley. Inside, a fierce-looking lion paced back and forth in obvious agitation.

"He'll calm down in a moment," one of the handlers was saying. "It's just all the excitement of the travel. He'll be fine once he's had his feeding."

"Can you believe it?" Bess asked. "A real lion! Whatever can Mr. Kellar be planning? Harry, have you ever seen the like?"

Even my brother appeared to be impressed. "A lion would make for a very splendid spectacle," he admitted. "Very splendid, indeed."

"Perhaps Kellar is planning to vanish it," I said. "Or maybe some sort of transposition?"

Harry did not appear to be listening. "I shall need something even more magnificent if I am to achieve the pinnacle of the profession," he said in a musing sort of way. "A tiger, perhaps? A panther?"

Bess turned to him in surprise. "Harry, whatever are you talking about?"

"An elephant!" he said, as if arriving at a sudden decision. "I shall cause an elephant to vanish!"

"A fine idea," said Bess facetiously. "And how do you propose to get this elephant from place to place? Do you suppose Bert will be able to give you and the elephant a ride on his milk cart?"

Harry appeared to consider the problem. "The elephant could walk from place to place on its own four legs," he declared. "However, it would require a special train carriage if we intended to take it on tour. That might be impractical."

"It might at that," said Bess with raised eyebrows. "Better to leave him behind in New York. No doubt your mother would be pleased to cook for an elephant." She turned away and swept her hand toward the enormous jumble of apparatus littering the back of the stage. "Look at all those crates! How does Mr. Kellar carry it from city to city?"

"Mr. Kellar has his own private train," said a man who had come up from behind. "The equipment alone occupies four cars."

We turned and found ourselves facing a lean, powerfully-built young man with rolled sleeves and an open collar. He had sandy hair, blue eyes and an affable, lopsided grin that made a striking contrast to my brother's dark gravity. "Name's Jim

Collins," the young man said, sticking out a bony hand. "I'm one of the stagehands, and I guess I know about as much as there is to know about breaking this show down and setting it back up again. I've done it often enough."

"I am the Great Houdini," said Harry, pumping Collins' hand. "This is my lovely wife, Bess, and my brother, Dash. We are here for our appointment with Mr. Kellar."

"You have an appointment with the old man?" asked Collins, frowning.

"Actually, our appointment is with Mr. McAdow," I put in.

"But Mr. Kellar will want to see us," Harry said firmly. "You may be certain of that. Tell me, Mr. Collins, how are the plans for the Floating Lady coming along?"

Collins recoiled as if slapped across the face. "The Floating Lady? How did you—" He took a step forward and gripped Harry firmly by the lapels. "See here, little man, if you've come snooping for Servais Le Roy, you can tell him from me that he can just pack up and go back to France or Belgium or wherever the hell it is he comes from! Furthermore, you can tell him—"

Smiling, Harry broke Collins's grip with a strength that clearly surprised the bigger man. "Calm yourself, Mr. Collins. I am not here on behalf of Mr. Le Roy or any other rival magician, though your loyalty to your employer does you credit."

Collins was not mollified. "Then how in God's name did you come to know anything about the Floating Lady? We run a tight ship around here, and there's no possible way—"

"A simple observation on my part," said Harry. "I am a regular reader of *Mahatma* magazine, as are all magicians of any worth, and I keep abreast of the news from England. I know perfectly well that Mr. John Nevil Maskelyne has created a sensation at the Egyptian Hall with his levitation illusion, and it seems only logical that Mr. Kellar should wish to follow suit in America."

"Now look," said Collins. "Just because—"

But Harry wasn't finished. "Moreover," he continued, "I am well aware that the design of Mr. Maskelyne's effect has been a closely guarded secret, so it stands to reason that Mr. Kellar would have to devise his own method of achieving the illusion. When I come upon a theater that is rigged with an oversized pendulum apparatus high above the stage—which is clearly designed to lift an assistant out over the heads of the audience—I think it is fair to conclude that plans are underway for a new Floating Lady. Is it not so?"

The angry red color had slowly drained away from Collins's face as Harry spoke. The easy-going grin had now returned. "What was your name again?" he asked.

"Houdini. The Great Houdini."

"Well, Mr. Houdini, I guess I owe you an apology for the way I spoke before. It's just that we've had trouble with spies before, and this effect—if we can just get a few hitches worked out—this effect will be the biggest thing since Pepper's Ghost."

Harry glanced at the elaborate pendulum device overhead. "I take it this swing-lever apparatus is not working as you'd hoped?"

"It's been a disaster," Collins admitted. "And that's not the worst of it. Mr. Kellar is determined to debut his Floating Lady here on this stage next week, after a four-day try-out in Albany. Then he's going to take it on the tour."

"On tour?" Harry asked. "But Mr. Maskelyne has been advertising that his Egyptian Hall is the only place in the world where the Floating Lady effect can be seen."

"Mr. Maskelyne is no concern to us," Collins said coldly. "Our method will be entirely different. We won't be affected by his copyrights."

"So I understand, but that's not what I meant. I had understood from Mr. Maskelyne's statement that his apparatus was too ungainly to be moved from place to place. I assumed that he could only perform it at the Egyptian Hall because it couldn't be moved from the theater."

Collins studied Harry's face closely. "You're right," he admitted, "although that is not generally known. In any case, it makes the

Maskelyne method useless for us. Mr. Kellar has always been a touring magician, and his latest itinerary is already set. We have to come up with a method that is easily moved over great distances."

"Couldn't you simply build a second apparatus in Albany?"

"No, Mr. Houdini, we're taking it all over the world. Allahabad, Lucknow, Delphi, Agra, Cawnpore, Bombay, Kurachee, Baghdad, Zanzibar, Mozambique, Durban, Capetown, to name a few."

Bess's eyes had grown bright. "Do you mean to say that if we should find ourselves employed by Mr. Kellar, we would be travelling to all of those places?" She squeezed Harry's hand tightly. "Think of it, Harry!"

Collins brushed a stray wisp of hair from his eyes. "To tell you the truth, Miss, I'm not sure any of us will be going anywhere. Not unless we get this thing off the drawing board."

Harry gave a shrug. "I wish you every good fortune, Mr. Collins, but I confess that I have little confidence in your pendulum." He took a step forward, craning his neck for a better view. "The assistant stands about here, yes? Then the pendulum swoops down—and she grabs hold of it in some fashion—whereupon it carries her high up over the heads of the audience and into the dome of the theater. Is that what you had in mind?"

Collins nodded.

"It would require a rather extraordinary young woman."

"We have one. Miss Moore. We hired her away from a team of aerialists. She's perfectly at ease on a circus high wire, so this will not present her with any difficulty. Quite a looker, too, I don't mind telling you."

"That may be the case, but how on earth are you planning to conceal the apparatus? Will it not be perfectly obvious that your young lady is clinging to an enormous pendulum?"

Collins frowned. "There's the rub, Houdini. We've been working with the lighting and various arrangements of drop curtains, but nothing has worked so far. We'd hoped that Francesca would appear to be—"

"Who is Francesca?"

"Miss Moore. We were hoping to use her costume to help with the concealment. We're calling the illusion "The Levitation of Princess Karnac" so that we can wrap her up in a great flowing Hindu-style outfit, complete with a veil and baggy pantaloons—just the type of thing to cover the apparatus. But the rehearsals have been terrible. It's meant to appear as if she's floating, gently, clear up to the dome of the theater, as if lifted by a gentle breeze."

"And this effect was not achieved?"

"Not by a long shot. It looks as though she's strapped to a barn door in a hurricane. The pendulum moves far too quickly, for one thing. And it creaks and groans like a rusty hinge. A child's rope swing would come closer to achieving the desired impression."

"I see." Harry's eyes were fixed on the strange-looking device. "You require a slow, steady ascent into the dome of the theater, is that it?"

"Yes," said Collins. "But once we manage that, there's the additional problem of concealing the pendulum from the audience."

Harry rubbed his hands together. "Your problem is intriguing."

"Have you tried counter-weighting the capstan?" I asked.

"We have."

"Have you tried gear notches in the fulcrum?" Harry wondered.

Collins looked at us with renewed interest. "We did try notches," he said, "though it took us two days to think of it. But it didn't work. The motion was too jerky."

Harry shook his head. "Then I don't see how your Floating Lady can possibly be ready for Albany."

Collins sighed. "It won't be. Mr. Kellar is dead set on having it ready when we return here in four days, but it won't be ready for Albany. That's why we've brought in Boris."

"Boris?" I asked.

"The lion." He gestured at the caged beast as it sent up

another mighty roar. "Mr. Kellar is going to try something new—an effect called the Lion's Bride. Quite a fascinating little trick, really, and it gives us a fine opportunity to make use of the skills of Miss Moore. She plays a young bride who is threatened by the lion. The curtain opens on—" He was interrupted by another energetic roar from the lion. "Damn thing is a real nuisance. Anyway, the curtain opens on—"

"Which one of you is Mr. Houdini?" We turned toward the house seats. Mr. McAdow, having apparently finished up his business, appeared to be ready for us.

"I am the Great Houdini," my brother said, stepping forward. "I am the eclipsing sensation of—"

"Houdini, huh?" asked McAdow, sizing up my brother's powerful build. "Are you a strongman, Mr. Houdini? We could use a strongman in the 'Circus of Wonders' illusion."

By way of an answer, Harry stepped over to the wings and returned with three heavy sandbags. "Strong?" he asked, as he began to juggle the sandbags in an overhand passing pattern. "Yes, I believe I am reasonably strong."

McAdow's eyes widened. "Yes," he agreed. "I should say that you are. And the young lady with you?"

"My lovely wife, Bess," Harry said proudly. "She is my capable assistant as well as a talented singer and dancer. You may have noted her performance in—"

"Very good," McAdow said. "And the tall fellow?"

"Dash Hardeen," I said, tightening my grip on the brim of my hat. "I do a bit of magic, a bit of juggling. A bit of everything, in fact."

"That's fine," said McAdow. "Leave your details with Collins. We'll be in touch if we require your services."

"Pardon?" said Harry.

"The girl and the tall one are presentable enough," McAdow continued. "If we need a strongman, there may be something for all three of you."

"A strongman?" Harry's voice bristled with incredulity.

"The Great Houdini is no mere strongman! You insult me, sir! I have come here prepared to show Mr. Kellar a miracle of epic proportions, a sensation of such magnitude that it will—"

"You've brought a magic trick, then?"

Harry's head snapped back as though he had scented a foul odor. "A magic trick," he repeated, as if amused by the impertinence of the question. "Yes, a magic trick."

McAdow glanced at his watch. "All right, then," he said. "Be quick about it."

"Now?" Harry asked, narrowing his eyes against the glare of the footlights. "Do you mean to say that I will not be performing for Mr. Kellar himself? The Great Houdini is to perform for a mere functionary?"

"Sir," came McAdow's measured response, "as Mr. Kellar's manager I am responsible for engaging his staff. Carry on, if you would."

Bess laid a restraining hand on Harry's forearm, but he would not be humored. "Are you a magician yourself, Mr. McAdow?" he called over the footlights. "I only ask because it requires a certain degree of refinement to appreciate the miracle you are about to see. It is said that only a true musician can appreciate the genius of Paderewski. So it is with Houdini. Houdini is entirely *sui generis*. So I must ask again—"

"I am in charge of the payroll, Mr. Houdini," came the blunt answer. "Carry on, please."

Harry sighed and shrugged his shoulders. "Very well." He turned upstage and helped me wrestle the trunk into position, frowning over the tumult of banging hammers behind us. "Harry," Bess whispered. "Remember what we discussed earlier. Perform. Don't talk." She slipped out of her overcoat to reveal her stage costume, a wispy confection of bows and puffs that I had come to regard as her "sugarplum fairy" outfit. It allowed her a free range of movement and also showed her legs to great advantage, a fact which was not entirely lost on Mr. McAdow, who made a side-of-mouth comment to the gentleman beside him. The younger man nodded, and made a note on his writing pad.

Much has been said and written of the Substitution Trunk Mystery, which is what we called it in those days. Soon enough the effect would be known throughout the world as "The Metamorphosis." The basic effect was simple: Harry, tied in a sack and locked in a trunk, changed places in the blink of an eye with Bess, who had been standing outside. Bess was then revealed to be locked inside the trunk and tied in the sack. It's quite likely that you have seen the Metamorphosis done by other, lesser performers. I'll promise you this—you've never seen it done better. To this day I carry a newspaper article I wrote at that time in which I tried to convey the novelty and excitement of this incredible transposition:

The clever Mr. Houdini and his lovely wife first submit their travel-worn trunk to a careful inspection by volunteers from the audience. The four sides of the trunk are sounded to demonstrate their solidity and to prove the absence of trickery. Next, a six-foot black flannel bag, a length of heavy tape, and some sealing wax are passed for examination.

Mr. Houdini then asks his volunteers to encase him securely in the previously examined sack, and tightly bind the mouth of the sack with the heavy tape. To ensure fair play, the knots are then sealed with wax. Thus bound and trammelled, Mr. Houdini is lifted into the trunk, which in turn is padlocked and trussed with stout ropes. The sounds of knocking from within the trunk give proof that Mr. Houdini is still imprisoned within. A small curtained enclosure is wheeled before the trunk. Mrs. Houdini, standing at the open curtain, offers a brief announcement: "Now, then, I shall clap my hands three times, and at the third and last time I ask you to watch *closely* for—the—*effect*!" At this, she swiftly draws the curtain closed and vanishes from view. Instantaneously the curtain is reopened to show Mr. Houdini himself standing before the trunk.

The volunteers are immediately called forward to unlock and untie the trunk. Inside, Mrs. Houdini, her loveliness undiminished, is found imprisoned within the same sack which a moment earlier held her husband. The exchange occurs with such lightning rapidity that it leaves the audience almost too astonished to applaud

I had been Harry's original partner in this effect, and I know from first-hand experience what a forceful impression this instantaneous transposition had upon our audiences. When Bess took my place following her marriage to Harry, the switch became even faster. The spectators literally could not believe their eyes.

This was to be the bedrock upon which my brother's remarkable career was built. In those earliest days, however, there was one slight hitch. For all his skill, Harry had not yet learned the golden rule of the stage magician. He had not yet learned to shut up and do the trick.

Facing Mr. McAdow across the footlights, Harry cleared his throat and pulled at the points of his bow tie, a gesture he invariably made before launching into a monologue. My heart sank. If my brother followed his usual pattern, we were in for a five-minute peroration on the genius of Harry Houdini. And if Mr. McAdow adhered to the example set by his brethren in theatrical management, the audition would be over before we ever saw the effect.

"My dear friends," said Harry, in that lulling drone of his, "this evening I am privileged to present a miracle of my own devising, an effect so stunning and original that there is only one man in the entire world capable of performing it. I ask you to steel your nerves against the frightful shock this effect may present, and do not look away even for an instant, or you are liable to miss the miracle that is the Substitution Trunk Mystery!" Harry threw one hand up toward the heavens, a gesture that traditionally invited applause. From his seat,

McAdow coughed discreetly into a pocket square.

Please, Harry, I muttered to myself. *Just get on with it.*

"From time immemorial, wizards and sorcerers have been captivated by the riddle of magically transposing one solid object with another. This afternoon, on this very stage, the Great Houdini will attempt this seemingly impossible feat with nothing more than a humble packing crate and a simple flannel sack. Is it possible, you ask? I assure you that it is."

Now, Harry. I pleaded under my breath. *Do the trick. And whatever you do, don't mention ancient Mesopotamia.*

"Long ago," Harry continued, "in ancient Mesopotamia, there was a plucky young wizard by the name of Ari Ardeeni. It was said that young Ari had the power to transport himself from one place to the next in the twinkling of an eye! One moment he might be frolicking in a stream, and at the next instant he could be seen dancing atop the highest mountain! Stranger still, it was believed that this handsome conjuror possessed the ability to change places with any being of his choosing, at the merest snap of his fingers! With such a skill at his command, it was thought that young Ari might even be able to switch places with the king himself!"

From my vantage, I could see Mr. McAdow consulting his watch—never a good sign. I caught Bess's eye and tapped the face of my own watch, a signal to hurry along. She raised her eyebrows and gave a barely perceptible shrug, indicating that matters were out of her control.

Please, Harry, I muttered. *Skip the part about the beauteous Wilhelmina.*

"Now this young wizard had a bride by the name of Wilhelmina," Harry continued, "and she was said to be—" he broke off momentarily at the sound of a collapsing sawhorse, followed closely by a mighty roar from the caged lion. He gathered himself and continued. "She was said to be the most pulchritudinous young woman in all the land. Her beauty was so great that even King Yar, with all his wealth and power, was known to be jealous of young Ari and his bride."

From his seat in the audience, McAdow began coughing more loudly, attempting to catch my brother's attention with a finger-twirling "hurry up" motion. Harry affected not to notice. "One day a dark passion seized the evil King Yar, and he ordered that young Ari be brought to him in chains. To keep his bride from harm, the wizard allowed himself to be bound tightly and placed within a sturdy box, which was carried back to King Yar's castle. When Wilhelmina learned of this, she hurried at once to—"

"Uh, Mr. Houdini," McAdow called over the footlights, "I wonder if—"

Harry took a step forward. "You are worried that I am being distracted by all the noise, are you not? The pounding hammers? The roaring lion? It is no matter, I assure you. I have wondrous powers of concentration."

"Actually, Mr. Houdini—"

Harry put a finger to his lips. "Do not trouble yourself. I will carry on. As I was saying, when Wilhelmina learned of her husband's imprisonment, she hurried at once into the presence of the king, and—"

"Mr. Houdini—" McAdow had risen from his seat now, and was standing at the edge of the orchestra pit. "Mr. Houdini, I really believe we've heard enough. I do thank you for coming to see us this afternoon."

"You have heard enough? But I haven't even reached the part about the mystical incantation! It is positively gripping!"

"I'm quite certain that is so, Mr. Houdini, but I'm afraid that Mr. Kellar will not be requiring your services after all. However, if Mrs. Houdini and Mr. Hardeen might wish to—"

"Will not be requiring my services? What can you mean?" I watched as a slow tide of comprehension washed over his features. For a moment he seemed to hover between anger and disbelief, with a rising note of tearfulness contending for the mastery. Then, with a sharp intake of breath, he regained his composure. "Mr. McAdow," he said in a voice heavy with injured pride, "I have just one thing to say to you."

As things turned out, we never got a chance to hear that one thing. At that precise moment, a carpenter at the back of the stage accidentally broke through the flimsy side-railing of a high scaffold. As he fell, he reached out and clawed at the rear curtain to slow his descent, knocking down a series of scenery flats like so many dominoes. Screams and cries of alarm filled the air as people jumped out of the way of the falling lumber, and for a moment the entire stage was engulfed in chaos.

"Is everyone all right?" shouted Collins, racing from the wings. "Is anyone hurt?"

His cries went unheeded. Everyone in the theater was transfixed by the sight of the dazed figure at the center of the stage, struggling to extricate himself from a tangle of debris.

Unfortunately, it was the lion.

3

THE LION'S BRIDE

DANGER, IT MUST BE SAID, ALWAYS BROUGHT OUT THE BEST IN MY brother.

Many times I watched him dangle at the end of a burning rope, high above a crowded city street. More than once he allowed himself to be tied to a set of railroad tracks in the path of a speeding locomotive. And on one occasion I saw him sealed up in a galvanized coffin and submerged in water for ninety minutes. But all of those stunts were carefully controlled and well rehearsed. There had been no rehearsals that day at the Belasco Theater. In the blink of an eye, my brother was suddenly standing nose to nose with an angry lion. The danger had never been so real.

Strange to say, this made my brother extremely happy.

Only seconds earlier, the entire theater had been alive with sound. Now, a silent chorus of stagehands, musicians and assistants stood at the edges of the scene, transfixed by the sight of the powerful lion ranging free at the center of the stage. It was clear that one of the falling scenery flats had crashed down on top of the lion's cage, shearing off the heavy locking handle. The beast, suddenly liberated, moved slowly forward, swinging its huge head from side to side as it surveyed the terrain. In its path were Harry and Bess. Bess, who had been standing inside the substitution trunk as she waited to be introduced, would not be able to take flight easily. Harry, standing next to the trunk, calmly stood his ground. He appeared relaxed and confident, perhaps forgetting that he was wearing a pair of shoes that had been smeared with beef fat.

I was still waiting in the wings, about ten yards away. An urgent conference was taking place behind me. Jim Collins, taking command of the situation, dispatched the animal wrangler to fetch a ball of ether-soaked rags at the end of a pole. Boris, it emerged, was rousing himself from the effects of a powerful sedative, which not only accounted for his slow and measured movements, but also for his extremely bellicose disposition. "For God's sake," Collins was saying in a frantic whisper, "it'll be five minutes before we're ready with that ether! Do you have any idea how much damage Boris can do in five minutes? He may be groggy, but he's just as vicious!"

I stepped forward into my brother's line of sight and touched my forehead to signal that I was working on the problem. Harry nodded and returned the gesture. Then he placed his hand behind his wife's head and firmly pushed her down into the trunk, as though guiding her through a low doorway. This done, he closed the trunk lid over her head. Whatever happened, Bess would be safe.

Turning away from the trunk, Harry moved cautiously forward, closing the distance between himself and the lion with short, measured strides, his hands open at his sides. Every eye in the theater—including those of Boris—was fixed upon this prim little man in the red bow tie who appeared to be inviting death. Taking another step forward, Harry cleared his throat and pulled at the points of his tie, the familiar pre-performance gesture. Then he opened his mouth and broke the ghastly pall that had settled over the theater.

"Here, kitty-kitty," he said.

I could not be certain whether to laugh or cry out. It seemed apparent that my brother had failed to grasp the seriousness of his situation.

"Here, kitty-kitty," he repeated. "I must commend you on your dramatic escape from that cage. I am a man who appreciates such things, and I must say that you did it very neatly. My compliments."

Harry inched closer, and even managed to smile pleasantly at the enormous creature. "I am reminded of a story," Harry said. "Long ago, in ancient Mesopotamia, there was a plucky young wizard by the name of Ari Ardeeni. It was said that young Ari had the power to transport himself from one place to the next in the twinkling of an eye!"

As Harry spoke, he continued to inch forward, almost imperceptibly. "At one moment," he continued, "young Ari might be frolicking in a stream, and at the next instant he could be seen dancing atop the highest mountain! Stranger still, it was believed that this handsome conjuror possessed the ability to change places with any being of his choosing—at the merest snap of his fingers! With such a skill at his command, it was thought that young Ari might even be able to switch places with the king himself!"

I knew my brother well enough to realize that he had some sort of plan in mind, but I couldn't for the life of me fathom what it might be. One thing was clear: the lulling monotone that had earlier threatened to send Mr. McAdow into a slumber was having the opposite effect on Boris. The lion had stopped prowling. Its eyes were locked on my brother. Worse, as Harry edged yet closer, the beast appeared to take a sudden interest in the fragrance of my brother's shoes. The animal lowered its head menacingly, sniffed the air once or twice, and emitted a low, steady growl. Incredibly, this appeared to be exactly what my brother had desired. He smiled, and backed away toward the forward lip of the stage. The lion took a lazy step toward him. *All right, Harry,* I thought to myself. *You have his attention. Now what?*

"One day," Harry continued, "young Ari learned of another wizard who made his home in the faraway land of France. His name was Bautier de Kolta, and he possessed many remarkable abilities."

My ears pricked up—this was a departure from the script.

"Young Ari particularly admired the innovative Monsieur de Kolta's Vanishing Lady illusion, in which one of the magician's comely young assistants seemed to disappear in the blink of an eye! If only young Ari could duplicate this feat, all might yet be well. Perhaps this would allow him to rise above his difficulties."

I turned to Collins, who had been standing behind me watching my brother with open-mouthed fascination. "This theater has a Pritchard hole, doesn't it?" I asked.

He turned and blinked rapidly, as though roused from a daydream. "Yes. Yes, of course!"

"Downstage center?"

Collins nodded.

"Where's the release?"

"Just—just over there," he said, pointing to a spot behind the curtain pulleys. "The red handle. Is that what he's trying to do? Do you think it could possibly—?"

"Tell the wrangler to get down there with the ether ball. The timing will have to be absolutely perfect. Everything will have to happen at once. I'll work the release. You get my brother out of there."

"Get him out of there? But how?"

I pointed upward toward the ungainly Floating Lady pendulum device. "Use that."

"That's crazy! You'll get him killed!"

"It was his idea."

"What? But—?"

" 'Rise above his difficulties.' That's what Harry said. I have no idea why he finds it necessary to speak in veiled references— it's not as if Boris can understand him—but that's his plan. He wants you to use the pendulum to lift him to safety."

"But the lion—how will—"

"Harry will manage it. Move along!"

Collins made for the rear exit, then turned back towards me. "We'll need a signal! How will I know when to spring it?"

"Harry will signal from the stage! He'll give the count of three."

Collins shook his head, his face filled with doubt.

"It'll work!" I insisted. "Get into position!"

I turned back to the stage. "What's that you say?" Harry was saying to the lion. "You wish to hear more about the bold young Ari and his astonishing abilities? Very well, my attentive friend. As it happens, this young wizard had a bride by the name of Wilhelmina, and she was said to be the most pulchritudinous young woman in all the land. Her beauty was so great that even King Yar, with all his wealth and power, was known to be jealous of young Ari and his bride."

Harry continued to edge backward. Boris, for his part, appeared to be growing more alert with each passing moment. Once or twice the lion jerked its head to the side, eyeing a group of assistants at the back wall, but each time Harry took a step toward the creature, recapturing its attention with his voice and his fragrant shoes. If Harry's intention had been to make himself the sole focus of the creature's predatory instincts, he was succeeding all too well.

"One day a dark passion seized the evil King Yar," he continued, "and he ordered that young Ari be brought to him in chains. To keep his bride from harm, the wizard allowed himself to be bound tightly and placed within a sturdy box, which was transported into the presence of the king. When Wilhelmina learned of this, she hurried at once to the royal palace and offered to marry the king in exchange for Ari's freedom."

Harry had now backed onto the forward lip of the stage, and indeed his heels were protruding over the edge into the empty space above the orchestra pit. For a heart-sickening moment it appeared as though he might lose his balance and topple into the pit, but with an effort he recovered himself.

I heard a tense whisper at my side. "Why doesn't he just jump?" asked Connell, the theater warden. "Why doesn't he just leap down into the orchestra pit?"

"The lion would jump in after him," I answered impatiently. "Harry would be trapped like a Roman gladiator."

From the stage, Harry kept up his steady stream of patter. "More?" he asked the lion. "Very well, but perhaps you might care to step a bit closer, in order to hear the tale more clearly." From backstage, I strained to keep track of the lion's every movement. The creature was not quite in position yet, but each step placed Harry in even greater peril. The merest swipe of the beast's enormous paw would have scattered my brother's insides across the stage. "Now, then," said Harry, mastering the alarm he must have felt, "perhaps it would be best if I demonstrated what happened next. As you'll recall, the lovely Wilhelmina was preparing to exchange her freedom for that of her husband. A brave young lady, certainly." Harry teetered a bit on the edge of the stage. "Pardon?" he asked, as if the lion had spoken. "What happened next? Well, perhaps you should step a bit closer. Just a bit more. You see, I wouldn't want you to miss even a fraction of the wondrous spectacle I am about to present. It is entirely *sui generis*."

I tied a length of rope around the red handle I had been clutching, then stepped forward onto the stage so that Harry would be able to see me without taking his eyes off of the lion. At last, everyone appeared to be in position. By now, Harry and the lion were all but touching noses, and he would later tell me that he could feel the creature's breath travel over him from head to toe. I glanced heavenward, wondering if his scheme could possibly work. My brother had the fastest reflexes of any man I have ever known, but could even he move faster than an adult lion, albeit a groggy one? I looked back at Harry. He gave a tight nod. I looked at Boris. He ran an enormous tongue over his lips.

"Now then," Harry was saying, "I shall clap my hands three times, and at the third and last time I ask you to watch *closely* for—the—*effect*. A little closer, if you would, kitty. Here, kitty-kitty."

Slowly, as though moving underwater, Harry raised his hands

and brought them together softly. "One," he said.

The lion, sensing movement from behind, bobbed its head twice in rapid succession. The creature's muscles tensed, sending a visible ripple across its back. Fixing its attention on the stagehands to the rear, the animal took a step away from Harry.

"He's out of position," I whispered. "Come on, Harry…"

"Two," said Harry. "Come along, kitty-kitty. Look at me now."

The beast turned its head back toward my brother and stepped forward.

"Three," my brother said.

"*Go!*" I shouted, tugging frantically at the rope in my hands. Everything happened at once.

First, from his vantage point at the rear of the stage, Collins released a sandbag cleat, sending the giant Floating Lady device into motion with a sudden grinding of wood and springs. The apparatus may have been ineffective as a means of causing a lady to float in mid-air, but it was a wondrously expedient method of removing my brother from the lion's clutches. The enormous pendulum cleaved through the air like a mighty scythe, describing a broad arc through the center of the stage at the precise spot where Harry stood. He calmly reached out and snatched at the heavy bag as it sailed past. In the blink of an eye it scooped him up and carried him heavenward into the dome of the theater. The motion, I noted, was decidedly jerky, but sufficient to our purposes.

At the same instant, I yanked hard at the rope I held in my hands, tripping the release lever in the wings. The drop of a fitted trap door—such as might once have been used to produce the ghost of Hamlet's father—fell open beneath the forepaws of the lion. The creature tumbled forward into a makeshift pen beneath the stage, where a leash-lead and ether-bag were deployed in a smooth coordination by a pair of wranglers. The lion roared once and lashed out with a vicious paw, but the powerful narcotic did its work almost instantly. The entire operation could not have lasted more than five seconds—about as long as it took for my brother to swing up to the dome of the theater and back again—but they were the longest five seconds I have ever known.

"Dash!" Harry shouted, as the pendulum brought him swooping over the stage like a trapeze artist. "I was marvelous, was I not?" He leapt from the pendulum as it passed over the stage and nimbly trotted to my side.

"Harry!" I cried. "You're not hurt? You're all right?"

"Why should I be otherwise?" he called, throwing open the lid of the substitution trunk. "There, there, my dear," he said, freeing Bess from the tangle of ropes and fabric inside. "I am perfectly all right, as you can see. Yes, the lion has been captured. Yes. No. No, I have not been eaten by the lion. He would have found me a bit stringy in any case. I'm quite all right."

"You—you're certain?" Bess stammered. "I couldn't hear—I couldn't make out what—" She was as pale as I have ever seen her, and her lips were trembling uncontrollably.

"Bess," my brother said, gently, "I am fine. Here, let me show you." He lifted her out of the trunk and carried her to the edge of the open trap door. Peering down, we could see the prostrate form of the lion and hear its labored breathing. "There you are," Harry said. "He's sleeping like a kitten. I don't see why—"

But Bess had thrown her arms about his neck and pressed her lips to his with such ardent force that his face went bright scarlet. At this, the scattered members of the company burst from the wings and swarmed onto the stage to offer Harry their congratulations, and it was some moments before the noisy back-slapping and hand-pumping subsided. At length Mr. McAdow forced himself into the center of the throng and threw his arm around my brother's shoulders.

"My boy!" he cried, thrusting a panatella between Harry's lips, "that was quite the most amazing thing I've ever seen! So long as Dudley McAdow has anything to say about it, there will always be a home for you here with the Kellar show!"

A loud cheer went up from the multitude.

Harry removed the cigar from his lips with obvious distaste. "Thank you," he said. "That is most kind. But I am afraid I cannot possibly accept that generous offer."

"Pardon?" cried Mr. McAdow, as dissenting noises were heard from the throng. "What are you saying, young man? You came here looking for work, didn't you?"

"Of course, but—"

"Well, then, that's all there is to it! You'll come with us to Albany on tomorrow's train!"

"But I—"

"If it's money, young man, I'm afraid I can't help you there. Mr. Kellar has very strict rules about salaries and compensations, and there's no room for negotiation. But if it's any further inducement, I can offer you a guarantee for the entire run of the current tour!"

"That's terribly kind, sir—" Harry began, but his remarks were drowned out by shouts of "Come on, Harry!" and "There's a good fellow!" from Collins and his band of stagehands. Harry held up his hands for silence. "You have all made entirely too much of the small role I played in subduing our lion friend," Harry said with a modesty that surprised me. "Please be assured that I would like nothing more than to join your company, along with my wife and brother. However, there is one condition that must be satisfied before I can possibly accept."

McAdow frowned and took his cigar from his mouth. "Condition? Mr. Houdini, I've already told you that Mr. Kellar's fees are set in advance. We can't possibly agree to any new conditions."

"This one is easily met, sir," Harry assured him.

"And what would that be?"

Harry smoothed his hair. "I must be allowed to complete my audition."

A wave of laughter swept through the assembly. Mr. McAdow gave a cry of disbelief. "But you've already got the job, man! Why on God's green earth would we need to see your audition?"

Harry folded his arms. "I am resolute on this point. Otherwise I would be accepting the job under false pretenses."

McAdow stared at my brother with frank incredulity. "That beats all, Mr. Houdini," he said as a wide grin broke across his face. He held up his hands for silence. "My friends, if I could ask that we all have a seat in the first row or two of seats, it seems that our friend Mr. Houdini here is going to show us his little magic trick after all."

"Thank you again, Mr. McAdow," said Harry, as a long line of stagehands, carpenters, dancing girls, lighting men and curtain-pullers made their way out into the front rows, "and may I thank you all once again for your kindness. Seeing you all here this afternoon, I am reminded of a story I once heard."

He tugged at the points of his bow tie. "Long ago, it seems, in ancient Mesopotamia, there was a plucky young wizard by the name of Ari Ardeeni…"

‍⟨ 4 ⟩‍

CURIOUS AND UTTERLY BAFFLING SURPRISES

"SO YOU'RE THE ONES WHO CORRALLED BORIS, ARE YOU?" SAID our host, extending a firm hand. "You must be Houdini, is that right? I'm very glad to know you."

"I am the Great Houdini," said Harry, shaking hands. "Allow me to present my charming wife, Bess, and my younger brother, Dash Hardeen."

"I'm delighted to meet all of you," he said, bringing his heels together as he bent to kiss Bess's hand. "I am Harry Kellar."

"We know who you are, sir," I said. "It's a great honor."

We were riding in the private compartment of Mr. Kellar's personal six-car train, which had departed moments earlier from New York City to Albany. The three of us had spent a hectic twenty-four hours preparing to join the tour, and had barely settled into the passenger compartment when we received a summons to join Mr. Kellar at the rear of the train.

Mr. Kellar's private car was furnished with exquisite care. A group of high-backed velvet chairs and a davenport were arranged at the center of the car, so as to command a view of the passing landscape through a leaded picture window. Crook-necked lamps and occasional tables were scattered throughout, and a revolving cherry-wood bookcase stood within easy reach of a worn Morris chair, suggesting that Mr. Kellar spent a great deal of his travel time with a good book. A heavy burgundy curtain marked off a corner of the compartment that I took to be the sleeping area, and an ormolu clock stood atop a glass display case filled with curios from our host's lifetime of travel. The effect was one of comfortable opulence, and but for the steady thrum of the train wheels clattering over the track, Mr. Kellar's parlor car might well have been the smoking room of a New York gentlemen's club.

Harry Kellar had been a boyhood idol for both Harry and me. We had followed the spectacular progress of his career as a headliner in the pages of *Mahatma* magazine, and whenever he came to New York we did whatever we could to attend as many of his performances as possible, usually from the five-cent gallery of the Lyceum. Mr. Kellar's splendid illusions and skilled sleight of hand, coupled with his engaging stage manner, had raised the standard for every aspiring magician in the country, and helped to elevate the art of magic from the sideshow to the legitimate theater. There would come a day when my brother Harry was considered a hero and role model for thousands of boys across the country, but at that time it was Mr. Kellar who received sacks of letters from young admirers, and whose photograph adorned the cover of countless magazines and pamphlets. For me, he was something of a cross between Thomas Edison and King Solomon. Even Harry, who acknowledged few equals and no superiors, held a special regard for the man who had come to be known as the Dean of American Magicians.

In person, Mr. Kellar was taller and perhaps not quite as slender as he appeared from the stage. His large, egg-shaped head was nearly bald now, with a fringe of white hair at the back. His pale green eyes and pinkish features gave an impression of fatherly benevolence, while his thick upper lip lent a touch of sibilance to his manner of speech.

"Do sit down," Kellar was saying. "Will you take a cigar? They're genuine Havanas."

"Thank you, no," said Harry. "My personal regimen of bodily conditioning and muscular expansionism forbids the use of tobacco."

"Is that so?" Kellar asked, with raised eyebrows. "What about you, Mr. Hardeen?"

I reached across and selected one. "My personal regimen is not quite so rigid as Harry's."

"Good man," Kellar said. "What about a drink?" He reached for a decanter on the sideboard. "I usually take a bourbon and soda at about this time."

"Alcohol is also forbidden if one wishes to achieve the proper balance of bodily humors," Harry announced.

Kellar glanced at me.

"Bourbon and soda would be fine," I said.

"Excellent. Mrs. Houdini?"

Bess allowed herself to be persuaded to accept a small sherry, which Kellar presented to her with another courtly bow. He then poured a measure of Harper's bourbon into a pair of crystal glasses and added a jet of soda water from a gasogene. Handing one to me, he settled himself in the Morris chair, opposite a long divan where the three of us were seated.

For a moment the four of us sat in a companionable silence, watching through the large window as the scenery flashed past. "Wonderful, isn't it?" asked Mr. Kellar, sending up a cloud of cigar smoke.

"The view is lovely, sir," said Bess.

Kellar sighed with satisfaction. "Our profession has been kind to me," he said, "though I was not always able to travel in such grand style. At your age, I was not above hitching rides on a baggage car, often barely a step ahead of my creditors. I once toured South America on the back of an ornery burro, then lost the proceeds in a shipwreck before I could enjoy them. No, sir, I wouldn't exchange places with you now, even if I could. But I do hope that in the end the profession will be kind to you as well."

"I am certain of it," said Harry firmly. "It is only a matter of time."

"You seem a very confident young man, Mr. Houdini." Kellar sipped at his bourbon. "That's all to the good. Confident and brave in the bargain."

Harry brushed aside the compliment. "As I have already said, Mr. McAdow has made entirely too much of my exploit at the theater. No doubt you would have done the same."

Kellar examined the white ash at the end of his cigar. "I doubt it, young man, but you are kind to say so. However, I wasn't referring to your little dust-up with Boris."

"Ah! You have seen me perform!" Harry's cheeks glowed with pleasure. "Perhaps you came to see me at Huber's Museum the last time you passed through New York? I thought I spotted you. Or perhaps you've had occasion to witness my turn with the Marco Company?" Harry jumped to his feet and began pacing the compartment, barely able to contain his excitement. "I assure you, those performances gave only the merest suggestion of the Great Houdini's talents. In the proper circumstances, there is no limit to what I might achieve. Why, with my skills and your resources, I might at last be able to—"

"Please, Mr. Houdini," said Kellar, holding up his palm, "I'm afraid I've not yet had the honor of seeing your stage act."

"No?" Harry's face fell. "Then how do you know of my remarkable skills and abilities?"

"I've had reports, my friend." Kellar frowned at his cigar, as if deciding whether it could be trusted with a confidence. "You see, I've made a few inquiries about you, Mr. Houdini. You and your brother."

"Inquiries?"

"Josef Graff was a friend of mine."

Harry's lips twitched. "He was a friend of mine, as well," he said, sitting down again. "Such a loss."

"Branford Wintour was also my friend."

"I did not have the pleasure of meeting Mr. Wintour before—that is to say—"

"Before his murder?" Kellar gazed through the picture window as the train slowed to pass through the Poughkeepsie station. "I suppose you wouldn't have. But you certainly came to know the circumstances of his death well enough, didn't you?"

Mr. Kellar was referring to an unhappy affair in which Harry and I had become entangled the previous year, when our friend Josef Graff, the owner of a New York magic shop, had been accused of the murder of a reclusive millionaire named Branford Wintour. Harry and I, through a combination of native cunning and dumb luck, had managed to stumble across the real killer, though the discovery nearly cost us our own lives.

"Mr. Kellar." I said, setting down my cigar, "the authorities were careful to withhold any mention of the role that Harry and I played in the Wintour murder. Our names never appeared in any of the newspapers."

"An outrage!" Harry grumbled. "The police would still be chasing their own shadows if I had not—"

"Be that as it may, Harry, the information was considered confidential. How did you come to know of it, Mr. Kellar?"

Our host studied my face closely for a moment, evidently finding something there that he had not noticed before. "It seems I am not allowed to keep any of my secrets these days," he sighed. "Very well, Mr. Hardeen. I play cards with Senator Bibbs. He was there at the resolution of the matter, I believe, and he's a rather indiscreet fellow once he's had a few bottles of wine poured down his throat. I made it my business to find out why Josef's death had been hushed up in such a strange manner."

I set down my glass and rose from my chair. "I'm afraid we can say nothing further on this matter, Mr. Kellar. Harry and I were sworn to—"

"Sit down, Mr. Hardeen," Kellar said with a dry chuckle. "I wouldn't think of asking you to betray a confidence. It pleases me to learn that you and your brother can be trusted to keep a secret. I wonder if I might presume to entrust you with one of mine?"

"For heaven's sake, Henry," came a woman's voice, "can't you set aside the theatrics even for a moment?" We looked up to see a tall, extremely elegant woman standing in the entryway. "Sometimes I think your talents are wasted as a magician. You should have been an actor in a melodrama!"

Kellar threw back his head with laughter. "Gentlemen, Mrs. Houdini," he said, rising to his feet. "Allow me to present my wife, Eva."

I had seen Mrs. Kellar often enough serving as an assistant to her husband when he was a younger man. Then as now, I was struck by her proud bearing and graceful carriage, but in person there was a pleasant sense of mischief playing about her features, as though she had just been told a rather wicked joke. The lovely auburn hair that I remembered from her touring days was now shot through with grey, and she wore it off her shoulders in the fashion of the day.

"It's fortunate that I came when I did," she told Bess as she took a seat near her husband. "Otherwise Henry might have spent the rest of the journey making those strange, cryptic remarks. He's a great one for dramatic pronouncements."

Bess gave a sidelong glance at Harry. "A professional hazard, I suspect."

My brother leaned forward. "Why does Mrs. Kellar call you by the name of 'Henry'? I thought—"

"My given name is Heinrich," Kellar said. "Never much cared for the name. What about you? You don't strike me as a man who was born 'Harry.'"

"No," my brother admitted. "I was born Ehrich Weiss."

"So you chose your stage name to echo that of a great performer from the past. Jean Eugene Robert-Houdin becomes Harry Houdini. Makes good—"

"Gentlemen," said Mrs. Kellar firmly, "there will be plenty of time to exchange pedigrees in the coming weeks. Before we reach Albany, Henry, I think you had better say what's on your mind."

Kellar nodded. "Eva has a habit of coming to the point," he said, making his way to the far end of the car. He paused before a framed handbill, from the early years of his career, announcing an exhibition of 'Curious and Utterly Baffling Surprises.' Beneath it stood a wide captain's desk with a number of wooden cubbyholes. Kellar fished out a key on the end of his watch chain and unlocked a drawer at the back of the desk. Reaching in, he withdrew a heavy Babson church lock which had evidently been prised from a wooden door.

"You say you're clever with locks, Mr. Houdini," said Kellar. "What do you make of this one?"

Harry took the lock and turned it over in his hands several times, examining it from all angles. Then he carried it over to one of the wall sconces and held it up to the light. "Interesting," he said, passing the lock to me. "What do you think, Dash?"

"It's obvious that the lock has been interfered with," I said, after a moment's examination. "I would say that at least five of the pins have been filed down."

"Exactly so," Harry agreed. "Rather sloppy work, by the look of it, but it would get the job done. One would have only to put his shoulder to the door and it would fly open. Probably the work of an amateur burglar. Was anything taken?"

"No, nothing is missing." Kellar folded his hands. "Gentlemen, I pried that lock from the bars of the lion cage only three hours ago."

Bess let out a gasp as her hand flew to her mouth. Harry and I merely stared at our host in disbelief, as though he might be playing some sort of prank. "You cannot be serious, Mr. Kellar," Harry said, his voice rising. "Do you really mean to say that the lion was set free deliberately?"

"That is precisely what I mean."

Harry took the lock from my hands and peered again into the keyhole. "But who would do such a thing?"

"I'm afraid I have no idea, Mr. Houdini." Kellar rose and began refilling his glass at the sideboard. He turned to me and raised his eyebrows. I passed over my empty glass.

"Mr. Kellar," I said, "if what you say is true, you are suggesting that someone intended for the lion to escape during yesterday's rehearsal. But what we saw was an accident. There can be no question about it. One of your stagehands fell from a platform and knocked a scenery flat onto the cage. It could hardly have been staged. It was just bad luck."

"Actually, I believe it was a stroke of good luck," he answered, handing me a fresh bourbon and soda. "I believe that it was a perverse good fortune that you and your brother happened to be there when Boris escaped. If what I believe is true, then whoever tampered with this lock did not expect that the lion would break out of the cage until tomorrow."

"Tomorrow?"

"During the performance in Albany. At the opening of the Lion's Bride illusion, I cause Boris's cage to appear in a puff of smoke. I use a pair of smudgepots to cover the workings, and the flash as the pots go off usually causes the lion to startle. In fact, we planned it that way so that Boris would roar and swipe at the bars of the cage—good, dramatic stuff—just to show that it wasn't a man in a lion suit or some such fakery. But if Boris had knocked against the bars with this lock on the door—"

"—The cage would have sprung open," Harry said.

"Exactly. And a ferocious, hungry lion would have been turned loose."

My sister-in-law made a curious noise and seemed in danger of fainting. Harry took her hands and rubbed them. "I'm all right, Harry," she insisted. "I just couldn't help but picture the scene in my mind. It was frightening enough when the theater was relatively empty, but a full house—"

"Exactly," said Kellar.

"But what about your safety measures?" I asked. "Surely you

have your handlers standing ready backstage in case anything goes wrong?"

"Of course," Kellar replied. "But you saw how long it took them to respond to your dilemma yesterday. If he had escaped during a live performance, the creature might well have been loose for two or three minutes before we could bring him under control."

"He might have killed as many as a dozen people in that time," said Harry. He turned to Kellar, as though considering an even more grim prospect. "Your career would have been ruined," he added.

"My *life* would have been ruined," Kellar said emphatically. "I don't see how I could have lived with the knowledge that I had caused such carnage."

Harry picked up the lock and examined it a second time. "When was the last time you performed the Lion's Bride?"

"We've not yet done it before an audience. We bought it from the Great Lafayette when it became clear that the Floating Lady wouldn't be ready in time. Lafayette can take it right back as far as I'm concerned."

"But you've rehearsed the effect?"

"Of course. The day before yesterday. We ran it seven times."

"I take it the lock was in working order at the time?"

"Unquestionably. Boris rattled the bars of the cage several times during each rehearsal. Boris is usually a very docile creature. Under normal conditions, the flashing of the smudge pots is required to rouse him to a show of anger."

"Falling scenery appears to have the same effect," Harry noted.

"Just so," Kellar said.

"When did the rehearsals end?" I asked.

Kellar glanced at his wife. "It must have been before six o'clock. Eva and I kept a dinner engagement in the city. Yes, six o'clock or so."

"So sometime between the end of rehearsals and the mishap

the following afternoon, someone must have tampered with the lock."

"So it would seem."

"Boris doesn't spend all of his time in the cage, does he?"

"No. At the end of rehearsals he was taken off to an exercise pen in Brooklyn."

Harry banged the lock mechanism against his open palm once or twice. "Who would have access to the cage once rehearsals had ended?"

"That's just it, Mr. Houdini. I run a very tight ship. You know what steps one must take to protect secrets in this business. My equipment is held under lock and key whenever it is not in use."

"At the theater?" I asked.

"Yes. Under guard. A fellow named Danbury. Been with me for some years. A very reliable person, you may be assured. Old army man."

I set down my glass. "Are there any members of your company who might get access to your equipment after hours without rousing the suspicions of the guard?"

"No, Mr. Hardeen. I trust the members of my company, but I find it best not to place temptation in their way. Danbury keeps me informed if there is anyone poking about where they shouldn't be."

"Have there been any unusual comings and goings?"

"None."

"So whoever tampered with the cage must have done so during the course of a normal rehearsal."

"Yes," said Kellar.

"But that means—"

"Yes, Mr. Houdini. Whoever rigged that lock is a member of my own company."

I stubbed out my Havana in a crystal ashtray. "You don't sound entirely surprised, Mr. Kellar."

He rubbed his forehead wearily. "I'm afraid I've been expecting something of the sort, now that we're so close to debuting the

Floating Lady. I've spent a fortune developing that illusion, and you can't imagine what Le Roy would do to get his hands on it. I must hold the copyright to the Floating Lady at all—"

Harry looked up from the locking mechanism. "I thought I understood that Mr. Maskelyne held the copyright to the Floating Lady. Was I misinformed?"

Kellar's eyes flashed with sudden anger. "Sir," he said with considerable heat, "Mr. Maskelyne is a fine magician, a clever inventor and an excellent showman. The Egyptian Hall in London is an ornament to the conjuror's craft and we would do well to emulate its success here in America. But for all his many talents, Mr. Maskelyne cannot claim to own the patent on inspiration. He has devised a very engaging little illusion called Asrah, and it is a commendable effort, so far as it goes. But it is not the Floating Lady that I have in mind. It is not the Floating Lady that I have dreamed of since boyhood. And by God it is not the Floating Lady that I plan to present in New York City in four days' time!"

Kellar's voice had risen steadily during these remarks, and by the time he concluded his face had turned an alarming shade of red. "You must forgive my husband," said Mrs. Kellar in a tone of mild reproach, as though he had dropped a dinner roll. "It is one of the few subjects upon which he has absolutely no sense of humor."

"Yes, of course," said Kellar, struggling to master his temper, "I—"

"Do you mean to say," Harry broke in, brushing aside the social proprieties, "that you have been working on a Floating Lady illusion since the beginning of your career?"

"I have. It was a lifelong dream of my mentor, the Wizard of Kalliffa." His eyes drifted toward a small portrait in a gilt frame. It showed a steely-eyed older man with mutton chop whiskers, a dimpled chin and a sweep of dark hair across a heavily-lined forehead. "He always said that this trick would bring fame and fortune to the man who perfected it. I believe that even he had no real conception of what the idea would be worth. I estimate that the man who introduces the Floating Lady to America stands to make well over one million dollars."

"One million!"

"It's true, Mr. Hardeen. My bookings have fallen off a touch during recent years, but a headline grabber such as this one would put me back in the money. Moreover, I could send out four or five touring companies, each one carrying an authorized version of the effect. Make no mistake, one of us is going to make a fortune—me or Servais Le Roy." He leaned back and drew on his cigar. "Fame and fortune does not matter to me so much as it once did," he continued, "but I confess that I will not consider my career complete until I have mastered this one last illusion. I feel that I owe it to my old mentor."

"He was really an Englishman, wasn't he? The Wizard of Kalliffa?"

"A Scot, Mr. Houdini. Duncan McGregor. I knew him as Mac. He and Mrs. McGregor were like second parents to me, and I have tried to honor their memory by becoming the kind of magician he wanted me to be."

Harry studied the face in the portrait. "How did a Scot named Duncan McGregor come to be known as the 'Wizard of Kalliffa'?"

"In those days, every Scottish magician had to take pains to avoid comparisons with the great John Henry Anderson. I think Mac might have done better without the exotic trappings, however. He was born too soon, really. He had brilliant ideas, just brilliant. The Floating Lady was like the holy grail to him. He nearly got there."

"But surely in his day there was little hope of perfecting such an ambitious illusion? It is only recently that we've developed the necessary mechanics."

Kellar chuckled. "It may amuse you to know that Mac created and discarded no fewer than five methods of floating a lady, including the one that Mr. Maskelyne is taking such great pains to protect. Mac simply wasn't satisfied with any of them. He invented the apparatus you may know as a 'levitation banquette'—the piece of furniture upon which the assistant is resting as she begins to rise. It's a wonderfully clever idea. The banquette appears to be so innocent, and yet—well, I suppose you know all about it. In any case, Mac discovered a means of causing the assistant to rise from the banquette and hover about five feet off the stage. I thought it was a thing of beauty, but he wasn't satisfied. He wanted her to float out over the heads of the audience. 'Got to get her off the stage and into the audience,' he would say. 'Knock down the artifice of the thing.' "

"Floating over the heads of the audience," Harry said, with a note of reverence in his voice. "That would be one for the ages."

"Exactly. Mac planned to debut the effect at the old Lyceum, which had a magnificent high dome, so that Mrs. McGregor could rise clear up to the top." Kellar paused, gazing long and hard at the framed portrait. "Mac even had his patter all scripted. 'Cast your eyes heavenward, my friends, and watch as she rises, rises, rises. Now she flings aside the high-flown theories of gravity and science like so much useless chaff. See how she floats, as though on a gentle zephyr, borne aloft by the hypnotic force of animal magnetism.' "

"What happened?" Bess asked. "Why didn't he show the effect?"

A dark cloud seemed to pass over Kellar's face. "He—he never got the opportunity. Mrs. McGregor passed away suddenly, and Mac couldn't bring himself to go on. The performance had been all set. The theater was booked, and the tickets sold, but Mac—he simply couldn't carry on. This coming Saturday night will mark the twenty-fifth anniversary of Mrs. McGregor's passing. I can't imagine a more fitting tribute than to perform the Floating Lady at long last." Kellar raised his glass to McGregor's portrait and threw back the rest of his bourbon. "I really think I'll get there this time," he said. "I've been so close so often, but now

I've almost perfected it. I'll make John Nevil Maskelyne look like a circus tout! If only—" his face darkened. "If only Le Roy doesn't beat me to it. Damn clever fellow, for a Frenchman."

"I believe Mr. Le Roy is Belgian," said Harry.

"Whatever. All I know is that he's smart as blazes, and he's let it be known that he plans to introduce a '*Lévitation Mystérieuse*' by the end of this season. If Le Roy beats me to the finish line, he may well take the bulk of next year's bookings out from under me. A magician is only as good as his latest miracle. I started out doing shadow puppets and producing cakes from a hat. Do I do those tricks any more? No, sir, I do not. Quaint. That's what those tricks are. And when one reaches my age, there is little distinction between quaint and antiquated. I'm going to be first with the Floating Lady, and there's nothing Le Roy can do to stop me."

"Mr. Kellar," I said, "you're not suggesting that Mr. Le Roy had anything to do with the sabotage of the lion cage?"

"I don't know, young man. I wouldn't rule it out. Not with a million dollars at stake."

"Yes," said Harry, considering the possibility, "he could have bribed a member of the company. If Boris had gone on a rampage, Le Roy's only true competitor would have been forced to withdraw."

"What you're suggesting is outrageous!" I cried. "That lion could easily have killed someone! I can't believe that anyone would sink to such a depth, not even for a million dollars!"

"Someone did," Kellar said, picking up the broken lock from the lion cage. "Someone filed these pins. Maybe Le Roy is responsible, maybe not. When I find out who did it, I'll have my answer. That's where the two of you come in."

I gripped the arm of the divan as the train clattered over a series of points. "You want us to find out who did this?"

"I suppose I could hire a private detective, but he wouldn't be able to mingle with the company as freely as the two of you can. He wouldn't know what he was looking for, in any case. You two are new to the company. I know I can trust you. You can keep your ears to the ground in a way that I cannot." He paused and laid a hand on Harry's shoulder. "Young man, you showed a remarkably cool head when Boris escaped. I could use a man like you just now."

As Kellar spoke, my brother's face lit up like a penny pumpkin. The older magician had not only appealed to my brother's titanic ego, but he had also placed him in a role he had come to relish—that of the amateur sleuth. Harry stood up and laced his fingers behind his back, pacing the parlor car as though considering whether or not to accept the request. "Your case is not without features of interest," he said.

"Harry—" I began.

"If it is a question of payment," Kellar said, "I would be willing to compensate you for whatever added burdens are placed upon you."

Harry frowned. "My fees are on a fixed scale, save when I remit them altogether."

"Harry," I said. "For God's sake."

I must explain something. Over the course of his lifetime my brother would acquire some 70,000 volumes relating to magic and its history, and he even found time to author one or two of them himself. Despite his vast library, however, my brother could not have been called a great reader, and many was the time I pressed a volume of Dreiser or Tarkington upon him, only to come across it some months later with the spine unbroken and the pages uncut. Even so, there was one type of book that he dearly cherished, and this was the detective novel. He especially enjoyed the adventures of Mr. Sherlock Holmes, who at that time was believed to have perished at the hands of Professor Moriarty. There were at that stage only two collections of short stories detailing the cases of Sherlock Holmes, and I can say with confidence that both of them were in my brother's travel grip that day. When Harry made his curious remark about remitting his fees, as well as the comment about the unusual features of the case, he was actually quoting from the great detective, heedless of how inappropriate these utterances were to the situation in which we found ourselves. Mr. Kellar had handed him an opportunity to play detective, and my brother dearly loved to play detective. Despite my sympathy for Mr. Kellar's position, I knew that if I did not make some effort to rein in my brother's enthusiasm, Harry would soon be making obscure references to Wilson, the notorious canary trainer, and the giant rat of Sumatra.

"Harry," I said, "I suspect that Mr. Kellar simply wants us to keep our eyes peeled. I don't think we shall be required to fight off any poisonous swamp adders."

Harry's face colored. "I only meant to say that we would be honored to give any assistance that we can."

"It's very good of you, Houdini," said Kellar. "You too, Hardeen. I really don't know what to make of this, and frankly I'm feeling a bit hard pressed."

"Is there anyone within the company who has given you cause to be suspicious in recent weeks?" I asked.

"I wouldn't say so. I'm embarrassed to say that I really don't know the members of the company terribly well. People come and go in an outfit such as mine. I take it you met Collins this afternoon?"

"Your head stagehand? He seemed a very solid type of person. You don't mean to say you suspect him?"

"Far from it. But Collins ought to be able to introduce you around and let you know if there are any rum characters in the bunch. Eva and I—" he paused, choosing his words carefully, "Eva and I have not been terribly familiar with the company for the past year or so."

"We shall start with Collins, then," Harry said.

"It might be useful to know the names of the most recent additions to the company," I said. "Perhaps Mr. McAdow might be able to provide—"

Mrs. Kellar, who had been sitting quietly with a bag of knitting through much of this exchange, now spoke up, having evidently anticipated the question. "There are only four who have joined us within the past year," she said. "First there is Francesca Moore, who is to be our floating lady."

"A wonderful acrobat," Kellar remarked. "A great ornament to the stage."

"Then there is Mr. Malcolm Valletin," Mrs. Kellar continued, "our new head carpenter."

"I hired him away from Maskelyne," said Kellar with a wink. "He—shall we say—he brought along some useful ideas for us. He's a clever performer, as well, though I must say he is quite possibly the worst juggler I have ever seen. We're badly in need of a juggler, as it happens. Does either of you gentlemen happen to—?"

"We are both quite adept at juggling," Harry said.

"Excellent!" Kellar cried. "When all else fails, a man can always fall back on his juggling." He turned to Mrs. Kellar. "Who else is there, my dear?"

"Miss Perdita Wynn came aboard in Chicago. A lovely girl."

"We needed a singer," Kellar explained. "The last one ran away with a tuba player."

"And finally there is Mr. Collins himself," added Mrs. Kellar. "But you've already made his acquaintance."

"Mr. Collins has only been with you a short time?" I asked. "I thought I understood you to suggest that he was above suspicion."

"He is," said Kellar firmly. "I've known him for years. He spent some time working for the Herrmann show, but it was only this past March that I was lucky enough to hire him. I trust the man completely."

I marked the names down on my note pad. "Who was the gentleman we saw sitting with Mr. McAdow this afternoon? The dark-haired man with a moustache?"

Mr. Kellar raised his eyebrows. "Not sure I know who you mean."

"He seemed to be jotting down a great many notes. We didn't catch his name."

"Ah! Old Lyman! He's a newspaper man who has been spending some time traveling with us. You needn't pay any mind to him. He's helping me with a bit of a project I have in mind. I'm afraid I can't say anything more than that, but he's a harmless fellow, I assure you." He glanced at the ormolu clock. "We'll be in Albany shortly, gentlemen. I hope that I may count on you to keep your eyes open?"

Harry stood up and thrust his index finger into the air. "Rest assured, the Great Houdini is on the case! I shall not cease my efforts until these evil-doers are apprehended! I shall—" He broke off momentarily as Bess, smiling sweetly, looped her arm through his and gently pulled him toward the exit. "—I shall hunt down these varlets wherever—"

"—We'll keep our eyes open, sir," I said, following Harry and Bess to the door. "And failing that, we can always fall back on our juggling."

5

I CHARM THE LADIES

"LET US BEGIN THE INVESTIGATION AT ONCE!" HARRY CRIED AS THE train pulled into the Albany station.

"Harry," said Bess, "you must try not to arouse suspicion. Mr. Kellar wants you to stay alert, nothing more."

"Very well," he answered. "but I shall be ready to pounce in an instant! Dash, we must make it our business to make the acquaintance of our suspects!"

"The other members of the company, you mean? I really don't think we should refer to them as suspects."

"Ah, yes! I see what you mean!" He gave a broad wink. "Mustn't put them on their guard! Very good—I shall seek out Mr. Valletin."

"I'm sure we'll meet him soon enough in due course, along with Francesca Moore and Perdita Wynn."

"I shall leave them to you. The fair sex is your department, Dash. I should be foolish indeed if I did not avail myself of your natural advantages."

Bess, pulling on her winter gloves, regarded her husband with a curious expression. "Just what do you mean by that, Harry?"

"Frankly, I'm not entirely certain," he admitted. "It was a remark of Sherlock Holmes."

We stepped onto the station platform just as a heavy snow began to fall. Harry and I fell in with the others as the heavy work of unloading the baggage cars began. Nearly two tons worth of magical equipment—some of it quite fragile—had to be transferred onto horse-drawn wagons for delivery to the theater, an operation that required a coordinated effort from every man in the company. Jim Collins directed the operation with the cool precision of a battle general, striding up and down on the platform as he barked out instructions and positioned the loading ramps. Harry's remarkable strength and agility quickly won the respect of the others, as did his willingness to shoulder the heaviest crates and swarm up to the top of the baggage cars to release the support nettings. I may say that I was scarcely less useful; I never possessed the raw power of my brother, but I compensated with a certain wiry puissance.

After the first car was emptied, Collins dispatched me to load a set of Chinese painted screens onto the forward wagon, instructing me to take care with the seal-cloth covering so as to protect the delicate material from the elements. I loaded the screens safely and lashed them into place, but as I turned to jump down from the wagon I somehow contrived to put my foot through a brittle Japanese paper lantern. Pulling my foot free, I lost my balance and pitched forward over the edge of the wagon, sprawling face first into the snow at the foot of the platform.

"Are you all right, sir?" came a woman's voice.

"How the devil do you think I am?" I snapped, wiping snow from my eyes as I pulled myself from the ground. "I've just made an absolute—good lord!"

It was perhaps the most beautiful face I have ever seen. In those days, I confess, my head was easily turned by a dewy cheek or a well-turned ankle, but this woman was quite beyond my experience. Even now I find it nearly impossible to describe the effect that her dark, exotic features had upon me. It was as if, in the words of a popular novel of the time, she possessed the power to cloud a man's mind. I felt my heart quicken and my limbs grow numb. An unsettling tightness gripped the base of my neck and began radiating outwards.

"Sir?" she repeated, in a voice accented with Italian rhythms. "May I assist you in some way?"

Too late, it occurred to me that I should perhaps bring myself to a standing position and venture a few words of conversation, but I found that the power of speech had fled.

"That was quite a nasty fall, sir. Shall I fetch Mr. Collins?"

"I—I'm quite all right," I managed to say, rising from the ground. "Quite all right."

"You're sure?" A sense of alarm was plainly evident on her features. "You've gone the most appalling shade of red."

"Er, yes. The snow, I expect. Very cold. Snow generally is."

"Yes," she said cautiously, apparently finding signs of dementia in my reply. "I believe that is an absolute rule."

"Well, just so. Very true."

"You're sure I shouldn't fetch Mr. Collins? I'm sure he has the name of a physician…"

"No. No, indeed." I clapped my hat upon my head, only to send a wet dribble of melting snow down my nose. I brushed it away, hoping she hadn't noticed. "Beastly weather here in Albany, wouldn't you say?"

"Yes, quite," she said, warily. "Well, if you're certain that you're not injured, I'll continue on my way." She moved off to join the other female members of the company, who were being shown into a pair of carriages by Mr. Kellar and Mr. McAdow. I watched helplessly as she stepped onto the running board with an anxious backward glance at the tall, crazed fellow wearing a hatful of melting snow.

" 'Beastly weather here in Albany,' " I muttered angrily to myself. "Of all the utter codswollop!"

"I see you've met Miss Francesca Moore," said Collins, coming up behind me.

"Oh, indeed," I said. "Made quite an impression on the young lady, I'm sure."

Collins gave a hoarse, rumbling laugh. "You're not the first to make an ass of himself over that one, Hardeen. Every man in the company is sweet on her."

"She's extraordinary!"

"Noticed that, did you? Mr. Kellar wanted a real stunner for the floating lady. She's supposed to be a princess, he said, so by God she should look like a princess." Collins stepped back and raised his hat as the two carriages rolled past. "Miss Moore has been working the small-time up to this point, but once those New York managers get an eyeful, we'll be lucky to hold onto her for the run of the season. Come on, Hardeen, we've got another car to unload. Why don't you grab that bundle of tent poles?"

"Of course," I said. "Sorry about the lantern."

"Happens all the time," he replied. "Oh, one more thing…"

"Yes?" I turned back toward him.

"I agree with you completely. The Albany weather *is* beastly."

After two hours, the baggage cars had been loaded onto a series of seven wagons. While Kellar's train was diverted onto a side spur, the procession of wagons started along a snowy track for the theater. Harry and I rode with Collins atop a pile of bundled costume trunks on the rear wagon, and after a distance of some five or six miles we arrived at the darkened theater. Another hour of hard labor saw the wagons unloaded into a backstage holding pen, where the equipment would wait until early the following morning for the unpacking and set raising. Once Collins had satisfied himself that the crates were dry and secure, he left them under the watch of Sergeant Danbury—a stocky older man with a military brush moustache—while the rest of the crew made its way to the hotel.

It must have been past 10 o'clock by the time we checked into our rooms at the Blair-Kendricks, a stately if dark establishment not far from the train station. Harry immediately joined Bess to retire for the night, while I repaired to a small attic room that had been reserved for me at the last moment.

I found that I was not in the least bit sleepy, and a volume of Bret Harte stories I had brought with me on the train offered little distraction in my agitated frame of mind. After half an hour or so, I threw on my jacket and tie and made my way downstairs to the gentlemen's lounge.

I saw at once that Jim Collins was already seated at the bar, along with a pair of my fellow stagehands. Collins looked up as I came through the doorway and waved me over. "Hardeen!" he called. "I was wondering where you'd gone! Did you have a chance to meet the others at the train platform? I thought not. Allow me to present the other members of the illusion crew— Casper Felsden and Malcolm Valletin."

"A pleasure," I said. "Is that seat empty, Mr. Felsden?"

"Sit down, Hardeen," Valletin answered when Felsden made no reply. "Don't bother about him, he doesn't say much. They call him Silent Felsden. Me, I'm quite the opposite, I'm afraid."

Malcolm Valletin was a broad-shouldered, bulky man of perhaps thirty years of age. His plump cheeks and toothy grin gave him the aspect of an overgrown, mischievous cherub. Casper Felsden, by contrast, was small and rail thin, with a serious and brooding cast to his pale features. His eyes, when he looked up at me over his beer stein, might have been cast of cold steel.

"Have a cigar, Hardeen," Collins said, pushing an ash-wood humidor towards me. "The selection is quite good."

"I'd best not," I said.

"Go on," said Valletin. "It all goes on Mr. Kellar's tab. He's quite decent about looking after us on tour."

"Well, in that case—" I reached for a tightly-rolled belvedere.

Valletin pushed over a bronze cutter that lay near him on the bar. "So, Hardeen," he asked, after I had ordered a Harper's bourbon, "tell us all about the big mystery."

"Mystery?" I stammered. "I don't know—"

"Come on, Hardeen," said Collins. "None of us have ever been invited into Mr. Kellar's private car. What did he want with you?"

"Ah. I was surprised myself," I said, as I warmed and lit my cigar. "I don't imagine that I'll ever be invited in again, unless another lion happens to escape. Mr. Kellar wanted to hear the details from my brother."

"Still can't imagine how that happened," said Valletin. "That cage looked to me as if it could hold a dozen lions and a gorilla besides. I'd have never gone anywhere near the thing if I'd thought otherwise."

"Boris must be even stronger than he looks," Collins said. He emptied his glass and pushed it forward for a refill. "You know, Hardeen, you're not a thing like your brother."

"Well, no," I allowed. "He's unique, as he would be the first to tell you."

"No offense to him," Collins continued, "he seems to be a hard worker, but I don't appreciate being told how to do my job."

"Pardon?"

"Down at the train station. He was watching me like a hawk. 'Just remember, Collins,' he said, 'I'm keeping an eye on you.' Just like that."

"He told me that, too," said Valletin. "I thought he wanted my job."

I sighed. "My brother—my brother has a peculiar sense of humor," I ventured. "He was trying to make a joke."

"Perhaps," said Collins. "How did he do that trick with his wife in the trunk, anyway?"

It was a familiar question and I gave the standard answer. "Very quickly," I said.

Collins smiled at the evasion. "Have it your way. I admit I'm flummoxed. We have the three men responsible for Mr. Kellar's latest illusions sitting right here at this bar, and we can't figure out how he did it."

"Just give us a hint!" cried Valletin, with the noisy enthusiasm of a man well along in the night's drinking. "Otherwise Silent Felsden here won't be able to sleep a wink."

I looked at the pale, serious Mr. Felsden. True to his sobriquet, he had not said a word since I entered the lounge. He nursed his ale and stared ahead into the mirror behind the bar. He did not appear to be overly concerned about the Substitution Trunk.

"I really can't help you," I said. "My brother is very chary with his secrets."

"Quite a bit of that going around," said Collins.

"Don't get me wrong," said Valletin, sipping at his gin and lemon. "I could manage the escape from the trunk. It's just the speed of the thing. I can't imagine how they made that switch so fast, him and that little slip of a girl."

"It suggests to me that Mr. Houdini is rather clever at coming up with new ideas," Collins said. "Seems to me as if Hardeen and his brother might just be able to get us back on track with the Floating Lady. We could use whatever help we can get, with only four days to go until the debut."

"We'll do our best."

"Little slip of a girl," Valletin repeated, by way of nothing in particular. "Too bad she's married, I say."

"Surprised you have eyes for another woman at all," Collins said, "not while Miss Francesca Moore walks among us."

Valletin raised his glass in salute. "Miss Francesca Moore!" he cried, sloshing a bit of gin onto the bar. "She walks in Beauty, like the night…"

"What an extraordinary woman!" I said. "And what an ass I made of myself!"

"… *Of cloudless climes and starry skies*…" Valletin struggled to remember the lines.

"You wouldn't be the first," Collins said to me. "There's hardly a man in the company who hasn't offered his heart on a platter to that one."

"… *And all that's best of dark and bright*…"

"She's not married, then?"

"She'd hardly be chasing across the country with us if she were married, would she? No, she was with the Kendall

Brothers for three years, walking the high wire. Then Mr. Kellar found her. She's never been married, so far as I know, though no doubt there have been offers."

"… *Meet in her aspect and her eyes…*"

Collins rolled his eyes. "You must forgive Valletin. Last night it was Keats." He turned and clapped Valletin on the back. "Why don't you save the poetry for someone who might return the sentiment? How about Miss Perdita Wynn? There's nothing wrong with her, not that I can see."

"Never you mind about Miss Perdita," said Valletin darkly.

"I've not had the pleasure," I said.

"Pretty as a spring day," said Collins. "And smart, in the bargain. Clever way of speaking. Always has a smile and a kind word. I'd have said you were making great strides with Miss Perdita, Malcolm. Trouble in paradise?"

"She's nothing more than a friend."

"Poor man is hooked and he doesn't even know it."

"I told you. She's just a friendly girl. I enjoy talking with her."

"Is that so?" asked Collins, winking at me in the bar mirror. "I don't suppose you'll mind if Mr. Hardeen here takes his chances, will you? He's a handsome enough sort. Our Miss Perdita might just take a shine to him."

"Now, look," I said, "the last thing I want to do is—"

"Just a friend," Valletin said, a little less confidently. "Nothing more."

I tapped the ash from my cigar. "Do you think there'll be any stage work for me?" I asked, eager to change the subject. "Mr. Kellar mentioned something about needing jugglers."

"I shouldn't wonder," said Collins. "Valletin here is the worst juggler in the world." He looked down the bar at Silent Felsden, who nodded in emphatic agreement.

"Well, perhaps not the absolute worst," Valletin said. "But I can't quite seem to master the overhand pass. I still say it wasn't my fault that night in Springfield."

"What happened in Springfield?" I asked.

"I dropped a flaming torch," he said. "Set fire to the forward curtain."

"Good lord!"

"It wasn't serious. Collins got there with a bucket of sand before any real damage was done. I swear the handles were too slick that night. I doubt if Bellman himself could have kept those torches in the air."

"Hell of a thing," Collins agreed. "If I didn't know better…" His voice trailed off as he stared down into his glass.

"What's that?" I said.

"Nothing. Not really. Just that there have been quite a few queer things going on lately."

"Such as?"

"Oh, nothing to trouble about."

I shifted my weight on the bar stool. "Come on now, Collins. My brother went nose to nose with an escaped lion yesterday. Now you're telling me that there have been other strange goings-on?"

Collins signaled the bar man for another drink. "I first began to notice it last month in Chicago. The old man's Vanishing Lamp began to go squiffy. One night it wouldn't vanish at all. After the show, he took an axe to it. Then there were the doves. Dying one right after the other. Thought there might be some disease running through them, so we split 'em up into three separate cages. Kept on dying. Every last one."

"Don't forget the smudgepots," Valletin said.

"What about them?" I asked.

"Well, they kept going off at the wrong times. There's nothing terribly complicated about a smudge pot—bit of powder, a length of fuse—makes a nice little flash and a puff of smoke. But for a week or so they kept going off too soon. Then one night one of them exploded into a million bits. Would have singed the old man's hair, if he had any."

"Mr. Kellar never mentioned any of this," I said.

"Half the things that go on he never hears about," Collins

insisted. "We keep things to ourselves, most of the time. After the smudgepot exploded, Mr. Kellar talked about shutting the show down for a couple of months." Collins swirled his drink in its glass. "He can afford not to work for a couple of months. I can't."

"You say there are things Mr. Kellar doesn't know about?"

Valletin nodded. "Plenty of things. Like the time I was breaking down the gimmicks for 'Through the Looking Glass.' The damn mirror shattered all over me! Could have torn me to ribbons! Then there was the time Felsden fell through the lighting platform in Wichita. Might have broken his neck. I'm telling you, it makes a man think." He examined his cigar, which had now burned down to a stump. "Makes a man think," he repeated.

"It sounds like a bad string of accidents," I allowed, "but surely nothing more than that?"

"I might have thought so," Valletin continued, grinding the cigar stump into a glass ashtray, "but there's too many of them. Too many accidents in a row. Too close together. Some of the fellows are talking about jumping ship."

"Is that so?"

"Sure. There's always the opera. I wouldn't mind settling down to a bit of culture."

"What about you, Collins? Will you be leaving for greener pastures?"

"I'll finish the season," he said. "Don't want to walk out in the middle of a job. Of course, that's assuming I don't get eaten by a lion in the—God! What's he doing here? Doesn't he ever sleep?"

"What?" I asked. "Who?"

Collins gestured toward a corner table where Mr. Lyman, the newspaper man that Kellar had mentioned, was sitting by himself scribbling furiously on a note pad.

"We call him 'Bartleby the Scrivener,'" said Valletin in a lowered tone. "Always writing in that pad of his. Makes me nervous."

"If you ask me, he's a strange bird," Collins said.

"How so?"

"Hard to say, exactly, but he's always making strange remarks. The other day he told me to instruct the company that from that day forward we were to refer to the old man as 'the great and powerful Kellar.' On stage and off. When I refused, he called me a 'nasty old humbug.' What can you do with a fellow like that?"

"To be candid, my brother constantly refers to himself as 'The Great Houdini,' and he has even been known to introduce me as 'the brother of the Great Houdini,' as though I had no name of my own."

"Well, I'm sure you and Lyman will get along famously, then," Valletin said. "He seems to have taken a shine to you already."

I glanced at the mirror behind the bar. Sure enough, Mr. Lyman was bent forward staring at the back of my head with an expression of the utmost fascination, while his hand moved in an unceasing motion over the pages of his notebook.

~6~

HARDEEN TO THE RESCUE

THE NEXT FOUR DAYS PASSED QUICKLY AS HARRY, BESS AND I FELL into the routine of life with the Kellar show. We set about to learn our performance roles as quickly as possible, and happily took on whatever backstage duties came our way.

As expected, I was given a turn as a juggler during the novelty interlude between acts, and I blush to recall that Mr. Kellar was greatly impressed by my ability to handle clubs, balls and sharp knives with equal facility. I also appeared in Japanese garb and make-up during a routine called 'The Mikado's Foulard,' which involved the production of a great many strange items from within the folds of an apparently innocent handkerchief. I made a second appearance—in evening dress, carrying a silver tray— during 'The Spiritual Decanters,' a clever puzzlement in which any spirit or liquid called for by a member of the audience was poured from a mysterious jeweled vessel.

My small roles suited me quite well, and I was honored to have the opportunity to watch Mr. Kellar perform at such close proximity. Bess, for her part, made no fewer than seven appearances each evening. It was discovered that she was of a similar size and build to a young lady named Mabel, the singer who had recently decamped with a tuba player, leaving behind a trunk filled with elaborate costumes. Bess happily assumed all of Mabel's vacant roles, most of which involved smiling and gesticulating at the successful conclusion of each effect. Within two days, Bess's fine, clear soprano voice had won her a leading spot with "Kellar's Kanaries," who stood before the curtain during scene changes to serenade the audience with popular songs of the day. "Isn't it wonderful, Dash?" she whispered to me one night as she came off stage. "And I don't even have to escape from handcuffs!"

Harry was somewhat less pleased with his role in the company. His appearance as Brakko the strongman in the 'Circus of Wonders' tableau required him to don a leopard-pattern loin cloth and make a series of grunting noises. Later, he would refine the role by swinging a knobbled club. "So it has come to this!" he would exclaim each night as he strapped on his leather sandals. "The Great Houdini is reduced to a mere carnival player!"

I did not share my brother's restiveness. Perhaps I am lacking in ambition, but I cheerfully admit that if things had evolved differently I might have been content to remain with the Kellar show until the great man retired. There would have been enough money to keep me, the duties were interesting but not overly demanding, and there was the prospect of travel to faraway lands. Even then, however, I realized that my fortunes were bound up with those of my brother, whose aspirations had already set him on a more difficult path, carrying lesser souls along in his wake.

I had never been in Albany before, and I found myself anxious to see something of the city. Our mornings were generally free, so I passed the time in taking long, exploratory walks, a habit I developed during our travels with the Welsh Brothers Circus. I believed—and I continue to believe—that there was something to be gained at each stop along the route of a traveling show. One never knew if the opportunity to pass through such places as Newburyport, Massachusetts, or Findlay, Ohio, would ever come again, and no matter how small the town might be I made some effort to get to know it. I always made a special point of trying to sample the local cuisine, a habit that had not yet taken its toll on my waistline. Some of the most pleasant memories I have of my touring days are of the beef and oyster sausages in Wisconsin, and the salty tang of Minnesota's lutefisk.

It was not an interest my brother shared. Throughout his life, no matter where he was in the world, Harry's movements seldom deviated. His tracks ran from the theater to the hotel and back again, with occasional side trips to visit the gravesites of famous magicians. I recall that on one occasion, when he returned from his first tour of France, our mother asked how he had enjoyed Paris. "Not so much," my brother replied. "The dressing room smelled of rotting fish."

Albany was a pleasant city to explore on foot, and a dusting of winter snow lent an especially picturesque aspect. At that time there were many handsome new buildings in various stages of construction—including, I believe, the state capitol—but on the whole the city retained much of the hardy character of its original Dutch founders. I seem to remember that Albany was unusually well supplied with stove manufacturing concerns, which interested me not at all, but also a number of breweries, which merited closer study.

Returning from my walk on our third morning in the city, I found Miss Perdita Wynn seated on one of the quilted pillar-benches in the hotel lobby. At that stage I had met her only once—a brief exchange of greetings during rehearsals, but she had made a forceful impression. She was, as Collins had noted, an exceedingly handsome woman—slim-waisted and fair-skinned—with flowing hair of an arresting shade of red. Her rich, throaty laughter made a delightful accompaniment to each day's rehearsal.

Miss Wynn's face brightened as I came through the revolving door. "Mr. Hardeen!" she cried. "My hero! My absolute hero!"

I lifted my hat, sending a swirl of melting snow onto the maroon carpet. "Miss Wynn," I said, "may I ask how I came to achieve such esteem in your eyes?"

"Because you're just in time!" She stood up and tugged at the hem of her fitted wool jacket. "I'm positively gasping for a cup of tea. And now here you are! Mr. Hardeen to the rescue!"

"But surely—"

"This isn't the city, Mr. Hardeen. I hesitated to go into the parlor without an escort. Would you deny me the pleasure of your company? I would hate to think of you as anything less than gallant."

I suppressed an urge to consult my pocket watch. "I should be honored, Miss Wynn," I said, extending my arm. "A cup of tea is just what I need."

She chatted gaily about a costuming mishap as we were shown to a table by the fire, and gave an animated account of the romantic woes of the property mistress while we waited for our tea. In the firelight, I could not help but notice lines of worry about her eyes and mouth, which seemed strangely at odds with her spirited personality.

"So tell me, Mr. Hardeen," she said when the tea had been poured, "have you and your brother figured out a way to save the season yet?"

"Pardon?"

"It's all over the company. The old man has brought you aboard to figure out the Floating Lady. He seems to feel it's his only hope of fighting off the rising star of Mr. Le Roy."

"Mr. Kellar has managed his career quite admirably up to this point. I'm sure that he would be able to carry on without us."

"But you are working with Collins on the Floating Lady?"

"Of course. Why not?"

"Have you cracked it yet?"

I leaned back and smiled. "So far the solution has eluded us. Perhaps Mr. Kellar has given us too much credit."

"I have every confidence. You and that funny little brother of yours are supposed to be geniuses of some kind. That's what Mr. Valletin says, anyway. And I don't mind telling you, Mr. Hardeen, I enjoy my position with the Kellar company, and I wouldn't want to see the old man get any strange ideas about retiring. I'd be right back with the Gaiety Girls. No, thank you."

"I believe you're exaggerating our abilities."

She tugged at the fingers of one of her gloves. "I doubt it, Mr. Hardeen. I was there when the lion escaped. I saw what your brother did—what both of you did."

"That was Harry's plan. I simply executed it."

She touched her lips with a linen napkin. "Why do you hide your light, Mr. Hardeen? For a man in show business, you're strangely unassuming. Silent Felsden seems to expect a government proclamation every time he figures out how to load a rabbit into a top hat. Malcolm Valletin once spent a good forty minutes showing me how he rigged the vanishing candelabra with two extra flames. But when you trap an escaped lion, you claim it was someone else's doing."

"I told you—"

"Yes. I know. I know how brave and clever your brother is. He's told me so himself, three or four times. But your brother isn't the one stifling an urge to be elsewhere while I drink a cup of tea, so let's talk about you."

"Miss Wynn, I—"

"It's a hobby of mine, you see. Gathering life stories. But you strike me as a bit of a challenge. You're a puzzle with a missing piece. Let's try to solve it, shall we? Are you married, Mr. Hardeen?"

"I—I have not yet had that good fortune, no."

"A handsome fellow such as yourself? You must surely have had your opportunities by now. Still, you're quite young yet. A bit shy, are you? Or perhaps you just haven't found the right girl."

"I'm sure I'm no more shy than the next fellow. As for finding the right girl—"

She wasn't listening. She had leaned forward to peer closely at my eyes, as though conducting a medical examination. "So that's it," she said softly. "Nursing a broken heart. I should have spotted it straight off."

"Miss Wynn, I have no idea what—"

"There, there, Mr. Hardeen," she said, reaching across the table to pat my hand. "Why don't you tell me all about it?"

"I assure you that there is nothing to tell!" I gave a laugh that was meant to sound carefree and worldly.

She favored me with a luminous smile. "Dear boy," she said, "you grow more intriguing by the moment! Now then, was it your childhood sweetheart? Yes, I think it must have been. Young Mr. Hardeen and his sweetheart."

"This is growing absurd."

"Humor me, Mr. Hardeen. In my own case, it was a childhood sweetheart. His name was Douglas Elliott, and he was as staunch and upright a young man as could be found in Yellow Springs, West Virginia. Of course, I was a perfect young lady. We never so much as took a stroll without a chaperone, and he came for dinner each Friday night with my mother and my brother. Afterwards we would sit on the back porch and drink lemonade. We were a perfect couple. Everyone said so."

"And what happened?" I asked, in spite of myself.

"Oh, he ran off with my cousin." She refilled our tea cups and replaced the cozy on the pot. "What about you, Mr. Hardeen? Did she run off with your cousin? No, I expect not. Was it a bible salesman, perhaps? Come along, Mr. Hardeen. I know a broken heart when I see it."

"I assure you that there is no dark secret to be told. I have had my broken romances, of course. But so has everyone else."

"All right, Mr. Hardeen. We'll leave it at that, at least until I can ask your sister-in-law."

"That won't be—"

"Oh, look! Here she is now! How convenient!"

"Dash?" came the familiar voice from the doorway. "There you are! We wondered where you were keeping yourself."

I turned to find Harry and Bess making their way toward us arm in arm. "Good morning, Miss Wynn," said Harry, with a courtly bow. "You are looking especially radiant this morning."

"You are kindness itself, Mr. Houdini." Miss Wynn nodded pleasantly at Bess. "Won't you join us?"

"Thank you," said Bess. "We thought we might have a coffee before Harry left for the theater. He has been up—do sit down, Dash, I'm quite capable—he has been up half the night jotting down things in his notebook."

"I've had a brainstorm!" cried Harry. "Dash, what do you think of this? While Princess Karnac is lying on the levitation banquette, Mr. Kellar reaches beneath his coat for a—"

"Please, Harry," said Bess. "Can we spend a few moments discussing something other than the levitation of Princess Karnac?" She turned to Miss Wynn. "You've slept well. I trust?"

"Oh, indeed."

"And your room is comfortable?"

"Exceedingly so." Miss Wynn's voice was bright but distant. "Quite remarkably comfortable."

"Perdita?" said Bess. "Are you all right? You have the strangest expression on your face!"

Miss Wynn gave a start. "Do I? You must forgive me. I have only just noticed that you bear the most startling resemblance to an old friend of mine, Mrs. Houdini. It really is quite extraordinary!"

"How very strange," said Bess, laughing.

"With respect, Miss Wynn," said Harry genially, "I don't see how your friend could possibly be as lovely as my wife."

"How very gallant," she replied. "Perhaps you and your brother are more alike than I imagined, Mr. Houdini." She bestowed another incandescent smile upon me. "It was so kind of him to sit with me this morning."

"I assure you that the pleasure was mine," I said, rising from my seat, "but I fear that I must now leave you in the capable hands of my sister-in-law. Harry, we really should be getting to the theater."

"Quite right," said Harry, leaping out of his chair. "A very good day to you, Miss Wynn."

"Mr. Hardeen?" she called after me.

"Yes," I said, pausing at the door.

"I'm so glad we had a chance to work on that little puzzle."

"Fascinating woman," said Harry, as we walked along Main Street toward the theater. "Quite attractive, as well."

"Harry…"

"Mama thinks you're getting too set in your bachelor ways."

"I'm not sure Mama is ready for Miss Perdita Wynn," I said. "I'm not sure any of us are."

Harry chuckled. "I hate to see you mooning over that Francesca Moore when there's a far more—how shall I say it?—a far more realistic possibility on the horizon. I think Miss Wynn is a peach. Did you see the way she and Bess hit it off?"

"I haven't been mooning over Francesca," I said, petulantly.

"No? I don't suppose that's a new necktie, either? I don't suppose that's a fresh collar and cuffs?"

I adjusted my collar pin. "I needed a new tie." I said.

"Oh, certainly, And I suppose you also needed to spend the better part of yesterday lounging in a chair near Miss Moore's dressing room, searching for occasions to strike up a conversation."

"It's a comfortable chair."

"As you wish, Dash."

"She said good morning to me yesterday."

"My dear fellow!" cried Harry. "My warmest congratulations! Have you selected a date yet?"

I ignored him. "Small steps, Harry," I said, echoing a favorite phrase of our mother's. "Everything in small steps."

We arrived at the theater to find Collins, Vallelin and Silent Felsden huddled over the fragile-looking levitation banquette. "Houdini!" called Collins, as we made our way through the empty house. "Hardeen! I think we may have something here!"

Harry and I climbed onto the stage. "We think we may have been going about this from the wrong angle." said Valletin, gesturing at the banquette. "We've been trying something new with Matilda here."

"Matilda?"

Valletin indicated a wooden mannequin, dressed to resemble Francesca Moore in her Princess Karnac costume, lying atop a thin padded surface. "Watch this."

Collins rolled the banquette to the front of the stage on its dragon-foot casters. "Here's how it will appear to the audience." he said, rolling back his cuffs. "Mr. Kellar will set the scene, speaking of the ancient miracle of levitation and so on. Miss Moore will step from the wings and allow herself to be placed into a hypnotic state." Collins waved his hands over the mannequin's face, as though placing it into a trance. "Next, we cover her with this large buckram cloth—"

"Why the cloth?" Harry asked.

"To hide the wires, of course."

Harry folded his arms. "I know that, Mr. Collins. I meant, what's the sell?"

"Harry's right," I said. "There should be a reason why the Princess is being hidden from view. Otherwise, when the audience sees her being covered up, it may break the spell. They're likely to ask themselves why she's being hidden. They'll assume that it's part of the secret of the trick. If we could—"

"There must be a story," Harry insisted. "If we could suggest a reason for the cloth without interrupting the story—"

"I see what you mean," said Collins. "All right. What about this? The beautiful Princess Karnac is fleeing from an evil Pasha who wants to make her his bride. You should like that, Houdini. It's just like your Substitution Trunk."

"A Pasha?" asked Harry.

"Why not?"

"Isn't that Turkish? I thought the Princess was Indian."

Collins sighed. "A travelling Pasha, perhaps. In any case, the princess is forced to flee to preserve her maidenhood, and seeks the protection of the powerful wizard—Mr. Kellar."

"Good," said Valletin. "He'll like that."

Silent Felsden nodded his agreement.

"We'll build the whole effect around it," Collins continued. "No sooner does the princess arrive than we hear the Pasha's men banging at the door. What does Kellar do? He throws his cloak over her, hiding her from view."

"Excellent!" cried Harry.

"But the Pasha's men storm in, and just as they are about to discover the hiding place of the Princess, the wizard waves his hands and causes her to float away to safety."

"Leaving the Pasha's men astonished and fearful," added Harry. "Very good, Mr. Collins."

"I'm sure Mr. Kellar will improve upon it," said Collins briskly. "He generally does. Now, have a look at what Silent Felsden has for us." Collins lifted the mannequin to show an intricate harness fashioned from leather, metal and whalebone. It looked like a cross between a corset and a suit of chainmail.

"How does it work?" Harry asked.

"Watch," said Collins, as Felsden threaded a thin hemp rope through the harness and ran it to a support beam at the back of the stage. "Silent has a wooden pulley back there. We'll run it through so that the rope forms a continuous loop. Of course, if this works, we'll lengthen the rope and run it into the dome."

Harry and I exchanged an incredulous look. "You mean to say that someone off stage will be lugging on the rope?" he asked. "Princess Karnac will be hoisted from the stage to the dome on a rope pulley?"

"Like a clothes-line?" I added.

"That's the general idea," said Valletin. "Of course, it will take two or three of us pulling at once to manage her weight."

"It's very ingenious," I said cautiously, "but has any provision been made to keep the audience from seeing the rope?"

"Yes," Harry put in. "It seems a bit conspicuous."

"We'll dye it black and keep the lights low," said Valletin.

"But still—" Harry began.

"Let's just try it," said Collins. "We'll worry about concealing the rope once we've satisfied ourselves that the harness works."

Collins bent over Matilda for a moment, fastening the harness into place and adjusting the angle and tension of the rope. "Pardon me, old girl," he said, patting the mannequin on the shoulder, "I just need to secure this one last—there we go! All right, Silent. Get into position."

Felsden scrambled up a ladder at the back of the stage and grabbed hold of the far end of the rope, which was cleated onto a pulley near the fly curtains.

"Right." Collins walked around the front of the banquette, talking himself through the sequence of events. "The curtain comes up to show Mr. Kellar in his wizard's lair. The princess arrives and begs for his protection. He places her under a protective hypnosis. She will begin to topple backward, but a pair of assistants will catch her before she falls." Harry and I stepped forward and went through the motions of easing the hypnotized Matilda onto the banquette.

"Very good," Collins continued. "Now Mr. Kellar hears a noise in the distance—it's the evil Pasha's men." He moved beside the banquette, snatching a tarpaulin from a nearby crate. "There's hammering at the door. Mr. Kellar hides Princess Karnac with his cloak just as the door flies open and the Pasha's men rush in. Mr. Kellar is undaunted, he gives a magical incantation, and the princess miraculously begins to rise into the air." Collins waved a hand. "Now, Silent."

At this, the wooden representation of Princess Karnac was meant to rise from the banquette and float gracefully through the empty space above the stage. Sadly, this was not precisely what happened. Matters got off to an inauspicious start when Matilda lurched down the length of the banquette with a sudden start, banging her head against the forward edge as she passed. The wooden figure then bounced up and down in the manner of a hooked fish while Felsden struggled to control the movements.

"Uh, Silent—?" Collins looked up at the top of the ladder.

"Give him a minute," said Valletin. "He's almost got it."

But Matilda had now turned head-down so that her legs were pointing to the heavens. As the covering cloth slipped to the stage, we could see her skirts slipping earthward in a most indecorous manner.

"I knew a girl like that in Paris once," said Valletin.

By now the creaking of the pulley-cleat could be plainly heard, and with each tug of the rope the mannequin seemed to strike a new and increasingly lurid pose. After a moment, by which time Matilda had succeeded in traveling only two feet into the air, Collins motioned for Silent Felsden to cease his exertions. "I think that will do," he said, unhooking the mannequin from its leather harness. "I guess we need to go back to the drawing board."

"We could always grease the pulley," said Valletin.

"Why bother?" asked Collins dejectedly. "Even if we could figure out a way to hide the ropes, we'll never manage to stabilize that harness. Miss Moore would be gyrating like a top."

"The gentlemen in the gallery might enjoy it," Valletin offered.

Collins ignored him. "Two days," he said. "Mr. Kellar wants to be ready to debut the Levitation of Princess Karnac in two days." He pushed a lock of hair from his eyes. "Houdini, if you have a suggestion, I'd be very happy to hear it."

"I'm afraid my brother and I are at something of a disadvantage," Harry said. "We've never seen any version of the Floating Lady."

"You've never seen the Maskelyne version?"

"We've never been to London," I said.

"Of course, I keep forgetting." Collins said. "Wait a moment." He darted into the wings and returned a moment later with a large tube of rolled broadsheets. "This is how Mr. Maskelyne's presentation appears to the audience," he said, displaying a colorful theatrical poster. It showed a gentleman in a riding jacket and breech leggings rising horizontally from a bare stage.

Nearby, a pair of performers in Japanese garb were waving a pair of fans, as though creating a gentle breeze to lift the floating figure higher into the air.

"Impressive," I said.

"Indeed," said Collins. "Read what it says there." He pointed to a small box of text in the lower corner.

" 'Trapped By Magic,' " I read. " 'Mr. Maskelyne's latest illusory sketch, introducing the most astounding mysteries ever witnessed, in one of which a performer rises into space in full light, and a solid steel hoop, which is examined by the audience before and after it is used, is passed completely over him from head to foot.' "

"How is that possible?" Harry asked.

"I'll show you," said Collins, unrolling a second broadsheet. "Here, as you can see—"

"Mr. Collins!" Harry cried. "Those are the blueprints for Mr. Maskelyne's effect!"

Collins looked up from the page with a bemused expression. "So they are, Houdini."

"But—but—how do you come to have them?"

"Professional secret, Houdini." He glanced at Valletin, who was whistling and glancing heavenward in a showy display of innocence.

"I take it Mr. Le Roy isn't the only one who has spies about?" I said.

Collins grinned. "You may be right about that, Hardeen. In any case, these plans aren't of much practical use. Take a look."

"Wondrous," Harry murmured, scanning the intricate markings. "The man who created this must be a genius."

"But it's even bigger than we imagined," I said. "The hoisting apparatus is the largest winch I've ever seen. I haven't seen such a device since the Brooklyn Bridge was completed!"

"Totally impractical for a touring magician," Collins agreed. "There's no possible way that this device will ever leave London. Even if we could recreate it here, the presentation would never satisfy Mr. Kellar."

"But why not?" Harry asked. "It seems to have done very well for Mr. Maskelyne."

"Mr. Maskelyne is content merely to present the spectacle," Collins said. "Mr. Kellar wishes to be the featured player. Look at this illustration—" he pointed to the two Japanese men crouched beneath the floating figure "—which one of them is the magician? Is it one of the two men waving the fans, or is it the one who's floating?"

"I see your point," Harry said.

"Now look at this," Collins continued. "It's Mr. Kellar's poster—just off the presses." He unrolled a large tube of paper and spread it across the stage. The image showed Mr. Kellar standing upon a curtained stage with his arms outstretched. The figure of Princess Karnac, draped in her loose-fitting Indian garb, hovered in empty space just beyond the magician's fingertips. In the foreground, a trio of men whispered excitedly to one another, presumably about the miracle unfolding before them. The single word 'Kellar' was splashed across the bottom of the illustration, in the familiar, upward-sweeping block letters that he had used for many years.

"Do you see the difference?" Collins asked. "In the Maskelyne poster, there's no focus. With Mr. Kellar's version, it's as plain as the nose on your face. Kellar waves his hands—the lady floats. That's the impression he means to convey, and that's what we have to create on stage."

"Very dramatic," I said.

"You don't know the half of it," Collins said. "Here's the description Mr. McAdow is having printed up in the program." He handed over a sheet of paper.

" 'The Levitation of Princess Karnac,' " I read aloud. " 'The most daring and bewildering illusion, and by far the most difficult achievement ever attempted. Absolutely new in principle. The dream in mid-air of the dainty Princess Karnac surpasses the fabled feats of the ancient Egyptian sorcerers, and it lends a resemblance to the miraculous tales of levitation that come out of India. It is the most profound achievement of either ancient or modern magic. Its perfection represents thirty years of patient research and obtuse study, and the expenditure of many thousands of dollars. The result of these labors is a veritable masterpiece of magic, the sensational marvel of the nineteenth century, and the crowning achievement of Mr. Kellar's long and brilliant career.'"

I handed the paper back to him. "I gather that Mr. McAdow is not one for understatement."

"Hardly," said Collins. "Of course, it's left to us to make certain that it actually happens. I don't know whether—"

"The dome," Harry said.

Collins looked up from the illusion plans. "Pardon?"

"I would be surprised if Maskelyne's floating figure is able to rise more than four feet above the stage," Harry said. "Not if this apparatus works in the manner that I believe it must. What's more, a conventional winch would lift the figure straight up above the stage. But Mr. Kellar has made it clear that he will settle for nothing less than a Floating Lady who rises out over the heads of the audience until she has reached the very dome of the theater."

"A winch doesn't help us," Valletin agreed. "Neither does 'thirty years of patient research and obtuse study,' apparently."

"The dome is the key to the entire effect," said Harry. "The dome at the Belasco must be a good seventy feet high!"

"Seventy-two and a half."

"Even better!" cried Harry.

"I can't imagine why you'd think so, Houdini," said Collins. "I've been trying to talk the old man out of it ever since he came up with the idea. I could just about see giving him a levitation roughly equal to the Maskelyne effect, but the dome is just too much. He's got his heart set on it because of—Houdini? What are you doing?"

My brother had wandered off into the wings and was pawing through an open crate of juggling props. "I'm just thinking," he said. "Carry on with what you were saying."

"He's got his heart set on it because of his kindly old teacher. The Wizard of Kansas, or whatever his name was."

"Kalliffa."

"Right. But every time we try to give him what he wants, we get buffaloed by—Houdini? What are you doing now?"

Harry had climbed onto the Floating Lady banquette and was holding a red juggling ball up to the lights. "Ignore me," he said. "Pretend you don't see me."

Collins looked at me and raised his eyebrows. I shrugged. "Well, as I was saying, I've now devised four or five perfectly acceptable methods of doing a levitation. Any other magician would be well satisfied. But unless we find a way to—unless we find a way—Houdini? That's quite distracting. Would you mind?"

Harry had begun bouncing the rubberized juggling ball off of the stage with such force that it bounced nearly into the curtain rigging. "Pay me no mind," he said, darting out his hand to catch the ball as it dropped. "Just go about your business, if you would." He hurled the ball at the stage once more, and watched as it bounced high overhead.

"Look, Houdini," said Collins, raising his voice a notch. "As much as I hate to interrupt, I believe Mr. Kellar would prefer that you assist us with our little problem."

Harry's hand darted out to catch the ball as it returned, though he nearly lost his footing as the platform shifted beneath his weight. "Oh, that," he said, leaping down from the platform. "I've solved it."

"Pardon?" Collins asked.

Valletin struggled to suppress a smirk. Silent Felsden merely folded his arms and glowered.

"Yes," said Harry. "Quite simple, really." He tossed the red ball to me. "Small steps, Dash," he said. "Everything in small steps."

I caught the ball and examined it as though it might hold some clue to Harry's strange behavior.

"I believe your mistake was in knowing how to approach the problem," Harry was saying. "You have concentrated entirely on devising a means of causing Miss Moore to float."

"Well, Mr. Houdini," said Valletin, "since that is the effect that Mr. Kellar has asked us to achieve, I would say that our approach has been rather sensible."

"Oh, I agree that we must achieve the *effect* of causing the lady to float. It is simply that we will not actually *cause* her to float."

"You've lost me there, Houdini." said Collins. "And I really don't have time for more puzzles right now."

"Harry," I said, trying to head off Collins's rising temper, "if you've really cracked the problem, now would be the time to let us know."

"Feed me the ball, Dash."

"What?"

"Feed me the ball."

"If you say so." He was referring to the throwing, or "feeding," of a series of balls to a juggler—one at a time—so that the performer could handle three or more at once. I drew back my arm and sailed the ball toward him in a gentle arc, so that it would reach him at waist level. Rather than catch it, Harry brought his palms together in a thunderous hand clap. The ball had completely disappeared. "Gone," he said, holding up his empty hands. "Vanished."

Valletin appeared genuinely startled. "Not bad, Houdini," he said, rubbing at his plump cheeks. "Where'd it go?"

"Ah!" Harry walked to the forward edge of the stage and pointed a finger upward. There, wedged between two arms of an ornate chandelier, was the red ball.

"Nice trick," said Valletin, "but what's that got to do with—"

"I get it." I walked back to the center of the stage. "Very good, Harry. Small steps." I ran my eyes from the banquette to the chandelier. "Small steps," I said again. "It might work."

"It will work," Harry said. "It's the only way."

Collins cleared his throat. "Gentlemen? Would one of you

mind letting the rest of us in on the secret?"

"I believe that even Mr. McAdow will agree that it is absolutely new in principle," Harry said. "One might even say that it is the most profound achievement of either ancient or modern magic, and that the result of my labors is a veritable masterpiece of magic."

"What he means to say," I added hastily, "is that he's come up with an interesting variation on the problem which might satisfy Mr. Kellar's requirements."

Collins fixed his eyes on the chandelier. "Time to tip the gaffe, boys."

"It's really very simple," I began. "Harry has just created the illusion of having caused that red ball to travel from the stage to the ceiling, as if it floated there. But in truth, the ball didn't go anywhere. It's actually a simple disappearance, followed by an equally simple reappearance. Harry made one red ball vanish from his hands, and at the same time he made another one appear in the chandelier. To the rest of us, it looked as if the red ball had traveled from one place to another instantaneously."

Collins stroked his chin. "He made one ball vanish and made another one appear."

"So the second ball was already up there in the chandelier the whole time," said Valletin. "Even before you started the trick."

"Exactly," said Harry. "But you had no reason to look until I pointed it out."

"And you're saying that we can work it the same way with Princess Karnac, is that it?"

Collins furrowed his brow. "It might work." He paced back and forth, talking it out to himself. "Princess Karnac comes out and lies down on the banquette. She's covered with a cloth. The audience doesn't realize it, but she's vanished underneath the cloth. Then we figure out a way to make it seem as if she's appeared up in the dome." His head snapped up. "Say, Houdini, how did you make that little ball appear up there, anyway? I never saw you go anywhere near the chandelier."

"Genius," Harry said.

"Foresight," I clarified. "While we were all ignoring him—when he seemed to be playing catch with the ball, he bounced one into the chandelier."

"I prefer my explanation," said Harry.

"Is there some means of causing Miss Moore to appear in the dome of the theater?" I asked. "The disappearance should be fairly straightforward, but I don't know how we'll manage the reappearance."

"I don't see too much difficulty about it," Collins said. "There's a catwalk running around the interior of the dome. We could lay a beam across the middle and have Miss Moore hidden beneath a black cloth. She's a trapeze artist, after all. She'll have no problem getting out onto the beam, so long as we have her attached to a safety harness. Once the house lights go down no one would ever be able to pick her out, even if they did happen to look up, which isn't terribly likely. All we'd have to do is attach some wires to the black cloth so that we can whip it away at the critical moment. It will seem as if she has appeared in mid-air!"

"That's fine for the Belasco," Valletin said, "but what about on tour?"

"I guess we'll have to bridge those domes when we get there. I think this is our best option. Houdini, let me be the first to—"

"Wait a moment," Valletin interrupted. "Aren't we getting a bit ahead of ourselves? Houdini's plan is very clever, I'll admit, but does it actually accomplish what Mr. Kellar wants? The way you've blocked it out, Princess Karnac will disappear from the stage and appear in the dome. It's a good effect, but will we ever actually see her floating in mid-air? It seems to me that unless we actually see the princess travel from the stage to the dome, then we haven't created a Floating Lady illusion."

I fished another red juggling ball out of the prop chest and tossed it to Harry. "Graveyard Ghouls?" I asked.

He nodded. "Exactly."

"You've lost me, gentlemen," said Collins.

"It's an idea we had a couple of years ago," I said. "We were travelling with the Marco Company, working as acrobats."

"You were an acrobat," Harry corrected. "I was an escape artist extraordinaire."

"Fine, Harry. In any case, sometimes the crowds would be a little thin, and Mr. Marco would lay on an added attraction for the late night shows. He'd do a ghost and goblin routine called 'The Graveyard Ghouls.' Harry and I would dress up in black costumes so that no one could see us against the black backdrop. Then we'd wave a lot of skeletons and tambourines in the air so that it looked as if they were floating around by themselves."

"Black art," said Collins. "We used to do a bit of that with the Herrmann show. But I don't really see how that helps us."

"It doesn't, but this part does. Mr. Marco began making a lot of money on the ghost show, so he added a special improvement mid-way through the tour. Marco had been a bit of an explorer in his younger days, and he always carried a lantern projector with him on tour, because whenever the opportunity arose he liked to earn a little extra by giving a 'mind-improving lecture' about his visit to Egypt with the Berrier expedition. He had a set of twelve slides painted onto glass—the pyramids, the sphinx, a couple of camels—and he spaced them out over forty minutes while he droned on about the ancient grandeur of Egypt. People sat through the lecture in order to marvel over the images, which were projected onto a large white wall. It was an amazing spectacle."

"I saw a lecture like that once," said Valletin. "Ancient Greece. The man had a lantern slide of the Parthenon. You'd have sworn it was right there. You could just about touch it."

I nodded. "The projector gives a remarkably lifelike effect. So when the ghost show caught on, Mr. Marco decided to use lantern slides to spice it up a little. He took three glass slides and painted them with images of ghosts, goblins and grinning skulls."

"Pepper's ghost," said Collins. "What you're describing is just a version of the old Pepper's Ghost illusion. You take a lantern projector and show slides of ghosts on a sheet of glass. The glass is angled so the audience never sees it, but the ghosts look very lifelike. If you get fancy, it doesn't even have to be slides. If you work it with a mirror, you can even dress someone up like a ghost and have them move around. Is that what you're getting at? We should project an image of a Floating Lady onto glass?"

"It'll never work," said Valletin. "The last time we had a Pepper's Ghost at the Egyptian Hall, the glass sheet weighed upwards of five hundred pounds. It took over a week to install. There's no possible way that you could tour with it. What if it fell?"

"We found a way to do it without glass," I said.

"No glass?" Collins took a look upward at the ceiling. "How?"

"The ghost show always had a lot of smudge pots going, to create a spooky atmosphere," I said. "The smoke also helped to hide what was going on behind the scenes. Harry and I discovered that if we added some extra potter's ash to the pots, they gave off a particularly thick column of white-colored smoke. If we then projected a lantern slide onto the smoke, it looked as if there were ghosts darting in and out."

Collins closed his eyes for a moment. "Is it possible? Could that actually work?"

"I'm telling you, the ghosts were very convincing. If we keep the lights low, and just show them a couple of glimpses—"

"I don't get it," Valletin said. "I'm sorry, but I don't see what you're driving at."

Collins walked to the center of the stage. "We're talking about doing the trick in three stages," he explained.

"Small steps," added Harry.

"First, Princess Karnac disappears from the banquette, right here at the center of the stage." He stepped forward and waved his hands over the orchestra pit. "Then the audience catches a glimpse of her floating in mid-air, right about here, on a column of smoke. We get ourselves a lantern slide of the Princess looking hypnotized, stretched out like she's on some kind of magic carpet." Collins trotted down the stage steps and moved halfway up the center aisle. "Then we see her again about there," he said, pointing over his head, "only she's farther away this time, as though she's actually moving upward."

"Exactly," Harry said. "And we use spotlights to control where the audience is looking at each phase."

"Until finally—" Collins moved further up the aisle. "She's all the way up in the dome. Hell, she could even look down and wave at us."

"Right," I said, "because it won't be a lantern slide by the time she appears in the dome. She'll have had time to get up there from the stage while the audience is busy looking at the projections. It'll really be her up there, suddenly popping into view."

Collins rubbed his jaw, reviewing each stage of the plan. "There's got to be a flaw," he said. "I can't believe that'll work."

"It'll work," Harry insisted.

"How can you be so certain?"

Harry took the red juggling ball, threw it hard against the stage floor, and watched as it arced upward into the branches of the chandelier. "Because," he said, "it's the only idea I have."

7

MR. KELLAR'S FINEST HOUR

"I ASSURE YOU, MR. LYMAN," HARRY WAS SAYING, "I AM NOT A humbug."

"You're sure?" Lyman asked genially. "I've heard you talking about all those things you can do. The handcuff escapes. Leaping from bridges while tied up in chains. Getting out of ropes. It all sounds like a lot of humbug to me."

"Dash," Harry caught my eye in the dressing room mirror, "what does he mean by that word?"

"Phoney," I said. "A fraud."

"Ah. A *shmegegge*." Harry turned back to Lyman. "Mr. Lyman, the Great Houdini is not a humbug. Of that you may be assured."

Harry and I were backstage donning our costumes for Kellar's return to the Belasco, back in New York City. The performance would feature the debut of the Levitation of Princess Karnac, and the last-minute preparations had left us pressed for time. My brother had barely found time to slip into his "Brakko the Strongman" costume as the five-minute bell rang, and I was busy hunting around for the floppy cap that I wore with my juggler's motley.

We had been working without pause for two days. Having secured Mr. Kellar's approval to develop the illusion along the lines Harry and I had devised, we spent an afternoon of frantic activity in Albany securing the necessary materials and props. Mr. Kellar himself supervised the staging and mechanical rehearsals, which continued until the very moment that it was time to strike the set and load the show back onto the train. Now, having installed the illusion at the Belasco, Harry and I had only a few moments to get into make-up before the curtain went up. For some reason, Mr. Lyman had chosen this moment to park himself in the dressing area and unleash a barrage of strange questions.

"Why are you so concerned about Harry's humbuggery?" I asked.

"I assure you that I mean no disrespect!" Lyman cried. "I've done a bit of humbuggery myself over the years. I've worked all sorts of angles—printer, crockery salesman, chicken farmer, small town newspaper man—I even sold axle grease at one stage. But I never thought of becoming a 'self-liberator.' That one got right past me!"

Harry smeared a bit of Tucker's paste onto his cheeks, hoping to make himself look ruddy and virile under the hot lights. "It's not an angle, Mr. Lyman. I am the world's foremost escape artist. There is no bond on earth that can hold Houdini a prisoner. One day my name will be as famous as that of Mr. Kellar. You may be certain of that, Mr. Lyman."

"Frank. Call me Frank." He pushed his spectacles up on his nose and flipped back a sheet of his note pad. "You see, that's just the sort of thing I wanted to know. 'World's foremost escape artist.' That's very good!"

I settled my cap onto my head and pushed the dangling balls away from my face. "May we ask which of your many professions you are pursuing at the moment?"

Lyman put a finger to his lips. "Can't say! Bit of a secret! But it's important that I come to know a bit about everyone who works for the great and powerful Kellar."

"You mentioned that you've worked as a journalist," I said. "Are you writing a story about Mr. Kellar?"

"Let's suppose I were," Lyman said carefully. "Let's suppose that I were gathering information for a story such as the one you propose. I would have to be very careful to cast the material into a form that his many admirers might care to read, wouldn't I? If I were writing a story about a politician, say, or a barrister, my path would be clear. I would take down the particulars of his accomplishments and the broad outline of his rise to the top, and then I would set it down on paper, largely without embellishment."

I glanced anxiously at my pocket watch. "Mr. Lyman—"

"Frank."

"Frank, the show is beginning. Harry and I are due on stage in a few moments."

"How very interesting!" He made a note on his pad. "Now, in Mr. Kellar's case there are a goodly number of events and happenings which would quite naturally make for interesting reading. Did you know, for instance, that he was once shipwrecked in the Bay of Biscay? He lost everything he owned—his props and costumes, his personal effects, and more than $20,000 worth of gold and silver!"

I glanced again at my watch. "A fascinating tale, but—"

"As fate would have it, Mr. Kellar was wearing a diamond ring when he struggled ashore on the island of Moleno. He sold the ring and managed to start over again from scratch! That is the measure of the man, wouldn't you say?" He thumbed back a few pages of his pad. "But where I would run into difficulty is in describing the actual things that Mr. Kellar does upon the stage. It is all very well and good to say that he causes a fierce lion to vanish, or that he brings about the magical blooming of a rose bush, but the plain words do not convey the spectacle, the grandeur. I would need to know the details of how he manages to accomplish these feats. Like the levitation of Princess Karnac, for example."

"You want to know how the tricks are done?" Harry asked.

"Well, yes," said Lyman. "I suppose I do. Mr. Collins gets terribly agitated whenever I inquire, and I hate to trouble Mr.

Kellar. I merely want to know for verisimilitude, you understand. It would help me a great deal."

I put a finger to my lips. "Can't say! Bit of a secret!" I cried, echoing Lyman's own words. "Mr. Kellar is most particular about that!"

"But in this case couldn't you—"

"It's against the rules!" I continued. "The penalties are exceedingly harsh!"

"Rules? Penalties?"

"Dash, why didn't you tell me that it had gotten so late?" Harry cried, snatching up his wooden caveman club. "Mr. Lyman, we shall be happy to speak with you after the performance, but right now Dash and I are in danger of missing the curtain." He grabbed my arm and pulled me toward the door.

"Can't have that!" he called after us. "Until later, then!"

"Harry, I'm quite capable of walking," I said as he dragged me down the corridor. "You can let go of my arm."

"That man is a spy!" he said in a fierce whisper. "Snooping around Mr. Kellar's secrets! It's just as bad as Collins said!"

"I think you're jumping to conclusions," I said as we slipped into our places behind the curtain. "After all, Mr. Kellar seems to be cooperating with him. If he were after secrets, he's had plenty of chances to dig around backstage."

"But he doesn't understand what he sees," Harry answered. "He needs someone who can explain the workings to him." He hefted his club as the orchestra music reached its crescendo. "I'm keeping my eye on Frank Lyman," he said, turning to face front just as the curtain began to lift.

I suppose there must be half a dozen or so of us left who were privileged to share a stage with Harry Kellar. More eloquent voices than mine have spoken of his grace upon the stage, his charming manner, and his consummate skill. I may only add that his presentations were no less miraculous when viewed from behind the curtain, and that the repetition of many nights of performance—together with matinees on Wednesdays and Saturdays—did nothing to diminish the wonder I felt each time the lights went up. "Once I gain the full attention of an audience," Mr. Kellar was fond of saying, "a brass band playing at full blast can march openly across the stage behind me, followed by a herd of elephants, yet no one will realize that they have passed by." He always spoke this maxim as a jest rather than a boast, but I would not be surprised if it were literally true.

Although Mr. Kellar was skilled at the presentation of large illusions, I must confess that I greatly preferred the effects he called his "one-handers"—the smaller-scale platform effects that relied on pure sleight of hand. Many years have passed since Kellar held a stage, and we have grown accustomed to bigger and more dramatic spectacles in our entertainments. In an age when it has become commonplace to see a gigantic gorilla cavorting across a movie screen, it is difficult to convey the excitement that a single man was able to produce with a few everyday props. If there was one effect that may be said to have captured the quiet glamor of Mr. Kellar's magic, I suppose it would be "Coffee and Milk," a trick of uncommon charm. The spectacle began as Mr. Kellar displayed a pair of nickel-plated containers that looked rather like cocktail shakers. Turning each container toward the audience, he rattled a magic wand around inside to prove that they were empty. Setting them aside, Mr. Kellar dipped his hand into a wooden box containing brown paper scraps, bringing out a handful and letting them drift back down into the box. He then filled one of the containers with scraps and set it on a stand some feet away. He repeated the procedure with a second box containing white scraps. At this, an assistant came forth holding a tray and two empty glass jugs. Mr. Kellar recited a few magic words as he tapped each of the two metal containers with his magic wand. Instantly, the brown shavings were transformed into steaming hot coffee, which he poured out into one of the glass jugs, while the second container was found to contain a great quantity of frothy milk.

As applause filled the air. the coffee and milk were promptly served out to members of the audience. This effect, and a great many others, passed in a smooth procession of wonder that night at the Belasco. From backstage, however, one could sense a perfunctory haste about Mr. Kellar that night, as though he were impatient to reach the new centerpiece of his act—the Floating Lady effect.

Harry and I watched from the wings as Mr. Kellar concluded his penultimate effect, in which an audience member's watch was borrowed, ground into useless bits with a mortar and pestle, and then miraculously restored. Acknowledging the applause with a deep bow, Mr. Kellar stepped forward into the footlights to introduce the levitation. "Ladies and gentlemen," he began in the crisp, familiar tones, "this evening's performance marks the culmination of a life's ambition. Since my earliest days on the stages of vaudeville and the burlesque halls, I have dreamed of presenting the effect you are about to witness. I ask for complete silence as the illusion begins, for even the slightest disturbance may disrupt the delicate atmosphere we are endeavoring to create."

As he spoke, the heavy front curtains closed behind him to allow for the final change of scene. Harry and I fell in with the rest of the stagehands to dress the stage. A scenery flat depicting a wizard's castle dropped down from the braces; the dragon-footed levitation banquette was rolled out on casters; Miss Moore's costume was checked by the wardrobe mistress; and various Indian-themed artifacts and pottery pieces were placed into position.

From the front of the stage, muffled by the heavy curtain, we could hear Kellar bringing his remarks to a close. "... And so it is my pleasure to offer you the crowning miracle of my career—my finest hour upon the stage—the Levitation of Princess Karnac!"

Harry and I darted back to the wings as the curtain slowly rose. The lights had fallen to one-third to create a suitably portentous atmosphere, and the musicians in the orchestra pit struck up a somewhat sinister melody. As he walked upstage,

Kellar snatched up a flowing buckram cloak and threw it about his shoulders, assuming the role of the powerful wizard.

The playlet unfolded much as we had outlined it with Collins and Valletin. Mr. Kellar was seen experimenting with a beaker of some powerful unguent while his apprentice, played by Mr. Valletin, attended in the background. We heard the sounds of a disturbance as Miss Moore, her eyes flashing behind a heavy veil, rushed onto the stage.

A brief exchange of dialogue established the dark intent of the evil Pasha, whose men were immediately heard to be hammering upon the door of the castle.

"Kind sir!" Miss Moore cried. "I beg of you! Hide me from the Pasha's minions!"

"You shall be safe, my child!" answered Kellar, waving his hands before her face. Miss Moore's eyes appeared to grow heavy and her head dropped forward. Kellar and Valletin gently eased her onto the ornate banquette.

"Summon my guards!" Kellar called to Valletin as the sound of hammering at the door grew louder. "Be quick!" With this he took off the heavy cloak and threw it over Miss Moore's recumbent form, hiding her from the view of the audience.

Harry tugged at my sleeve. "Perfect," he said in hushed tones. "It's working perfectly."

On stage, Kellar stepped behind the levitation banquette and began moving his hands in slow passes above Princess Karnac's sleeping form. The music increased in intensity as the sounds of splintering wood were heard. Silent Felsden, wearing an embroidered tunic and gold sash, rushed onto the stage in the guise of the evil Pasha. He brandished a scimitar while a pair of his henchmen rushed toward the banquette.

"Here we go!" Harry cried, rocking back and forth on the balls of his feet. "This is it!"

The Pasha and his men were momentarily staggered by a brilliant flash of light from Kellar's outstretched hand. Then, as the music reached a fevered crescendo, the shape beneath the buckram cloak began to stir.

"Please," Harry whispered, "don't let anything go wrong."

Slowly at first, then gathering a strange momentum, the draped figure rose from the platform and hovered in empty space, as though lying on an invisible palette. Silent Felsden and his henchmen dropped to their knees and averted their eyes, too overcome to look upon the spectacle. By now the form of the princess had risen just to the level of Kellar's head. He moved underneath the floating figure and swept his hands back and forth, urging the figure to rise higher still.

"Excellent," Harry murmured. "There can be no possibility of any supports or props beneath her. Not with his arms flailing around like that."

"So far so good," I agreed.

Just then, the evil Pasha appeared to gather his resolve. With a shrill cry, he charged forward, waving his scimitar high over his head. Kellar thrust out his hands and a second burst of flame shot forth.

"Now!" Harry cried, caught up in the moment in spite of himself.

The stage lights fell dark, replaced by a circle spotlight showing Kellar at center stage. Felsden lay at his feet, stunned into submission. Reaching upward, Kellar brushed the trailing edge of the cloak that covered the floating form of the princess as a pair of smudgepots erupted at the foot of the stage. When the flash subsided, Kellar stood alone at the edge of the stage, his arms raised toward the empty space above his head. The princess had vanished in mid-air. Thunderous applause greeted this miracle, but Kellar did not acknowledge it. Instead, he shielded his eyes like a sailor on lookout, fixing his gaze on a point in the middle distance.

Harry's hands were clenched with excitement. "Now! The smoke column!"

Above the heads of the audience a sudden burst of flame erupted. Shrieks of alarm and surprise could be heard as a thick column of white smoke drifted upwards, highlighted by the glow of a tracking spotlight. Kellar's voice filled the hall. "Cast your eyes heavenward, my friends, and watch as she rises… rises…rises… Now she flings aside the high-flown theories of gravity and science like so much useless chaff. See how she floats, as though on a gentle zephyr, borne aloft by the hypnotic force of animal magnetism."

The sounds of astonishment rose like steam from a kettle. There flickering amid the billows and curls of smoke was the draped figure of Princess Karnac floating high above the crowd, still lost in the grip of Kellar's trance. For a moment she seemed to waver and undulate, then she vanished as the light dimmed.

Kellar spoke again from the stage. "Now she is almost beyond our earthly grasp, ascending like Icarus himself toward the sky. Surely the gods themselves must watch in wonder as she floats up toward the vault of heaven."

More shrieks were heard as a second geyser of flame burst forth. "There she is!" came a cry from the balcony, in a voice that sounded suspiciously like that of Connell, the theater warden. "I see her!"

The audience craned to get a look as a second column of white smoke hovered in the air. Once again the spectral image of Princess Karnac could be seen—more distant this time— nearing the high dome of the theater. "Can we believe our eyes?" came Kellar's voice from the stage. "Can we trust our senses when they behold that which is plainly impossible? Still she rises…higher and higher…borne aloft by a power we mortals cannot begin to comprehend."

Again the lights went dim. "This is it!" Harry whispered, as we peered through a gap in the curtains. "Miss Moore has had time to get into position! They will see that she has really been transported to the very pinnacle of the theater! I made this happen!" His face was shining with excitement. "It is all due to Houdini!"

From the stage, Kellar's voice took on a sepulchral tone.

"Prepare to disbelieve the evidence of your own eyes, for now the lovely princess has neared the end of her strange journey. Soaring to the heavens, lifted by forces we cannot fathom, she completes her wondrous ascent. Behold!" Kellar thrust his hands up toward the dome.

"Now!" Harry cried. "The lights!"

To my dying day, I shall never forget what I saw when the lights came on. For the briefest moment, it appeared as if all was well. The draped figure of Miss Moore could be plainly seen suspended at the very apex of the dome. Slowly, as we had rehearsed, the corners of the buckram cloak lifted so that we would be able to see the recumbent form of the princess sleeping peacefully beneath. The effect had been magnificent in rehearsal that afternoon. "It is the best finish to any illusion I have ever seen," Kellar had said. "It will be the talk of New York!"

Indeed, the great man had been correct, though not in the manner he had foreseen. As the corners of the cloak lifted upward, we heard a strange creaking sound, punctuated by a tremulous scream.

"Good lord!" cried Harry. "That sounds like—"

His words were cut short as the figure of the princess suddenly twitched and writhed beneath the cloak. Another scream was heard. I glanced at Kellar. His face was ashen.

"No!" Harry shouted. "She's going to—"

It happened too quickly for action. As we watched in horror, the hovering form of the princess dipped and tossed, as though it were a marionette whose strings were being snapped one by one. *My God!* I thought to myself. *Seventy-two and a half feet!*

Harry burst through the curtains and made for the center aisle, with me close on his heels. "Hurry, Dash!" he shouted, racing to the forward lip of the stage. "Hurry!" Harry took a running leap off the forward edge of the stage, barely clearing the orchestra pit as he landed in a heap at the feet of the front row of the audience. He regained his footing in an instant, while I followed as closely as possible down the side steps of the stage.

Cries of alarm could be heard from every corner of the theater, but the audience melted into a faceless blur as Harry and I raced up the center aisle. We had travelled only a few yards when our path was blocked by panicked audience members rushing toward the exits.

"Please!" cried Harry, squeezing between a pair of beefy tuxedoed gentlemen. "Let me pass! Let me—!"

A long quavering scream cut through the tumult. We froze in our tracks and looked upward. For a moment it seemed as though she might right herself as the gyrations beneath the cloak ceased.

"Dash!" cried Harry. "Look!"

Then she fell, hard and fast, with folds of fabric billowing outward like a useless sail.

I suppose everyone in the theater must have looked away at the moment of impact—everyone except me and Harry. We watched in open-mouthed horror as she fell, perhaps hoping for some last-minute miracle. There was none. The falling figure struck a brass railing with a sickening thud, then caromed into a null space behind the seats.

The entire theater had fallen silent now, and all movement ceased. Harry and I picked our way through the patrons standing stock still in our path. Harry's face was pale and grim, and I suppose my own must have reflected the dread feelings churning within me.

The body lay at a downward angle on the short flight of steps leading to the lobby. Harry crouched beside it and pulled away the tangled cloak. Francesca Moore's lifeless face stared back at us in a rictus of shock, blood trailing from her nose and mouth.

Harry looked away, brushing at his eyes with one hand, steadying himself against a wall with the other. When he spoke, his words were so hushed and labored that I could not be certain I was meant to hear.

"I made this happen," he said, his voice coming in a bitter rasp. "It is all due to Houdini."

8

THE CURSE OF KALLIFFA

"HOUDINI," SAID LIEUTENANT MURRAY, RUBBING AT HIS RED-rimmed eyes. "I might have known you'd be mixed up in this. Dead lady at a magic show. Who else would I expect to find?"

"I assure you I would rather have it otherwise," Harry said quietly.

"Yeah," the lieutenant said with a nod. "I suppose you would at that."

Less than two hours had passed since Miss Moore's tragic fall from the dome of the theater. Somehow Mr. Kellar had summoned the composure to address the audience from the stage, calming them with the crisp authority of his voice as he directed them to depart through the side exits of the theater. It took perhaps twenty minutes for the last of the patrons to file out, by which time the first representatives of the New York City Police Department were on the scene.

Heading the delegation of officers was Lieutenant Patrick Murray, whom Harry and I had come to know the previous year when he investigated the macabre murder of the millionaire Branford Wintour. Tall, red-faced and burly, Lieutenant Murray was sporting his familiar rumpled brown suit and green, egg-stained tie. I noted with relief that he appeared to have changed his shirt in the intervening months. "Hardeen," he said, after he had surveyed the scene, "why don't you fill me in on the particulars?"

I sketched out the details of the tragedy, such as I could, while a pair of leatherheads moved among the company, writing down names and taking statements. My colleagues were scattered throughout the empty theater, leaning against the walls and slumped into seats in postures of shock and disbelief. Collins and Silent Felsden, still in their costumes, were sitting on the edge of the stage with their legs dangling into the pit, passing a flask between them. Valletin and Miss Wynn were side by side in the front row, clutching one another's hands in transparent grief. Harry stood at the top of the center aisle, watching with a stony expression as the police physician examined the body. Bess, carefully averting her eyes from the unpleasant scene, tried in vain to pull him away.

Of all the members of the company, the one who appeared to have been most severely affected was Mr. Kellar himself. He sat with his shoulders sagging in one of the ludicrously jewelled sedan chairs from the 'Circus of Wonders' pageant, looking for all the world like a once-mighty monarch whose kingdom had fallen. Mrs. Kellar stood beside him, curling a protective arm around his shoulders.

Lieutenant Murray listened carefully while I reviewed the details of the evening's performance, and I was struck by his immediate grasp of the salient details. "How long did this Miss Moore have to get from the stage up to the dome?" he asked.

"About nine minutes," I said.

He raised his eyebrows. "It took her nine minutes to go up a few flights of stairs?"

"No. She could easily have made it in two. But Mr. Kellar didn't want the trick to be over too quickly. He wanted it to last twenty minutes from end to end, so there was a lot of business with the evil Pasha's men and so on."

The lieutenant made a note. "I talked to witnesses who said she was in plain sight the whole time. And they say it only took a minute or so for her to float up to the dome."

"That's how it looks from out front,"

"I take it that's not quite how it works?"

"Not quite." I pointed to the levitation banquette. "Once she lies down on that thing and Kellar covers her with the cloth, all bets are off."

"You mean the audience thinks she's there, but maybe she's not really there?"

"You didn't hear it from me."

He nodded, figuring the angles. "So while Kellar was out here doing battle with the forces of evil, she was already on her way up to the dome."

"That's right."

"She go by herself, or was someone with her?"

"Mr. Collins led her up to the catwalk and helped her into the safety harness."

"Collins? Which one's he?"

I pointed to the stage.

"We'll need to speak with him." Murray looked back toward the body, then jerked his thumb at the spot where Harry was keeping his vigil. "Your brother's taking this hard, wouldn't you say?"

"He and I helped to create the illusion—or this particular method of achieving it. If her death was the result of some negligence on our part, I don't know how either one of us will be able to live with it."

By way of an answer, Murray coughed twice into his fist. "He was telling me some cock-and-bull story about an escaped lion. You know anything about that?"

"For once he wasn't exaggerating. He risked his life to help capture it."

"He seems to think it wasn't an accident, the lion getting out like that."

"It appeared as if someone had tampered with the lock on its cage."

"So he said. He seems to think maybe somebody tampered with this Floating Lady rig, too. What do you think about that?"

In spite of myself, I found my eyes drifting back up to the dome. "I don't know, Lieutenant," I said. "It seems—"

"Far-fetched? That's what I said. It seems to me that every time some magician stubs his toe in New York, your brother is out looking for some big sinister conspiracy. This trick you dreamed up, it looks dangerous. I think maybe she just slipped. An accident."

"My brother will have a hard time accepting that. It would be easier on him to have someone to blame. Someone besides himself, I mean. I can't say he's entirely alone."

"Accidents happen. You're not to blame."

"How can you be so sure of that?"

"I'm not. I said it to make you feel better. I don't want you drowning in grief until I'm done with you." He turned again to the back of the theater. "Doc Peterson?" he called.

A round-faced man with an impressive mane of white hair emerged from behind the brass railing. "Yes, Lieutenant?"

"Finding anything interesting?"

"Well, sir, I can't say anything conclusively, but it looks to be about what you'd expect of a fall from such a great height. Contusions, broken limbs, shattered collar bone, concussive—"

Murray held up a hand to stop the litany. "You almost done?"

"Nearly. I'll finish back at the laboratory."

"See me first before you leave. Hardeen?"

"Yes?"

"Let's take Collins and have a look at the dome. We'd better get your brother, too."

I led the lieutenant to the spot where Collins and Silent Felsden were seated and explained what was wanted in a low voice. Collins nodded grimly and stood up, leaving Silent staring gloomily into his glass flask. We headed up the center aisle to where Harry was standing.

"Come on, Houdini," said the lieutenant. "Let's take a look at the catwalk."

Harry looked up from Dr. Peterson's examination of the

body. His face was chalky. "I would prefer to remain here."

Lieutenant Murray rested a hand on the brass railing behind the seats. "I just can't figure you, Houdini. Last year I couldn't get you out from underfoot. Now I'm giving you a chance to stick your nose into a police matter, and you'd rather keep watch down here. I just don't get it."

Harry had returned his attention to Dr. Peterson. "I should stay with Miss Moore," he said.

I looked at him in surprise. It was our father's custom, when one of his congregants passed on, to sit with the body until the proper arrangements could be made. Apparently Harry was heeding the same impulse. I stepped forward and knelt beside him. "Harry," I said quietly, "Dr. Peterson will be taking her away in a few moments. We can be more useful if we try to help Lieutenant Murray. You're just in the way here."

His eyes lingered a moment longer on the broken form of Miss Moore, then he sighed heavily and got to his feet. "Very well," he said. "I shall try to be useful."

With Harry trailing behind, Collins led us out through the lobby and up a flight of steps.

"What's on this level?" Lieutenant Murray asked.

"Business offices and the manager's suite," Collins answered. "Toward the back is the ladies dressing room."

The lieutenant stopped walking. "The ladies dressing room? They have to go through the lobby to get to the stage?"

"No," Collins answered. "There's a back stair. The manager prefers to keep the men and women on separate floors. Says it encourages 'overly familiar congress' otherwise."

" 'Overly familiar congress,' " Murray repeated. "We have a different word for it down at the precinct house."

Fetching a lantern from one of the offices, Collins pushed through an unmarked door and continued the climb along a bare wooden staircase with open slatting. The chamber was oddly-shaped and heavy with cobwebs. Only the light of the lantern kept us safely on the stairway.

"Where the hell are we?" asked Lieutenant Murray."

"This puts us onto the catwalk running along the inside of the dome," Collins said. "Only the riggers ever use it." He flicked the latches on a low hatchway and ducked through onto the catwalk.

The catwalk was actually a circular balcony running along the inside rim of the massive theater dome. Both shallow and narrow, it allowed only about a shoulder's width of space between its low railing and the rising wall of the dome. Seen from below, it blended smoothly with the gilt striping of the interior decor, so that the average patron would not have realized that it existed. From our vantage, the drop was dizzying.

"Lord," said the lieutenant, gripping the low railing.

"Are you all right?" I asked.

"Fine," he said gruffly. "I just—Miss Moore wasn't subject to fear of heights, was she?"

"Hardly," said Collins. "She was a trapeze artist. Seventy feet wouldn't have troubled her much."

"Seventy-two and a half," Harry said.

"Besides," said Collins, "all she had to do was climb out there and wave." He pointed to a makeshift scaffolding that we had rigged the previous afternoon. It was nothing more than a narrow length of planking stretched over the open drop of the dome, supported at each corner by a braided wire. Each wire ran to an eyehook secured by a stout bracket. A black rope ladder stretched from where we stood to the edge of the planking. "You see?" Collins asked. "Simplicity itself. There shouldn't have been anything to it."

"It looks awfully precarious to me," Lieutenant Murray said. "I sure couldn't have made it out there."

"Nor I," said Collins. "But Miss Moore is—Miss Moore was a professional wire walker. When I showed her the rigging, she chided me for making it too easy for her. Still, something was bothering her this evening. Maybe it was just opening night nerves, but she definitely seemed out of sorts."

"How so?" the lieutenant asked.

"She was awfully pale. Barely said a word. Almost as if she had a premonition of some kind."

I reached out and fingered the nearest eyehook and bracket, feeling a jolt of self-recrimination.

"Everything where it should be?" Murray asked, reading my mind.

"I think so."

"The wires look pretty strong," he said.

"They were. Each one of them was strong enough to support her weight. Together they could hold seven hundred pounds. Even if one of them had broken or come loose from its moorings, the other three should have been more than adequate."

The lieutenant reached out and plucked at the nearest support wire. "No slack," he said.

"There isn't supposed to be any," said Collins.

"I take it you helped her onto the platform?" the lieutenant asked.

Collins nodded. "Not that she needed it. She moved like a cat."

"And were you still here when she fell?"

"Don't you think I'd have tried to save her if I had been? I had to get back down to the stage for the finale. I was backstage when she fell."

Murray tightened his grip on the catwalk railing and peered over the edge as far as he dared. "This has to be the strangest accident I've ever worked," he said, shaking his head. "Falling from the top of a theater. During a show, for God's sake." He leaned back and pressed his shoulders against the wall of the dome. "Houdini, you've been unusually quiet. What do you make of it?"

Harry did not appear to be listening. "You say she was wearing the safety harness?" he asked Collins.

"Of course."

"And it was properly attached?"

"I helped her with it myself. Of course she might have unfastened it after I left, but I can't imagine why she would have done so."

"How does this harness work?" Lieutenant Murray asked.

"It's just a safety wire attached to a pair of crossed leather straps," Harry explained. "Many trapeze artists use them. It's supposed to catch the performer in case of slips. Here, I'll show you—"

"Harry!" I cried. "Don't—"

"Houdini! What are you—?"

My brother was making out over the open drop toward the narrow platform, travelling across the black rope ladder as easily as if he were climbing a set of stairs. "I'm merely demonstrating how the harness should have worked, Lieutenant," said my brother carelessly. "It's easier this way."

"Harry," I insisted, "you saw what happened this evening! The platform may not be safe!"

"That may be true," he returned, "and what better way to find out? Now, Lieutenant, what you must understand is that Miss Moore was wearing a harness beneath her costume, and there was a safety wire attached to one of the supports, like so." Harry peeled off his suit coat and unbuttoned his leather braces, threading them in a loop around one of the four support wires. "Now, Dash, if you'd be so good as to toss me your braces, I'll show the Lieutenant how the harness would have been fastened."

"Harry, this is a ridiculous—"

"Do it, Hardeen," the lieutenant said. "This is getting interesting."

I shrugged and stripped off my coat, removing my braces with one hand while I gathered the waistband of my baggy trousers with the other. "Here you go, Harry."

"Thanks, Dash. Now I'll—good God!"

"Harry! No!" I reached forward as he lost his footing on the narrow planking, tumbling forward into the empty space high above the audience seats. For a ghastly moment he flailed helplessly in mid-air with one arm, but an instant later he caught himself with the makeshift safety wire he had fashioned from his leather braces. "You see?" he called up as his feet dangled in the empty space below the dome. "I'm perfectly safe!"

"That was a damned reckless thing to do, Houdini!" cried Collins, whose face had turned a sickly green. "Especially after what's happened!"

"Not at all," said Harry, hauling himself back up onto the platform. "I was never in danger so long as I held onto the strap. That's what doesn't make sense about this evening's tragedy. If the harness was fastened, she couldn't have fallen. The safety wire would have saved her. She didn't even need to hold on."

I turned to the lieutenant. "My brother's methods may be a bit dramatic, but he's absolutely correct. The wire should have caught her when she slipped off the platform."

Lieutenant Murray turned to Collins. "You saw her attach the wire?"

He nodded. "I did. It fastens with a spring-loaded clip."

"The clip is still attached to the harness," Harry said, anticipating the lieutenant's next question. "It seems to be in perfect working order. Somehow the precautions failed."

"But how?" Collins asked. "We went over it dozens of times!"

Harry's face clouded. "I wish I knew."

"Maybe she unfastened the harness for some reason," the lieutenant said. "Maybe she was having some sort of trouble."

"It's possible," said Harry, crawling back across the rope ladder to join us on the catwalk, "but—"

A voice from below interrupted him. "For God's sake, Houdini! Get down off of there!"

"Who's that?" asked Lieutenant Murray, pointing over the edge of the catwalk at the figure glaring up at us from the center aisle.

"That's Mr. McAdow," I said. "Mr. Kellar's business manager."

Lieutenant Murray watched as McAdow climbed onto the

stage and began speaking to Kellar, his hands cutting sharply through the air as he spoke.

"I guess I'd better have a word with him," the lieutenant said. "I've seen just about all I'm going to see from here."

"But why do you want to speak to Mr. McAdow?" my brother asked. "What about Miss—?"

Lieutenant Murray held up his palm to cut Harry off. "Please, Houdini. You've been very helpful, but this is a police matter."

"But—"

"It's a matter of routine, Houdini. I need to speak with everyone present."

"Come on, Harry," I said. "We'd better check and see how Bess is doing."

Lieutenant Murray waited while Collins and Harry ducked through the low hatchway. As I made to follow, he reached out and grabbed my elbow. "Hardeen," he whispered with a sudden urgency, "what do you know about that guy Collins?"

"Collins? Not much, I—"

"Anything queer about him?"

"No, I wouldn't say so. He seems very trustworthy."

"But he was alone up here with Miss Moore? Just before she fell?"

"Yes, but only because he wasn't needed on stage just then. It could just as easily have been me or Harry."

Collins poked his head back through the hatchway. "Is there a problem, gentlemen?"

"No," said the lieutenant with an airy nonchalance. "I was just admiring the view." He ducked his head and climbed back onto the staircase.

We followed Collins past the office suites until we were once again in the theater lobby. While Harry went off to find Bess, Lieutenant Murray pushed through the studded leather doors that opened into the house and strolled down the center aisle, his hands in the pockets of his suit. He looked very much like a man who had concluded his work. "Mr. Kellar?" he called when he had reached the stage steps. "Might I have a word?"

"Mr. Kellar has no statement at this time," said McAdow stiffly. "He will answer all inquiries through his attorneys."

"Dudley," said Kellar wearily, "don't be ridiculous. I intend to cooperate with the police in every way I possibly can. How can I help you, young man?"

Lieutenant Murray mounted the steps and pulled out his notebook. I listened as he posed the same set of questions he had asked me, taking careful note of where Kellar had been standing, and whether he had noticed anything unusual in the moments leading up to the accident. After marking down Kellar's replies, the lieutenant turned to McAdow. "Your overcoat is covered with snow," the lieutenant noted. "You weren't here for the performance this evening, sir?"

"I was not," McAdow answered. "What possible difference would that have made?"

"None, I'm sure, but—"

"I have had the honor of serving as Mr. Kellar's business manager for nearly seventeen years. In that time I have had the pleasure of watching him perform many thousands of times. You cannot imagine that I am present at each and every—"

"Tonight was a big night, wasn't it?" Lieutenant Murray interrupted. "I mean, unveiling this big new trick, right? But I guess you had some urgent business elsewhere."

"If you are suggesting—"

"Mr. McAdow generally leaves the magic side of things to me," said Kellar. "And I leave the business end to him. So you would do well to direct all questions about tonight's misfortune to me. I bear sole responsibility for this tragedy."

Lieutenant Murray scratched lazily at the back of his head. "It's funny. People are just about tripping over themselves in the rush to take the blame for this thing. Houdini. Collins. Hardeen, here. You, Mr. Kellar. Isn't it possible that nobody's to blame?"

"Miss Moore came to harm under my care," Kellar said. "It was I who placed her in harm's way, and it is I who must bear the burden."

Lieutenant Murray snapped his notebook shut. "Have it your way," he said. "Naturally I'll want to hear what the doc has to say in his final report, but I wouldn't be surprised if he points me toward death by misadventure."

"Death by misadventure?" I asked.

"An accident," he clarified.

"But the safety harness?"

"Maybe it came loose. Or maybe she never fastened it in the first place."

"Collins says she did."

"Maybe so, maybe not." He leaned toward me and lowered his voice. "Say, Hardeen, do you happen to know if Collins and this Miss Moore, by any chance were they, uh, were they—"

"Not that I've heard, Lieutenant."

"And what about your brother? He seems to be taking this awfully hard. Were he and Miss Moore—"

"Certainly not."

"I suppose not," the lieutenant said. "Not with the wife watching over him morning, noon and night. All right," he turned back to Kellar. "I'll be in touch in the morning to wrap up the details. I would ask you not to speak to the press until then."

"I will not be speaking to the press at all," said Kellar listlessly. "Perhaps never again."

"Just don't speak to them tonight or tomorrow. I take it I can reach you at your hotel?"

Kellar nodded.

"Fine. Hardeen, I suggest that you take your brother home and pour him a stiff drink."

"If only he would drink it," I replied.

"Well, maybe you should have it for him, then." The lieutenant moved off to see how Dr. Peterson was proceeding.

"Dudley," said Kellar after a moment, "dismiss the company.

Mr. Hardeen, may I presume upon you and your brother to join me in my dressing room?"

Harry and I put Bess in a cab as the rest of the crew dispersed. Collins and Valletin invited us to join them at the hotel bar, but we begged off with an excuse about answering further questions for the lieutenant. I couldn't be certain what Mr. Kellar wished to see us about, but it seemed pointless to excite further speculation among the other members of the company.

Harry and I circled around to the back of the theater and made our way to Mr. Kellar's spacious dressing room. We found the magician seated on a wicker stool, removing his make-up with the help of a large lighted mirror. McAdow was hovering at his shoulder as we entered, speaking in insistent tones. "But there's no reason for that, Henry!" McAdow was saying. "No reason at all! You're being too hasty!"

"My mind is set upon the matter," Kellar said as he caught sight of us in the mirror. "Gentlemen, do sit down."

Harry and I perched on a leather chaise longue. Naturally I felt curious to hear whatever Kellar might say. My brother, on the other hand, might just as well have been locked away in his substitution trunk. His features were still pale and grim, and he stared at the opposite wall as though hoping it might fall on him.

"Harry," McAdow continued as if we weren't there, "think of the enormous sums of money involved! I've made deposits on theaters! I've signed contracts in seven languages! We must go on! We must!"

Mr. Kellar wiped his face with a towel and turned away from the mirror. "Dudley, I am resolved. Mr. Houdini, Mr. Hardeen, as you may have gathered, I have elected to cancel the remainder of the tour."

Harry nodded slowly, but did not speak. "Mr. Kellar," I said, "Lieutenant Murray seems to feel that tonight's tragedy may have been an accident. I know that we are all shocked beyond expression, but I think it would be unwise to make such a decision until we have all had a chance to recover our senses. You are far too upset."

"Listen to the boy," said McAdow. "He's talking sense. Certainly we must go dark for at least a week, out of respect for Miss Moore. But what you're suggesting is nothing short of—"

"I am retiring from the stage," said Kellar. "I have given my final performance."

"Henry!" cried McAdow. "You can't! You'll be ruined!"

"I am already ruined," said Kellar. "This disaster will haunt me until the end of my days. My glories as a performer will be forgotten, and I will be relegated to a grim footnote in history as the man who killed the Floating Lady."

"Ludicrous!" cried McAdow. "You will see reason in the morning, I assure you!"

"It is only now that I have come to my senses," Kellar insisted. "I should have known enough to call a halt the other day—after Boris escaped. Miss Moore would still be alive, and I might have preserved something of my professional dignity."

I leaned forward. "Sir," I began, "when we spoke aboard the train the other day, you mentioned a series of accidents that had plagued the show. You seemed to feel that some member of the company had contrived to set these accidents in motion, possibly to force you to close the show before you were able to perfect the Floating Lady illusion. Do you believe that this same person—whomever it might have been—was responsible for tonight's tragedy?"

"In a sense, Mr. Hardeen." Kellar stood and walked to an occasional table where a number of wooden boxes were arranged. "I'm afraid I was not entirely candid with you the other day."

"How do you mean?"

"The truth is that I should have been able to predict every last thing that happened here tonight. I suppose I hoped that you and your brother might help to forestall the inevitable."

McAdow wrinkled his forehead. "You're speaking in circles, Henry."

"You don't understand, Dudley. You couldn't possibly understand. You see, this has happened before. Every last bit of it."

"What can you mean?"

Kellar picked up a silver memory frame and snapped it open. For a moment his eyes rested on the daguerreotype inside. "My mentor. The Wizard of Kalliffa. Duncan McGregor. This was made during his prime, but already one senses an air of gathering doom." He turned the frame towards us. Although I had seen an oil portrait of the man in Mr. Kellar's parlor car, the daguerreotype seemed to capture some quality of inexpressible sadness that I had not noticed before.

"I told you that it was his lifelong dream to perform the Floating Lady illusion," Kellar continued, "but it would perhaps have been more accurate to say that it became his obsession. His life had been a very comfortable one. His services were in demand. His home life was contented. His reputation with the public was of the very highest order. All of this changed, however, as his preoccupation with the levitation took hold. The quality of his performances began to slip. He let things run down. He could scarcely wait to get off stage each night to resume his work on the levitation."

Kellar dabbed at a patch of rouge on his cheek. "I did what I could to keep the show on its feet, but Mr. McGregor's neglect began to take its toll. Soon, every performance was marked by some minor mishap. A trained bird would die. A prop would break during a performance. A costume would go missing. At first, it all seemed very much a matter of routine, the sorts of things that will bedevil any large enterprise. Over time, however, the mishaps became more grave. An assistant suffered a terrible broken leg. A sandbag came down during a performance, nearly striking a spectator. We began to acquire a reputation for calamity. At first there was only a half-seriousness to it, a sort of gallows humor in which we all shared. 'Beware the curse of Kalliffa,' we would say. Soon there came a time when we could no longer afford to be so cavalier. Theatrical managers began to fight shy of us. Our receipts dropped off. Mr. McGregor, who had been an abstemious man, began to console himself with alcohol, and from that point forward our decline grew even more precipitous."

Kellar drew back and regarded himself in the dressing room mirror, as though searching for signs of his own incipient dissolution. "Then one night, after an especially ill-favored performance in Missouri, Mr. McGregor gathered the remaining members of the company into the darkened theater to make an announcement. At last he had perfected the Floating Lady illusion, he told us. The decline of our fortunes would be halted, and we would ascend to heights of glory we had never dreamed possible."

Kellar drew a deep breath, apparently steeling himself to continue. "I allowed myself to believe that it might be true," he said, "but the apparatus that Mr. McGregor unveiled that night did not inspire confidence. It was little more than a crude swing, supported by an intricate lattice-work of thin wire. Individually, the wires were too thin to be seen from below. Together, they would support the assistant's weight as she swung from the stage to the top of the theater and back again." Kellar winced at the memory. "I had no faith in the contrivance, and I tried to stop him from proceeding. Mr. McGregor would not be dissuaded. I appealed to Mrs. McGregor, but she wanted only to please her husband. She cheerfully climbed onto the contraption and waited for McGregor to set it in motion." Kellar sighed heavily and closed his eyes before continuing.

"For a few moments, it appeared as if all might be well. Mrs. McGregor sailed high over our heads, with the swing device concealed beneath a flowing robe. The motion was a bit too fast, and perhaps too unnatural, but we might have worked out those difficulties. But then, as she began to descend, the wires started to snap, one by one. She did not fall so much as tumble, as though pitching down a flight of stairs. She plunged headlong into the footlights." Kellar's hands clenched. "There was a ball of fire, and a spray of glass and hot oil. We rushed forward with blankets, but—but we were not in time." Kellar's eyes were moist, but his voice was firm. "That was twenty-five years ago, gentlemen. Twenty-five years ago this very evening. I suppose I hoped that if I were able to achieve the effect successfully, it would lay the memory to rest. But now the curse of Kalliffa has claimed another victim."

"Henry," said McAdow gently. "It was a terrible thing, I won't deny it. But you cannot begin to compare the McGregor tragedy to our own. By your own admission he was reckless and foolhardy. You were not. We took every precaution that could be imagined. It was an accident. A terrible one, surely. But an accident all the same."

"A tragic accident," Kellar repeated. "Do you imagine that I did not try to console Mr. McGregor in exactly the same fashion? But he knew better. He caused his wife's death, and he took the full measure of blame. The Wizard of Kalliffa never performed again. I can do no less. I am responsible for the death of Miss Moore. It would be best if I withdrew from public life."

"You did not kill Miss Moore," said Harry, speaking for the first time since we entered the room. I turned to him in some alarm, hearing a strange note in his voice. His entire aspect was flat and enervated, as though he could scarcely rouse himself to speech. "At worst you are the general who ordered his troops into battle, but you are not the one who killed her." He sighed and looked down at his empty hands. "I am."

"Harry…"

"Dash, you know as well as I do that Miss Moore would still be alive if I had not suggested that particular method of performing the effect."

"We don't know that, Harry."

"It is foolishness to think otherwise. It appears that the curse

131

of Kalliffa has claimed yet another victim."

"Harry, this is not a time for—"

He silenced me with a look. "You think that I am being dramatic. I am not. You think that Mr. Kellar is a superstitious old man. He is not. He is simply accepting the consequences of his actions. So must I. Houdini is finished."

I stared. "You can't mean that."

"Young man," said Kellar, "you are at the very beginning of your career. I see great promise in you. You must not let—"

"One week," I blurted out. "That's all I ask."

"What do you mean, Hardeen?"

"When you brought us into the company you spoke of these accidents as being the work of some malicious enemy. I believe this may yet be the case. Mr. McAdow has suggested that we lower the curtain for one week to honor Miss Moore. Let me use that time to uncover whatever truth may lay behind this tragedy. If I find that we are at fault, then we must all share in the consequences. But if there are other agencies at work, it would be well to discover them."

Mr. Kellar looked again at the daguerreotype in his hand. "One week," he said, snapping the case shut. "But no longer. You are very persistent, Mr. Hardeen. I hope that this is not merely wishful thinking on your part."

"So do I, sir."

"Who knows? If you are right, perhaps I can still avoid the remainder of the curse."

"The remainder?" Harry asked.

Kellar fingered the memory frame. "I said that the Wizard of Kalliffa never performed again. But Mr. McGregor did not have enough money to allow him simply to stop working. He began to appear in dirt shows and carny calls. I saw him once more, performing on a haywagon at a county fair. He was calling himself John Henry Anderson IV, pretending to be the nephew of the Wizard of the North. The lavish props were gone, sold to support his drinking. He had become a shadow of his former greatness. His hands shook so badly that he dropped a Chinese rice bowl. The crowd jeered at him. When it was over I tried to speak with him. I had begun to have some success on my own by that time, and I tried to give him money, but he wouldn't accept. He pretended not to recognize me."

Kellar stood up and reached for the frockcoat hanging on a nearby peg. "I have always been haunted by it. I know that I could have done more. I should have pressed the money on him for the sake of his children. Perhaps I never should have left him in the first place, but I was young and I wanted to make my own way."

"What are you suggesting?" asked McAdow. "Do you really think that Harry Kellar is going to end up in some backwater tent show? You're the most famous magician in the world!"

Kellar turned toward us as he slipped into his frockcoat. His eyes, it seemed to me, were now touched by the same sadness that I had noted in the daguerreotype. "I am grateful for your reassurances," he said, "but I said much the same thing to Mr. McGregor."

~9~

THE MARK OF KENDALL

"THE CURSE OF KALLIFFA," SAID BESS AT BREAKFAST THE FOLLOWING morning. "It sounds like the latest novel by H. Rider Haggard."

"It does," I agreed. "All it requires is a hidden treasure."

"But there is a hidden treasure," she answered. "If Mr. Kellar is to be believed, the secret of the Floating Lady is worth one million dollars."

"Last night I believe he would have cheerfully surrendered that much and more never to have heard of the Floating Lady illusion. He believes that it is the source of this ludicrous curse."

"That is not precisely what he said," Harry insisted. "He merely pointed out that the Floating Lady had been the ruin of his mentor, and that now it was threatening to bring ruin upon him as well. Besides, you know perfectly well that many entertainers are superstitious. I have known actors to be so leery of the Scottish tragedy that they will not even speak the title in a theater."

"*Macbeth*, you mean?" said Bess.

"Well, yes," said Harry uneasily. "*Macbeth*."

We were not in a theater. We were again gathered around the breakfast table in my mother's flat on East 69th Street. Although Mr. Kellar had arranged for the company to stay at the Tilden, Harry and Bess had decided to lodge at home during the New York run, in anticipation of the lengthy tour to come. For my own part, I had opted for the relative luxury of the hotel, with its modern shower-baths and fresh bedding.

"I must say, Dash," said Bess. "You're looking even more spruce than usual this morning."

"Am I?" I rubbed at my chin. "Well, I had a shave and haircut from the hotel barber."

"Shoes polished, too, I see."

"Well, yes."

"And what's the scent?"

"A new hair tonic. Mitchell's Lime Root."

Harry snorted. "Availing yourself of all the amenities of the hotel, are you?"

"It seems a shame to let the opportunity pass," I said. "No, thank you, Mama," I added, as she placed a dish of salted herring before me. "I—well—I had a rather hearty breakfast in the hotel."

Harry regarded me with interest. "With anyone in particular?"

"Miss Wynn asked for my company," I explained. "She doesn't like to dine alone."

"Ah, the charming Miss Wynn!" said Harry. "You seem to be enjoying a great deal of her company."

"She was quite devastated by the events of last night," I replied. "I tried to lend some comfort."

"Is that all it was?" Bess asked, smiling.

"You are wasting your time with him, my dear," Harry said. "He seems determined to remain a bachelor. Miss Wynn is just another of the names on his list of suspects to be studied and questioned."

"Surely not!" Bess cried. "You can't seriously believe that Miss Wynn could have been responsible for last night's tragedy!"

"Someone tampered with the lock on the lion cage," I said. "Is it really so impossible to believe that this same person might have tampered with the Floating Lady apparatus?"

"Perhaps," said Harry. "Perhaps not."

"Harry, I won't hear any more superstitious claptrap! If you insist on going on about Mr. Kellar's so-called curse—"

"You admit that there is such a thing as coincidence?"

"Of course."

"And perhaps you have experienced the strange sensation of déjà vu?"

"Naturally."

"Then your mind is beginning to open toward the possibility of senses and sensations beyond the normal realm. Small steps, Dash. Small steps."

"Harry, you don't believe in such things yourself."

"No, but my mind is supple," he said. "I am open to possibility. At least for the present."

It must be said that these were strange words to have come from the mouth of Harry Houdini, who in his later years would acquire a reputation as the most outspoken anti-spiritualist crusader of his generation. There would come a time when he would devote the better part of his time and resources to the unmasking of fraudulent spirit mediums, whom he regarded as nothing more than sideshow hucksters. "Mine has not been an investigation of a few days or weeks or months but one that has extended over thirty years," he was to write shortly before his death, "and in that thirty years I have found not one incident that savored of the genuine."

By that time my brother had grown so accustomed to fraud on the part of the spiritualists that it was no longer possible for him to keep an open mind. With his vast knowledge of magic and its techniques he easily saw through the paper-thin deceptions of the séance room. But in his younger days, he was of a far more liberal frame of mind. "I wish to believe," I often heard him say. "I *long* to believe. Yet I must have evidence that I can see and touch."

But to my way of thinking, my brother's "supple" mind was bringing us no closer to a plan of action. "Harry," I said, impatient to return to the matter at hand, "we have only a short time in which to act. For the moment, shall we restrict our attentions to the earthly plane?"

"I appreciate what you are trying to do, Dash. You are trying to ease my conscience over my role in the death of Miss Moore. You are hoping to prove that it was the work of some enemy of Mr. Kellar's, but I shall carry—"

"Harry, you and your conscience can do whatever you like. I'm on my way down to the theater to see if I can shed any light on this matter. I intend to do so without recourse to the psychic realm. I would welcome your company, if the spirits will permit it."

"There is no need for sarcasm, Dash," he said in an injured tone. "Besides, aren't you forgetting something?"

"No, Harry. Mr. Kellar has given us the full run of the theater. We have only to—"

"I was referring to your salted herring," he said. "As Mama says, you can't hope to put in a full day without a little something on your stomach."

Within the hour, the Brothers Houdini, their stomachs warmed with herring and numerous cups of tea, made their way back downtown to the Belasco. To our surprise, the front doors were bolted and we found a police padlock on the stage entrance. "Odd," said Harry, "I thought Lieutenant Murray had finished last night. Well, no matter." He took out the leather wallet containing his pick locks and held it up to the door. "Quite routine, really. A Glickson two-pin. Have it open in"—there was a sharp click as the padlock fell open—"less time than it takes to say."

We pushed the stage door open. Inside, we felt our way through the darkened corridors toward the main stage. As we rounded a corner, we could make out the faint outlines of a figure seated on a stool near Mr. Kellar's dressing room. "Hello?" Harry called. "Who's there?"

The figure didn't stir. "Dash, I don't like the looks of this." Harry edged closer, reaching out to shake the figure by the shoulder. As he did so, the familiar face of Matilda the mannequin pitched forward into the light, smiling placidly.

"Keeping watch, are you, Matilda?" Harry asked. "We'll just put you back where we found you." He propped the mannequin back onto the stool and we edged further along the dim corridor. As we drew near the stage we found that the house lights were illuminated.

"Hello?" Harry called. "Is anyone there?"

"Someone has been here," I said. "The lieutenant's men, most likely. McAdow would have a fit if he knew these lights were left burning."

"Somehow I think Mr. McAdow has other things weighing on his mind at the moment. Now, Dash, what is it that you're expecting to find?"

"I want to take a closer look at the rigging up there in the dome. We worked out every detail of that illusion, including the safety features. Assuming that Miss Moore's harness was attached properly, there's no possible way that she could have fallen. You know that as well as I do." I hopped down off the stage and made my way through the empty house with Harry at my heels.

"I agree that it's unlikely," he said, "but not impossible. After all, the bullet catch trick is also supposed to be fail-safe, but there are a number of dead magicians whose widows could attest to the contrary."

"That's different, as you know perfectly well. The bullet catch involves a loaded gun. We weren't using anything more dangerous than a smudge pot."

"And an enormous height," Harry said, looking up into the dome. "Don't forget that."

"I haven't forgotten, Harry. But Miss Moore had training as an aerialist, remember? Collins tells me that she spent three years with the Kendall Brothers. Heights held no terror for her."

"The Kendall Brothers?" Harry asked. "Miss Moore worked with the Kendall Brothers?"

"Of course, even the best wire-walkers have accidents," I

allowed. "Perhaps she unfastened the harness after he left her. Maybe she needed to change position for some reason." I paused at the spot behind the seats where Miss Moore's body had lain the previous night. A heavy cloth covered the spot. "After all," I said, "Collins said that she seemed out of sorts. But why would she have taken any unnecessary risks? It doesn't make sense!" I pulled the cloth aside and instantly regretted having done so. A sickly smell rose from beneath. "Come on, Harry," I said, hastily replacing the cloth. "Maybe we're wasting our time here."

He was staring into the dome. "You say that Miss Moore worked with the Kendall Brothers as an aerialist?"

"That's what Collins tells me."

"I knew Bartholomew Kendall," Harry said. "A very fine fellow. Also very much in the thrall of what you would call superstitious claptrap. He and his brothers were very much creatures of habit."

"Harry, what are you getting at?"

"Did you examine the catwalk last night?"

"You know I did."

"So did I. But I was looking for anything that seemed out of place. I should have been looking for something that wasn't there at all."

"Pardon?"

"I wonder…" For a moment or two he seemed lost in a trance. "Wait a moment, Dash," he said, suddenly snapping to attention. "I'll be right back."

He darted off into the lobby before I could even frame a question. In the hush of the theater I could hear the drifting sounds of footfalls and doors slamming. Then, very faintly, I heard a sound from overhead, as though a cat were clawing at the ceiling.

I looked up and immediately wished I hadn't. My brother was blithely hopping about inside the dome, without any manner of safety wire or harness. The previous evening he had made use of the rope ladder; now for some unfathomable reason he was walking along one of the support wires that held the suspended platform. I fought back the impulse to shout a warning, as I did not want to risk startling him. For several moments he paced back and forth on the slender wire, then hopped onto the platform at the center of the dome. To my horror, he then repeated his reckless wire-walking on each of the remaining three supports. He appeared to be studying the wires with extraordinary care, as if he expected to find something clinging to one of them. As he neared the far edge of the final support, he glanced back and saw me staring up at him.

"Dash!" His voice reverberated in the dome. "Did Lieutenant Murray—"

"Harry! Be careful! At least put on a harness!"

"Why bother? It didn't do Miss Moore any good. Tell me, did Lieutenant Murray find any strange markings up here last night? Anything at all?"

"You saw as much as I did. He didn't mention anything."

"It's very important. No matter how trivial it might seem."

"I'm quite certain that he didn't, Harry. Now get back on the catwalk!"

"Honestly, Dash," he called. "You can be such an old woman." He extended his arms and continued his journey along the final wire while I watched with my heart in my throat. He took a minor stumble as he neared the far edge, but recovered smoothly with a minimum of arm-waving. He hopped onto the catwalk and I lost sight of him as he slipped through the hatchway. A moment later he had returned to my side.

"What was that all about?" I asked.

"I'll tell you in a moment. First we must venture into forbidden territory."

"Oh?"

"The ladies dressing room." He led me up the stairs and past the offices on the second floor. We knocked at the entrance to the ladies dressing area and, receiving no answer, pushed open the door. Although larger than the male dressing room, the ladies suite was laid out along much the same lines, with rows of dressing mirrors on either side, and an array of seating couches running down the middle. While not nearly so grand as the private rooms reserved for the star attractions, the chamber was airy and pleasant, a welcome contrast to the arrangements we often encountered on the road.

"This must be where Bess was sitting," Harry said, gesturing to a mirror near the door. "Those are her dancing slippers."

"And I believe those yellow gloves belong to Miss Wynn," I said, pointing to the next seat over. "Could this be—yes! I recognize the scarf she was wearing when I first saw her. This must be Miss Moore's dressing table."

Harry sat down at the mirror and examined the surface of the table. "It should be here," he said, lifting up a square of linen. "Where would she have—ah!" He pulled open a shallow drawer. "Here! Do you see this, Dash? Isn't it lovely?"

"Harry, it's a piece of ordinary chalk."

He cradled the little nub of chalk as though it were a precious jewel. "Dash, it is the key to everything! This tiny piece of chalk may well absolve us of any blame in the death of Miss Moore! More importantly, it sets us down the path of a great mystery, one that shall require all of my remarkable gifts to solve! This may well be the greatest puzzle ever placed before the Great Houdini!"

"All that from one little piece of chalk?"

Harry regarded me with narrowed eyes. "Do you not see? You know my methods! Apply them!"

"You've lost me, Harry."

"You said that Miss Moore played with the Kendall Brothers for three years, did you not?"

"Yes…"

"Do you not remember the Kendall Brothers? We shared a bill with them when the Welsh Brothers passed through Illinois and Indiana."

"I remember, but Miss Moore couldn't have been with them at that time. I wouldn't have forgotten her."

"She wasn't. But I came to know Bartholomew Kendall quite well during that period. He was a very charming man, and had a great deal to teach me about the discipline of high-wire work."

"I remember him. Very sturdy, muscles like steel cords."

"Yes, he was a great believer in muscular expansionism—as am I. He also had a number of the odd quirks and customs that are so common in our profession."

"He was superstitious, you mean?"

"If you will. In any case, there was one tradition that had been handed down to him by his father, and which was observed by every member of the company, from the walkers to the riggers." Harry turned the chalk nubbin over in his hand. "Before every performance, each of the walkers made a pair of chalk marks on the wire. Two marks—just like this." He reached out and made two sharp vertical strokes on the edge of the dressing table. "These marks were meant as a tribute to Zeke Kendall and Emma Bigelow, two members of the company who had fallen from the wire."

"Killed?" I asked. "Both of them?"

"Yes. In separate accidents. The chalk marks were meant to honor their memory, and to ward off the bad luck that caused their deaths."

I fixed my eyes on the little nubbin of chalk. "Harry, you're saying that—"

"How could it be otherwise?"

"You're saying that Miss Moore should have made two chalk marks on the wire across the dome, before she attempted the Floating Lady."

"Exactly."

I let it filter around in my brain for a minute. "She was in a terrible hurry," I said. "Collins said she seemed distracted. Perhaps she didn't have time—"

"Dash, you have spent all morning berating me over the quaint beliefs of show folk. Do you mean to tell me that a member of the Kendall Brothers company couldn't find two seconds to scratch out a pair of simple chalk marks?"

"Perhaps she forgot the chalk. That must be it! What's her chalk doing here in the drawer? She must have left it behind in her haste to get ready for opening night!"

Harry dipped his hand into the drawer and removed three more pieces of chalk. "I think we can safely say that she remembered to carry a piece with her," he said. "No doubt Lieutenant Murray will confirm that a piece of chalk was found on her person. Furthermore, I think it's plain that the tradition had considerable importance to her."

"Incredible," I said. "You're suggesting that—"

"I'm suggesting that Miss Moore should have left a pair of chalk marks before she climbed out onto the wire, but for some reason she did not."

"Then you're saying that she didn't fall at all."

"No, indeed. She must have been pushed or thrown from the catwalk. One thing is certain." He stood up, his eyes gleaming. "Dash, it is murder!"

I took the chalk from his hand and stared at it. "Collins," I said. "He saw her crawl out onto the platform. He didn't say anything about any chalk marks. Unless—"

Harry nodded. "He says that he saw her mount the platform, but we have only his word for it. He was the last to see her alive."

"Collins! That bastard! That four-flushing—"

"Dash," my brother said stiffly, "you know that Mama does not approve of such language."

"All right, Harry," I said with a sigh. "Then shall we go and see if we can find this—this blackguard? I have some questions for him."

"As do I." Harry took the chalk and tightened his fist around it. "As do I. Come along, Dash. Mr. Collins has much to explain."

We had gotten no further than the stage when a voice

stopped us in our tracks. "What are you two doing here?" came the familiar growl.

"Lieutenant Murray!" cried Harry. "For once I am glad to see you! I have the most remarkable news! It seems Miss Moore—"

"She was murdered," he said. "Yes, I know. I wondered how long it would take the pair of you to work it out."

"You already knew? But how?"

The lieutenant clasped his hands behind his back, walking toward us. "Had my suspicions last night. Her hair was wet, for one thing. I pointed it out to Doc Peterson, and he found something sort of unusual when he examined the body down at the morgue."

"What was that?" I asked.

"Well, her injuries were severe, as you would expect in a fall from that height. Lots of broken bones and I don't know what all. But what really got the Doc's attention was the cause of death."

"The cause of death? The woman fell seventy feet!"

"So she did." The lieutenant's eyes were fixed on the wire suspended high above his head. "But that's not what killed her."

"Then what did?"

Lieutenant Murray met my gaze and held it for a moment. "Water in her lungs," he said.

"It can't be," I said.

"I'm afraid it is, Hardeen. It seems that your floating lady drowned in mid-air."

10

A VISIT TO COUSIN CHESTER

"SHE DROWNED? IN MID-AIR? HOW IS THAT POSSIBLE?"

"Well, Mr. Houdini, that's something I'd very much like to know."

We were seated in a police interview room at the thirteenth precinct station house on Delancy Street. We had driven over from the theater in a horse-drawn calash, and Lieutenant Murray spent the journey quizzing us on our experiences with the Kellar company. I don't know that we added anything new to what we had already told him the previous night, but by the time we reached the station house he had filled five pages of his note pad.

"It seems to me that we're wasting valuable time here, Lieutenant," said Harry, leaning across the interview table. "Shouldn't you be putting these questions to Jim Collins? After all, he was the one who claimed to have escorted Miss Moore safely up to the dome. I don't see how that could possibly be true."

"It can't," Murray said. "Not unless the lady somehow slipped from that wire and drowned while falling to her death. She must have been dead before she fell."

"Which means that Collins was lying," I said. "Surely you've questioned him by now?"

"Extensively." The lieutenant rubbed his eyes. "He's in a cell

145

downstairs. But he insists that Francesca Moore was alive when he helped her into the harness." The lieutenant riffled through a stack of loose pages on the table in front of him. "Here's what he told me: 'It all went like clockwork. We ran up the stairs to the dome, I helped her get strapped in, and I gave her a hand getting onto the ladder. She was all set for the lights to come up for the big finale. When I left, she was absolutely fine.'"

Harry drummed his fingers on the table. "He's describing the sequence of events as it would have been under normal circumstances, but that can't possibly have been the case last night. If she had slipped—if she had unfastened the harness for some reason and fallen—then certainly it might have happened as Mr. Collins says. But the woman drowned! How does he explain that? How does a woman take water into her lungs while falling to her death?"

"I put that same question to him myself, Houdini. Many times. Some of my colleagues have been a little overly zealous in their questioning, I'm afraid. But he still insists that it happened just that way."

"Can I have misjudged him so badly?" Harry asked. "He seemed such a solid fellow."

"It seems clear that he's lying, or covering for someone else," the lieutenant said. "Can you think of anything that might help us wear down his story?"

I searched my memory for anything he might have said over the past few days. "Mr. Kellar seems to have placed a great deal of faith in him," I said. "Apparently he used to work for Professor Herrmann."

"Who?"

"Another magician."

"Great. Just what I need. What about Felsden and Valletin? Is there any reason to think he might be covering for either of them?"

"It's difficult to say. Silent Felsden hasn't spoken a word to me since we joined the company. Valletin came over from the

Maskelyne troupe, and there was some talk that he——"

"Maskelyne? Would this be yet another magician?"

I nodded. "Valletin worked as a carpenter in his illusion shop."

"I can tell you another thing about Valletin," Harry said. "The man is a terrible juggler. Couldn't keep three balls in the air if his life depended on it."

"I'm sure that will be very helpful, Houdini. I'll be certain to confront him with that immediately."

"I don't know if this will be any more useful," I said, "but Valletin may have liberated a few of Maskelyne's secrets when he came to work for Mr. Kellar."

"That has to be the reason why he was hired," said Harry. "It couldn't have been his juggling."

"Great. So that's one more magician who has a reason to want to see Kellar fold his tent. Collins spent half the night telling me about spies working for Serge Le Roy."

"Servais."

"Whatever. Collins wanted me to think that Le Roy might have arranged to sabotage the stunt."

"There is a great deal of money at stake, according to Mr. Kellar," I allowed. "But it still doesn't explain how Miss Moore came to drown."

"No, it doesn't." said Lieutenant Murray, making a note in his pad, "but Collins is keeping to his story as though it were cast in iron. I'll check his background and see if I can find anything to loosen the rivets. You're sure you don't have any idea why he might have wished to kill this woman?"

"None," I said.

"Think carefully, Hardeen. The victim was a surpassingly beautiful woman. Was there anyone in particular who developed a passion for her, and perhaps had his advances spurned?"

"That could be said of nearly every man in the company, myself included."

"That's just what Collins said."

"I will grant that Miss Moore was an exceptional woman,"

said Harry, "but I do not believe that whoever hatched this plot harbored any grudge against her. She was merely another unfortunate victim of the curse."

"Harry," I said, "the lieutenant doesn't want to hear about the curse of Kalliffa."

"The what?"

"The coincidence is far too great," Harry insisted. "A woman is killed performing the Floating Lady effect. Twenty-five years later—on the same exact date—a second woman dies in the same manner. There must be a connection."

"A second woman?" said Lieutenant Murray. "The curse of Kalliffa? What's this about?"

Lieutenant Murray listened closely as Harry gave him a summary of what Mr. Kellar had told us the previous evening. "So you see," Harry said when he had finished, "these are very deep waters indeed."

"Perhaps not quite so deep as all that, Houdini. I'm not a great believer in curses. I'll grant you that it's a hell of a coincidence, and it certainly explains why Kellar was so keen to push ahead with the trick, but the real victim here is Miss Moore. When I investigate a murder, I look for people who wanted the victim dead. It's as simple as that."

"But—"

"Harry, the lieutenant is making a lot of sense."

"Perhaps so," Harry said glumly. "Either way, the tragedy may serve to end the career of a great man. This matter must be resolved promptly, and with a minimum of publicity."

"Too late for that, I'm afraid." Lieutenant Murray pushed a copy of the *New York World* across the table. The third column had a bold headline: SHOCKING EVENT AT THE BELASCO. A sub-head continued the theme: TRAGEDY ATTENDS KELLAR PERFORMANCE.

Harry snatched up the paper and scanned the article. "This is really unconscionable," he said, tossing the paper aside. "How could they do such a thing?"

"Mr. Kellar will be very distressed," I agreed. "But we could hardly expect the press to ignore the story. The house was full of reporters last—"

"Once again there is no mention of my name!"

Lieutenant Murray looked at me and raised his eyebrows. "Indeed, Houdini," he said, "the situation is even more grave than I thought."

"Lieutenant Murray," I said, "is there any chance that Harry and I might be permitted to question Mr. Collins for a moment or two? After all, we have a more intimate knowledge of the—"

Murray held up his hands. "It's impossible, Hardeen," he said, but there was something in his face that I couldn't read. "As an officer of the New York Police Department, I can't allow civilians to get in the way of a murder investigation. However, I think you'll find that we brought in your cousin Chester last night. Had a snootful, Chester did."

"I see."

"What?" cried Harry. "We have no cousin Chester! I don't—"

"You remember him, Houdini. Your cousin Chester. He's drying out in the lock-up."

"Very good," I said. "We'll look in on him before we go."

"Just across from Collins, as it turns out."

"Yes. Come along, Harry."

"But this is absurd! I am well acquainted with the family tree on both sides, and there is no—"

Exasperated, the lieutenant explained it to him in terms that might have brought a blush to the cheeks of Matilda the mannequin.

"Ah!" said Harry, as recognition slowly dawned. "I see! Our cousin Chester!" He gave a broad wink. "Let us go visit our cousin Chester, Dash!"

Lieutenant Murray rolled his eyes. "Yes, Houdini. I'll just tag along and listen, if I might." He led us down a wide central stairway to the dispatcher's desk. "I'm taking these boys on a tour of the hoosegow, O'Donnell," he told the desk sergeant.

"Any objections?"

"None," said O'Donnell, handing over a heavy ring of keys. "Shall I stay here and attend to my desk work?"

"That might be best."

"We're visiting our cousin Chester," said Harry, unable to help himself. "He's our cousin."

"Is that right?" asked O'Donnell.

"Come on, Houdini," said Lieutenant Murray testily. "Let's see if we can make it down the stairs without you telling the chief all about it."

"Why are you being so accommodating, lieutenant?" I asked as he led us past the sergeant's desk.

"Collins hasn't budged an inch from his story. I figure he might let something slip to you."

"We are pleased to be of assistance," Harry said.

"I'll be happy if you just stay out of my way," he answered, leading us down a set of dank steel-beam steps. "You can talk to your friend, then I want you to clear off."

Murray stopped in front of a metal-studded door with a heavy iron cross-bar. He lifted the bar and fitted a large key into a reinforced panel-lock, turning it three times clockwise. The door rolled sideways on rusty casters. Murray held it open as we passed through, then slid it shut behind us once we were inside.

The lock-up was comprised of only four cells, two on each side, with a wide corridor running down the center. Four bare light bulbs dangling from ceiling cords provided the only illumination. Collins was sitting in the cell on the far right, leaning forward on the narrow bench, his hands clasped between his knees. A muscular Chinese man lay asleep in the cell opposite, snoring contentedly.

Collins rose from his bench at the sound of our approach, blinking in the dim light. "Hardeen? Is that you? Houdini?" He stepped forward and gripped the bars at the front of the cell. "Good lord, have they arrested you, too?"

"Not just yet," I said, facing him through the bars. His right eye was badly swollen and there were dark bruises covering the left half of his face. "The police did this to you?" I asked.

Collins's eyes darted toward Lieutenant Murray, who was leaning against the sliding entry door. "I slipped," he said. "Listen, you have to give Mr. Kellar a message for me! I had nothing to do with Miss Moore's death! I would never do such a thing! I can't believe that anyone would believe that I'm capable of murder!"

"I wouldn't have thought so," I said, "but the police don't see any other explanation. How could she possibly—"

"I know," Collins said, nodding his head vigorously. "How could she possibly have drowned? How could she be alive when she fell off the wire and dead by drowning when she hit the ground? I've been thinking of nothing else since it happened."

"Collins," Harry said, "you're certain she was alive when you left the catwalk?"

"Was she alive? Of course she was alive, Houdini! She waved at me from the platform!"

"How much time passed between the moment you left the catwalk and when she fell?"

"Not more than two minutes, Hardeen. You know that perfectly well. It went exactly according to plan, just like in rehearsal. I left her all set for the final reveal, then I ran down the steps to the backstage area to get ready for my final entrance."

"Miss Moore gave you no indication that anything was wrong?"

"None whatsoever."

"Think carefully, Collins. Did you observe anything different from rehearsal?"

"No, Houdini. It was right on the money. Exactly the same."

"What about the chalk marks?" Harry asked.

"What chalk marks?"

"Harry expected her to make a couple of chalk marks on the wire before she climbed out," I explained. "It's something the Kendall Brothers used to do."

"You did not observe a piece of chalk in her hand?" Harry asked.

"No, Houdini, but I didn't see her make any marks during rehearsal, either."

"She wouldn't have," Harry said. "It was something they only did for performances."

I stepped closer to the bars of the cell, studying the bruising on Collins's face. "Are you quite certain that the woman you helped into the harness was actually Miss Moore? After all, she was wearing heavy Indian robes—even a veil."

"I've been in the magic business for a long time, Hardeen, and I know a great deal about working with doubles. This was no double. Besides, she wasn't wearing the veil backstage. I saw her face clearly before the curtain went up for the levitation. It was her, I'm absolutely certain."

"What about afterwards, when you led her up the stairs to the dome?"

"You're thinking that someone else might have taken her place, wearing an identical costume?" Collins paused to consider it. "I don't see it, Houdini. We hired that woman because she was a gifted wire-walker. When we got to the dome, I saw her climb out onto that wire as though she'd been born on a trapeze. Anybody else would have crawled out on that rope ladder on hands and knees. Miss Moore skipped across that ladder like it was a set of stepping stones in a river—just like rehearsal. Nobody else could have done it."

"I could have," my brother said. "I'm quite adept on the high wire."

"But I think I might have noticed you in an Indian princess costume, Houdini." Collins tightened his grip on the bars of the cell. "It was her. It was Francesca Moore. Next thing I knew, I was watching her fall to her death."

"Or so we thought."

"Or so we thought," he repeated. "Only that can't be what happened because it turns out that somehow she managed to drown after I left her." He let his arms dangle through the bars. "Tell me something, Houdini. Do I strike you as an unusually stupid man?"

Harry lifted his head in surprise. "No. No, you do not."

"I'm actually pretty clever, wouldn't you say?"

"I would."

"So don't you think that if I were responsible for the death of Miss Moore, as the police seem to believe, I would have come up with a better alibi?"

"Yes," Harry acknowledged. "I suppose you would have."

"I tell you, Houdini, this thing has got me beat. I'm clever enough to help to create the Levitation of Princess Karnac, but I can't figure out how Francesca Moore drowned in mid-air."

"Yes," Harry agreed. "It is a bit of a knotty problem."

"From your side of the bars it's a knotty problem, Houdini," Collins said. "From my side, it's rather more serious."

"Do you believe him?" I asked Harry, as Lieutenant Murray led us back up the steel stairs.

Harry spent a moment considering his answer. "I suppose I do," he said, "though I can't exactly say why. There are so many questions unanswered. Still, I consider myself a good judge of character, and there is something about his story that rings true."

"I'll grant you that he seems like a solid citizen," said the lieutenant, pausing in front of the dispatcher's desk, "but it still doesn't explain how Francesca Moore came to be dead."

"I know," Harry admitted, "and yet..."

"What?" I asked.

"Well, it's exactly as Collins said. If I were planning to drown Miss Moore and then throw her from the highest point in the Belasco Theater, I like to think that I'd do a better job of covering my tracks."

"You fell for that, did you?" asked Murray, leading us toward the front doors. "Hell, that one was already old when St. Paddy was a boy."

"What do you mean?"

"Houdini, we were never meant to discover that Miss Moore drowned. When a woman falls from a great height— with hundreds of witnesses, mind—and has a broken neck to show for it, most people wouldn't think to check for water in the lungs. But Doc Peterson isn't most people." The lieutenant pushed open the front doors and led us outside onto the marble steps. "Think about it. So long as we believed that she died in the fall, Collins's story would have held good. We'd have concluded that the whole thing was an accident. The drowning is what knocks his story to pieces. He never figured on us finding out about that."

"I'm still not convinced."

"That bothers me, Houdini. That worries me a lot."

"Lieutenant, you have to admit—"

"Look, Houdini," the lieutenant said sharply, "I appreciate the fact that this Collins is a friend of yours. And I can understand how it might come as a bit of a blow to find out that he's a murderer, especially with you being such a fine judge of character and all. But he's the killer, and I'm going to prove it—one way or another. If I were you I'd find something else to worry about, like finding a job. I don't think Mr. Kellar will be taking his show out on the road any time soon. Good morning, gentlemen." With that, he stepped back into the precinct house and closed the door behind him.

Harry and I walked along Delancy Street in silence for a few moments. "Small steps," he said, after a moment. "Everything in small steps."

"What?" I asked.

"We have a busy day ahead," he announced, starting off briskly in the direction of the elevated train.

"Harry, Lieutenant Murray wants us to stay out of the way."

"Lieutenant Murray has already made up his mind that Collins is guilty. I have not. Therefore, our paths are not likely to cross."

"But what can we do?"

"If we proceed from the hypothesis that Mr. Collins is telling the truth, then it stands to reason that someone else is responsible for the death of Miss Moore."

"You're no longer blaming the restless spirit of Kalliffa?"

"I am compelled to set that theory aside for the moment." He turned a corner onto Orchard Street. "I believe that if we were able to discover how Miss Moore was killed, we should soon find out who killed her."

"Makes sense."

"Lieutenant Murray laid out two very distinct possibilities—a jealous lover or a rival of Mr. Kellar's. Since he believes Mr. Collins is the villain, he is obviously leaning toward the former. I favor the latter. There can be no other explanation for the sensational manner in which she was killed."

"I'm not sure I entirely agree."

"I thought you might not. That is why I am assigning you to look into the young lady's background."

"Her background?"

"We know very little about Miss Moore. I believe there may be some clues to be had in a thorough investigation of her past. Are you still acquainted with that newspaper fellow? What was his name again?"

"Biggs. Harry, you know perfectly well that his name is Biggs. Are you never going to forgive him for that bad review?"

He pretended not to hear me. "The newspaper archive at the *New York World* is perhaps the finest resource of information in the city. I want you to see what you can discover about Miss Moore—particularly her years with the Kendall Brothers."

"Harry, it seems unlikely that there would be much information in the newspaper morgue. The Kendall Brothers are strictly bottom-rung."

"It is a fool's errand, actually. But I see no other means of convincing you that Miss Moore was simply a pawn in a larger plot against Mr. Kellar. Therefore I must allow you to eliminate the hypothesis that she was the sole victim. At the same time, you might look through the Kellar file and discover if you can isolate anyone who might be harboring a grudge against him."

"Kellar's file will be massive! It could take all day!"

"That will give me just enough time," Harry said.

"Enough time for what?"

"Enough time to deal with this," he said, stopping abruptly before a large theatrical poster. It showed a trim, dapper man in a tailcoat, gesturing extravagantly at a ghostly figure that appeared to be hovering above the heads of an enraptured audience. "Servais Le Roy presents his greatest mystery yet!" the poster announced. "The Mystery of Lhassa—a woman floats in the empty space!" A slash-panel pasted along the lower corner read: "Debut tomorrow evening!"

"Well, I'll be a fish on a bicycle," I said.

"Indeed."

"Servais Le Roy is in town, performing a Floating Lady illusion."

"Indeed."

"He and Kellar usually avoid each other like the plague."

"Indeed."

"So the timing is…suggestive."

"Indeed."

"Harry, what are you going to do?"

"Me? I am going to do exactly as Lieutenant Murray suggested."

"What's that?"

"I am going to ask Mr. Servais Le Roy for a job."

~⚬ 11 ⚬~

KARNAC IN FLAMES

I SPENT TEN MINUTES GRILLING HIM, BUT HARRY REFUSED TO elaborate on this curious remark. We parted in front of the courthouse after arranging to meet at the end of the day. I rode the elevated train to the offices of the *World,* convinced that an afternoon of fruitless labor lay before me. The prospect was not entirely unpleasant, as my friend Biggs could usually be relied upon for the name of a good pony or two.

I found Biggs slouched over an angled compositor's desk, as always. He wore his customary grey tweed suit with an open waistcoat and carelessly knotted wool tie, along with the ragged expression of a man perpetually three days behind on his sleep. His wavy red hair seemed to be fleeing in all directions from a bald patch at the back of his head, and dark smudges clung to his pale blue eyes.

"Dash, you old pepperpot!" he shouted when he saw me lounging in the doorway. "Just the man I need to see! Where have you been? Your landlady hasn't seen you for a week!"

"I've been on the road," I said, tossing my Trilby onto a battered stand in the corner. "We only got back to town yesterday."

"Yes, yes," he said impatiently, "you've been working with the Kellar show. I know all about that, of course. That's why I've been looking for you. The death of the Floating Lady! The tragedy of the falling star! It's the biggest story of the year, and somehow you and the ape man have wound up right at the center of it!"

"You really must stop calling him that."

"Oh, but I will, dear boy. Just as soon as he stops dragging his knuckles on the ground."

I sighed. Biggs and my brother had nurtured an intense dislike for one another since boyhood. Biggs had been a sensitive and somewhat fragile boy, while Harry had been a bit of a show-off and a bully. It made for a poor combination. My friend had matured into a fine journalist and a promising writer, while Harry had turned his youthful braggadocio into the cornerstone of his act. It remained a poor combination.

"Pull up a stool and tell me everything you know," Biggs was saying. "Don't leave out anything, especially if it's gruesome."

"To be candid, I'm not certain that I can add anything to what appeared in your newspaper this morning. The account of Miss Moore's injuries was rather shocking in its detail."

"Well, yes. We have a man at the city morgue. But I need you for the background. Come on, young Hardeen. Tell me everything about the accident. From the beginning."

I sat down and passed twenty minutes or so giving him an account of our actions from our first day with the Kellar company, carefully omitting any reference to the fact that Miss Moore's death had not been an accident. I took particular care to lavish attention on Harry's encounter with Boris the lion, which sent Biggs's pen flying over the pages of his notebook.

"Finally came up against a mouth bigger than his own, did he?" Biggs chuckled. "It was bound to happen one day."

"It's not a laughing matter, Biggs. That lion could easily have killed half the company."

"I know, Dash. I know. And I'll be certain to cast the Great Houdini in a properly heroic light when the time comes. Tell me, how is Mr. Kellar bearing up? I understand he's taken it all rather hard."

"He feels responsible for the death of Miss Moore, as one

might expect," I said carefully. "She came to harm in his employ."

"Yes, but I understood that he was thinking of closing the show for good. Leaving the field to men like this Le Roy character."

"That would be a great loss," I said, "but I would not presume to speak for Mr. Kellar."

Biggs eyed me carefully, a wide grin spreading across his face. "Why, Dash Hardeen! You're holding out on me! When did you get to be so crafty?"

My cheeks reddened. "Mr. Kellar requires confidentiality from his employees," I said.

"Well, well. Then it can't be a desire to tell everything that brought you to the offices of the *World* this morning. How may the fourth estate be of service, may I ask?"

"I want to find out a bit more about Miss Moore if I can."

He gave me a suspicious look. "Why?"

"It may help me to understand how the accident occurred."

"Balderdash," he said. "I didn't just fall off the turnip truck, Dash. What are you hiding?"

"Nothing, I assure you. I just—"

"Can't help you, in any case. She's a complete blank. Not a thing in our files."

"I may have a better idea of where to look."

"Oh, really?" Biggs asked, hopping down off his stool. "Are you willing to share?"

I nodded.

"Then let's head down to the crypt."

He led me through a warren of offices to a dim basement chamber arrayed with row upon row of dusty wooden file cabinets. "I've already been down here this morning," he said, pulling open a creaky file drawer. "There's nothing here under the name of Francesca Moore. The unfortunate woman is a bit of a puzzle. Quite an eyeful, I understand."

"You've no idea," I said. "These are the footlight files?"

"From here to that wall, yes. Everything we have on drama

and the arts, going back forty-two years."

I reached for the drawer marked with a "K."

" 'K' for Kellar?" asked Biggs.

"No, 'K' for Kendall Brothers. Miss Moore received her acrobatic training with them."

"Never heard of the Kendall Brothers."

"I'm not surprised. They're small-time."

"How did Miss Moore happen to cross paths with Kellar, then, for all of her surpassing beauty? It's been some time since he played anything less than the Palace."

"Mr. Kellar doesn't engage his own staff. He leaves that to his manager, Mr. McAdow. I can only assume that McAdow keeps an eye on the variety circuits, looking out for rising talent. Let me see…" I thumbed through the sheaves of yellowing documents until I came across the file on the Kendall Brothers. The packet was notably slim, and when I opened it a single newspaper clipping fluttered out.

"Not much of a legacy," Biggs observed. "What's it say?"

" 'Kendall Brothers Top Bill at Hogarth Fairground.' " I scanned the article. "Let's see… 'The youthful acrobats delighted the citizens of Hogarth with their aerial wizardry' … 'the human pyramid was an especial highlight, causing much astonishment' … ah! Here we are! 'The fetching Miss Francesca Moore drew much appreciative applause during her solo turn upon the high wire, which concluded with a stunning backward somersault.' " I passed the clipping over to Biggs.

He read it through and then looked up with feigned amazement. "Good God, Hardeen! What a scoop! We'll have to re-make page one!"

I sighed and replaced the clipping in the file. "Hardly the revelation I was seeking. No doubt there will be more material on Kellar."

Indeed, Mr. Kellar's file was so extensive as to require seven packets to contain it all. Biggs left me alone to work my way through it while he returned to his desk. In all I spent the better part of three hours sorting through the various reviews, advertisements and press announcements. The clippings presented a fascinating overview of the magician's long career, beginning with his modest appearances in vaudeville, where his efforts were usually described as "engaging" and "competent," through the long years of his worldwide travels, when the label of the "wandering wonder-worker" appeared with great frequency, and concluding with the period of his greatest success, during which he was referred to almost without exception as "the Dean of American Magicians." I noted a few familiar names running through the articles, including that of Dudley McAdow, whose appearance in Mr. Kellar's life appeared to coincide with a dramatic upturn in the magician's fortunes. Try as I might, however, I could find nothing to suggest a reason for anyone to wish harm upon Mr. Kellar, far less a motivation for the murder of Francesca Moore.

Upon finishing, I closed up the final file and replaced it in the cabinet, then went off to find Biggs. He looked up at my approach. "You didn't find anything, I take it?"

"How can you tell?"

"That fancy manicure of yours. You always chew your thumbnail when you take notes, but today it's positively pristine."

"You should have been a detective, Biggs." I reached for my hat.

"Come clean, Hardeen. What exactly are you digging for? The woman's death was an accident, wasn't it?"

"There's certainly nothing in the files to suggest otherwise," I said.

"That didn't exactly answer my question, Dash."

"Look, Biggs, I just wanted to find out a bit more about the poor woman who died last night. That's all."

He studied my face. "You really are a terrible liar, Dash. It's quite endearing, actually."

"You see? I was never cut out for journalism."

"Promise me one thing, then," he said, as I made for the door.

"Promise that when the story breaks—"

"Don't worry, Biggs. You'll be the first to know."

A heavy snow was falling as I left the offices of the *World*. Even so, I decided to make my way back to the hotel on foot. My finances were precarious at best, and the events of the past few days had left my prospects uncertain. A long walk in the frigid air, I told myself, would do me a world of good.

I had learned nothing to shed any light on why anyone should wish to harm Miss Moore or Mr. Kellar. From all that I had seen, Mr. Kellar was a generous employer, and most of my fellow crew members were openly grateful for the terms of their employment. Most, like myself, had worked in far less pleasant conditions, and enjoyed the little comforts and fripperies that came with a front-rank touring company.

Miss Moore, for her part, remained a troubling question mark. She had been with the company only a short time before the tragedy occurred, and no one seemed to have come to know her terribly well. Apart from her European birth, and her years with the Kendalls, I knew almost nothing about her. How had she come to be murdered in such an astonishingly dramatic fashion? I felt no closer to finding the answer.

By the time I neared the hotel, my face and hands had gone numb in the biting afternoon wind. My route happened to take me past the Belasco, and I was just thinking to myself how pleasant a roaring fire might be when I saw a column of dark smoke rising from the dome of the theater. Fearing the worst, I ran forward only to find that the black plume was coming from a trash fire in the back. I hurried down the access alley and came upon Silent Felsden and Valletin stoking an enormous bonfire.

"Hardeen!" cried Valletin as I emerged from the alley. "Just in time! Join the party!" The biting cold had reddened his cheeks, making him seem even more cherubic than usual. He took a bundle of scrap wood from Felsden, who was taking a long swig from his glass flask. "Come along! You can toss in the drapes!"

"What—what's going on?" I asked.

"Isn't it obvious?" Valletin asked, taking the flask from Felsden. "It's a funeral pyre for Princess Karnac!"

I peered into the inferno. Sure enough, I could just make out, amid the cracking wood and peeling paint, the outlines of the dragon-footed levitation banquette.

"The costumes and screens are already gone," said Valletin merrily, "but look, we've saved you the cloak!"

"I—I don't understand," I said. "This illusion cost Mr. Kellar a fortune! How could you just toss it onto a fire?"

"The old man gave the order himself," Valletin explained. "Says he never wants to lay eyes on the Floating Lady ever again."

"But the police! They may yet need to examine the equipment!"

Valletin waved aside a wisp of smoke. "Mr. Kellar said they were done with it. 'Throw it on the fire, boys,' he told us."

I hesitated. "It just seems such a waste, that's all."

"Hell, I once saw Mr. Maskelyne toss away an entire Temple of Benares illusion. Said he didn't like the way it creaked."

I watched as a pair of boards collapsed, sending up a shower of sparks. "That illusion cost more money than my father made in his entire lifetime," I said. "Just throwing it all on a fire like this, it doesn't seem right."

"Come on, Hardeen. It's just a pile of wood! You look as if you've lost your best friend!" He took another swig. "Who knows? Maybe this will drive out the evil spirits. Send the curse of Kalliffa across town to plague Mr. Servais Le Roy. Have a drink with us! Give the princess the send off she deserves!"

I took the flask from his hand and stared into the heart of the flames. "Rest easy, old girl," I said. I raised the flask in a salute and took a swallow.

"That's the spirit, Hardeen," said Valletin. "Come on, here's another piece of the braceworks, why don't you—oh, good afternoon, Miss."

We turned to see Perdita Wynn standing at the mouth of the

alley, dressed in a fur collar and muff. Her eyes were wide and gleaming in the reflection of the fire, and an expression of utter dismay was stamped upon her features. She took a step closer, but halted. Tears were streaming down her face.

"What's the matter, Perdita?" asked Valletin.

"How could you?" she sobbed. "How could you do such a thing?" She turned and fled into the alleyway.

"What's she off about?" asked Valletin. By way of a reply, Felsden shrugged and tilted the flask to his lips.

I dropped the wooden slat I was holding. "She seems rather upset," I said. "Hadn't you better go after her?"

"Why me?" Valletin snapped. "Miss Perdita Wynn is none of my responsibility."

"But—"

"See here, Hardeen," he continued, "if you're so concerned, you can go chasing after her yourself."

"As you wish." I turned and set off down the alley.

I caught sight of Miss Wynn hurrying along Broadway in the direction of the hotel. She did not seem to hear my shouts, so I ran a short distance to overtake her, grasping her by the arm as I reached her side. "Miss Wynn!" I said, catching my breath. "Perdita, what's the matter? You're trembling!"

"It's nothing, Mr. Hardeen," she said, taking the pocket square I held out to her. "I'm sure I'm being very foolish."

"Your cheeks are flushed with the cold," I said, clasping her hands, "and your fingers are like ice. Come on, let's get you inside." I led her a short distance across Broadway to Mickelson's tea room, and soon we were installed at one of the marble tables near a gleaming brass samovar.

"Is there no end to your capacity for chamomile, Mr. Hardeen?" she asked, smiling bravely through her tears. "It seems that you are forever obliged to ply me with cups of tea and endure my tales of woe. You're terribly brave."

"I would gladly drain a hogshead of chamomile for the pleasure of your company," I said, draping my coat around her shoulders, "though I would find it far more warming to see you restored to your better humor."

"Forgive me. I really don't know what's come over me."

"We are all distressed by the events of last night," I said, warming her hands with my own, "but you should not have been out in this foul weather. You might well have exposed yourself to pneumonia or worse."

"I've been walking for hours," she admitted, waving aside my ministrations. "I barely noticed the snow."

"Where were you going?"

She tilted her head as though trying to remember. "To be honest with you, Mr. Hardeen, I wasn't going anywhere. I've just been so upset since—since last night. I couldn't sleep at all. Every time I closed my eyes I fancied I could hear Francesca's scream. And then to come upon the three of you having a jolly time over the wreckage, it seemed..." She let the thought trail off. "I'm being foolish."

"Not at all," I said.

She waited while our tea was served, then leaned forward as the server withdrew. "Mr. Hardeen, I beg that you will be frank with me. Is it true that Mr. Collins has been imprisoned?"

"Who told you that?"

"I was sitting near Mrs. Kellar at breakfast when Mr. Kellar returned from speaking to that policeman. I couldn't help but overhear."

I considered my answer carefully. "The police seem to believe that Mr. Collins has not been as forthcoming as he might."

"But he's not to blame! He just happened to be the one who helped her onto the wire. It could have been any one of us! Surely the police understand that?"

"They appear to have formed a different view."

Her eyes filled with tears once again. "Mr. Collins is in jail, Mr. Kellar is thinking of closing the show. Yesterday everything seemed as bright as could be. Now it seems certain that I will have to rejoin the Gaiety Girls after all." She raised her tea cup.

"Do you know why I was coming to the theater just now?"

I shook my head.

"I wanted to speak to Mr. McAdow. I wanted to offer my services as the new Princess Karnac. I'd have happily taken over the role to prevent the show from closing, but then when I saw you burning the apparatus—well, I suppose there's no possibility of that now."

"You say you would have been willing to do the levitation?"

"Of course. I had been looking forward to a long period of employment before yesterday's unhappiness. I thought that if I could do something to help the show regain its footing—"

"What about the danger? The effect cost Miss Moore her life."

"I—I know that, Mr. Hardeen. There is no need to remind me, I assure you. But I was certain that you and your brother and Mr. Collins would discover what went wrong and take steps to be sure it wouldn't happen again. I have great confidence in you."

"But what made you think you would be able to assume the role so easily? Have you any experience on the high wire? Miss Moore was a very extraordinary young woman, and even she—"

Something flashed in her eyes. "I am well aware that Francesca was a woman of exceptional gifts, Mr. Hardeen. I have been reminded of this fact every hour of every day that I have been with the Kellar company. You and Malcolm and everyone else simply couldn't wait to tell me about how the sun rises and sets upon Miss Francesca Moore and her transcendent loveliness. Well, Mr. Hardeen, it may interest you to know that—" Her tirade broke off as quickly as it had begun. She snatched up my pocket square and pressed it to her mouth, her eyes wide with astonishment and self-reproach. "What am I saying?" she asked, lowering the napkin from her lips. "How could I think such things, especially now? I'm sure you must think me quite the worst person in the world, Mr. Hardeen."

"Not at all. You're just upset."

She twisted the fabric in her hands. "My God! I've been saying horrible things!"

"You make too much of it," I said, sipping my tea. "We are all in shock today. My brother has been spouting nonsense about some ludicrous curse all day long. We are not ourselves."

She fell silent over her tea for several moments, apparently trying to muster her composure. "What I meant to say, Mr. Hardeen—what I should have said—was that I am well aware that Francesca possessed many special talents that made her ideally suited for the role. However, I have come to believe that with the proper training, I might have made a passable substitute."

"Your willingness to do so is a great credit to you. I would only suggest that your lack of experience as an aerialist might have been an obstacle."

"Francesca seemed to think that the high-wire work was not so difficult as you and Mr. Collins had made out. She told me that she could have done the conclusion of the Floating Lady on one foot. She even promised to take me up to the dome one night and show me how much fun it was out there."

"With respect, I imagine that this is the sort of thing that seems simple enough to someone with her long experience, but very difficult to the uninitiated."

"I'm sure you're right. In any event, it hardly matters now."

"No. Mr. Kellar seems resolved that the effect will not be revived."

"He's a dear man, but it was just an accident. He can't possibly think that he could have prevented it, any more than Mr. Collins—" She looked into my eyes, and for the second time I had the uncomfortable notion that she was reading my thoughts. "It *was* an accident, wasn't it, Mr. Hardeen?"

"That's what Lieutenant Murray said last night," I offered.

She lifted her tea cup and studied me very carefully. "You're a good deal more clever than you pretend to be, Mr. Hardeen."

"You give me more credit than I deserve."

"Perhaps." She set the cup down and covered my hand with her own. "I suppose I'm feeling sorry for myself. As I said, I rather hoped that I might spend a year or two with Mr. Kellar.

Now, who can say? It hasn't always been easy to find work, you know."

"I've had some experience along those lines."

"No doubt. But it is so much harder for a woman, I expect. At least you needn't worry about lecherous advances from every booking agent and manager that you meet."

"Seldom," I agreed.

"I just couldn't go back to the burlesque houses, Mr. Hardeen. I'd sooner pack my bag and go back to Illinois." She withdrew her hand. "But there I go again, feeling sorry for myself. Perdita, you really have become the most extraordinary bore!"

"Perdita," I said. "It's quite an unusual name."

"My father was quite a Shakespeare enthusiast. Do you remember *The Winter's Tale*, Mr. Hardeen?"

"Dimly. Miss Becker was quite a demon for Shakespeare."

"Miss Becker?"

"My seventh form instructor. I preferred the historicals. I found *Henry V* rather stirring."

"I imagine you would have," she said. "Once more unto the breach, dear Hardeen. God for Harry! England! And Saint George!" She smiled. "That's you to the last detail, Mr. Hardeen."

The conversation continued in this vein as I settled the bill and escorted her back out onto Broadway. She gripped my arm tightly as I helped her over the mounting drifts of snow, and laughed at my remarks with rather more energy than they deserved.

"Thank you again, Mr. Hardeen," she said as we paused outside the Tilden. "You are quite possibly the most charming man in New York." She leaned forward and pressed her lips to my cheek, leaving me quite red-faced with surprise. "Oh, and don't forget this," she added, pressing the pocket square into my gloved hand.

"Er, Miss Wynn," I began, suddenly tongue-tied, "I wonder if—that is—I wonder if—"

"Yes?"

"You're quite fond of Shakespeare, are you?"

"Indeed, Mr. Hardeen."

"Of course you are. I happened to note that there is a production of *Cymbelline* at the Lyric. I wondered if, by any chance, you might wish—"

"Yes, Mr. Hardeen?"

"I wondered if you might care to—"

"Dash! There you are!" My brother burst through the front doors of the hotel and hurried down the snow-covered steps. "Come along! We have urgent business this evening!"

"Urgent business? This evening?"

"Ah! Miss Wynn!" Harry lifted his hat as he joined us at the bottom of the steps. "You grow more radiant each time I see you."

"How kind, Mr. Houdini."

"Harry, this is not the ideal moment—"

"There has been a stunning turn of events!" Harry cried. "It concerns—" he glanced at Miss Wynn, measuring his words, "—it concerns our cousin Chester! You remember Chester, don't you? Our cousin?"

"Yes, Harry," I said evenly. "I remember Chester."

"He requires our assistance at once! It is most urgent!"

"It sounds terribly serious," said Miss Wynn. "I won't detain you, Mr. Hardeen."

"I—"

"Thank you again for the tea. It was very warming." She took a step toward the front door of the hotel.

"Wait—"

She turned. "I understand that the tea at the Lyric is also quite good, Mr. Hardeen."

I let my hands fall to my sides. "I've heard that as well," I said.

"Next time, then." She turned and climbed the rest of the stairs. "And Mr. Hardeen—" she called, pausing at the door.

"Yes?"

"Do give my best to your cousin Chester."

12

A PONDEROUS CARPET

"HARRY," I SAID, "WHAT YOU'RE PROPOSING IS ILLEGAL. IF WE'RE caught, we'll go to jail."

"Why should that trouble you?" my brother asked with a grin. "Jail cells have never held us before."

"It would be different this time. If we broke out, they'd put us back in again. It could get tiring after a while."

We were sitting over the remains of a light supper in Mother's kitchen on East 69th Street. Harry had listened attentively as I reviewed my movements for the afternoon, and expressed little surprise that my search of the archive at the *World* had produced no revelations. "Dash gets these ideas in his head," he told Bess. "Sometimes it's best just to let him have his way."

Harry's own afternoon, as it turned out, had been no more fruitful. "Would you believe it?" he asked indignantly. "Mr. Servais Le Roy has never even heard of the Great Houdini!"

"Imagine," I said.

"Will wonders never cease?" asked Bess.

"It seems that I am not the first member of the Kellar company to come looking for work, either," Harry continued. "Can you imagine?"

"Who else?"

"Mr. Le Roy's representative would not say, but clearly

there had been several. Mr. Kellar has not even announced his retirement yet, and already the members of his company are fleeing like rats. It offends my sense of decency!"

"Well, Harry," said Bess, clearing away his dinner plate, "you were also there looking for employment."

"Ah! But I was in disguise!"

"In disguise?"

"Well, I was acting in a confidential capacity. Yes. A confidential capacity. Behind enemy lines."

"Harry, we don't know that Mr. Le Roy is an enemy."

"We do, Dash. Why else should he have hurried to New York with his version of the Floating Lady? How else could he have been ready with his posters and bookings?"

"Because he's smart? Because he's hoping to take advantage of all the publicity surrounding Mr. Kellar's misfortune?"

"It is more than that. Far more. The man is a horrible ghoul, at the very least. Possibly he is much worse. We must discover whether his method of achieving the Floating Lady illusion is the same as our own."

"What would that prove?"

"It would prove that he has a spy within the Kellar organization. And it would prove that he has a powerful motive for seeing the Kellar show closed for good."

I lifted my spoon as Mother placed a shallow bowl of currant pudding before me. "Do you really suppose that any magician would stoop so low as to commit murder to drive a rival out of business?"

"Of course. Besides, who else would have been clever enough to manage it?"

"But if Mr. Le Roy is a murderer, as you seem to believe, why wouldn't he simply kill Mr. Kellar? Wouldn't that be rather more direct?"

Harry plunged a spoon into his currant pudding. "The publicity, of course! Mr. Kellar's tragedy has generated a great deal of interest from the public. Mr. Le Roy's 'Mystery of Lhassa' is certain to open to a sold-out house. This is far more valuable to him than the death of Kellar."

"Harry," said Bess, "you are being utterly absurd!"

"Am I? Well, we will know soon enough—as soon as we put my plan into effect."

"Your plan is preposterous," I said. "You're suggesting that we—"

"—Steal Mr. Le Roy's Floating Lady." Harry spooned up a mouthful of pudding. "What's so preposterous about that?"

"Where shall I begin?"

"Dash, it's really very simple," he said, as though explaining simple arithmetic to an especially dull pupil. "It is vital that we ascertain the method by which he intends to perform the Floating Lady. If it is the same as ours, then he has stolen it from us. One could hardly blame us if we should then take back what was ours to begin with."

"Harry, you and I came up with the Kellar method in a single afternoon. Surely Mr. Le Roy might have hit upon the same method independently?"

"I find that very unlikely. The genius of Houdini is quite unparalleled." He scraped the bottom of his bowl with his spoon. "You know that I'm right, Dash. If Mr. Le Roy's method is the same as ours, then he is surely our villain."

"Why don't we simply wait until tomorrow, buy a ticket, and enjoy his performance of the Floating Lady when the rest of New York City sees it—at his opening performance?"

"That will be too late. Jim Collins is to be formally charged with murder tomorrow. That is what I came to tell you at the hotel. I wish to prevent that from happening if at all possible. I grow more convinced of his innocence with each passing moment! So we must not delay. I have discovered that Le Roy's apparatus is arriving this evening by train and will be stored in a holding facility at Grand Central. This is our opportunity."

"Grand Central?"

"Yes. We cannot afford to dawdle. Tomorrow the apparatus

will be transferred to the Forsythe Theater and held under guard. I am going to infiltrate the Grand Central storage facility at 3:17 this morning. You are welcome to join me, but I am going in any case."

"At 3:17? In the morning?"

"Or possibly 3:18. It may be dangerous, and the task would be considerably easier with your assistance."

Bess, hovering behind Harry's chair, fixed me with a pleading expression.

"You're certain there's no other way?"

"Do you believe that Jim Collins killed Francesca Moore?"

I sighed. "No," I said. "No, I suppose I don't."

"Then there is no other way."

"Very well, Harry," I said with an air of resignation, "but if we're caught, I'm going to insist on separate cells."

In those days, the sumptuous Grand Central Terminal of today was still some years off. Mr. Vanderbilt's smaller and far more modest structure occupied the site on 42nd Street. I can still recall the open cut of the railway tracks of the New York Central along Park Avenue, and the furor that attended the decision to charge them with electricity. Even then, the terminus was thriving with travelers, and it was already apparent that the needs of the city would soon necessitate a larger station.

Harry and I had elected to catch a few hours of sleep before setting off, so as to make our approach under cover of darkness. He insisted that we leave the flat at 2:30 precisely, so as to be "ready for curtain," as he phrased it, at the appointed hour. Harry had also insisted that we don our special dark clothing, the remnants of our 'Graveyard Ghouls' act.

I felt that the attire made us more than usually conspicuous. "What are we supposed to say if we run into a roundsman?" I asked as we made our way down Park Avenue. "We might as well be wearing domino masks and carrying a bag marked 'swag.'"

"You worry too much, Dash. I have decided that we won't wear masks."

"How prudent of you."

"What's the time?"

I hauled out my Elgin and peered at the face under a flickering street lamp. "Seven minutes before three," I said. "Why are you marking the time so carefully?"

"Look," he said, "there is the back gate of the station." He pointed to a high brick wall topped with sharpened slatting. "Formidable, is it not?"

"Harry, we can't climb that."

"No, indeed. The front is just as heavily fortified."

"What about the gates? Can we pick the locks?"

"Alas, no. There are guards posted at both entrances. They would surely object."

"Then how are we supposed to get in?"

"What's the time now?"

"Harry—"

"The time, Dash."

"Five to three."

"Good, there is just time enough. Come along, Dash."

"But Harry, how are we supposed to—"

He put a finger to his lips. "Small steps, Dash. Everything in small steps."

Twenty minutes later, a wagon rolled up to the rear gates of the station. It was a flat-back four-wheeler pulled by an aging draft horse named Bill. Heaped in the back was a pile of nine regulation U.S. Postal Service mailbags. Seven of them contained mail that would be shipped out by train in the morning. The other two contained the Brothers Houdini.

Harry managed it brilliantly, I have to admit. The previous afternoon, posing as an inspector from a mysterious "Weiss Agency," he had quizzed the station guards about security practices and schedules. He quickly fastened on the nightly mail delivery as the weak link in an otherwise solid chain, and set about devising a means of exploiting the fact. When he learned that Malachi, the delivery driver, generally stopped beside a briarberry bush at the corner of Madison and 43rd to perform a necessary, Harry's plan fell into place. That morning, while Malachi attended to his business in the bushes, Harry and I scrambled onto the back of the cart. By the time our driver's fly was buttoned, we had slipped into a pair of empty mail sacks.

From within the sack, I tried to follow our progress as Malachi flicked the reins and the cart moved toward the rear gate of the station. The cocoon of heavy canvas made it difficult to pick out movement and sound, but I could dimly hear a muffled exchange of greetings between the driver and the guard, followed by the sounds of the heavy gate swinging open. Our wagon lurched forward, and a sudden brightening of light told me that we had entered the station. I barely had time to register this fact when I felt a sudden thudding pain in my side, followed by the sensation of falling through empty space. Apparently Malachi had climbed onto the back of the cart and was kicking the bags onto the floor. Swathed in canvas, I could do nothing to break my fall. I came to land on a grunting mass that I took to be my brother. I rolled off and lay still for a moment. The sound of retreating horse hooves told me that the wagon was moving off.

For a considerable length of time I lay motionless, straining to hear any sounds of movement. It was decidedly close within the canvas sack, and it required something of an effort to breathe. Although I do not generally suffer from claustrophobia, I had the impression that my supply of air was thinning with each breath, and I had to fight an overpowering urge to struggle.

Straining to control my breathing, I listened for any sound that might indicate that Harry was slipping out of his sack. If Harry was lying low, I reasoned, perhaps we were still in danger of discovery by the guards. Several moments passed, and with each one my sense of suffocation intensified. I was now coated in a sheen of perspiration, and waves of needle-like heat were spreading across my skin. My legs had begun to cramp, and spots were swimming before my eyes.

Why had Harry not freed himself? There had been no sounds of movement that I could discern. All indications pointed to the fact that the storage facility was empty. A second thought struck me; perhaps Harry had been knocked unconscious when we had been unceremoniously dumped from the cart. Maybe he had struck his head and was now in danger of suffocating within the canvas sheath! I listened again for the sound of movement, but heard nothing. At last I could stand it no longer. I decided to free myself from the mailbag.

It proved to be more difficult than I had imagined. The durable canvas not only restricted my breathing, it also limited my movement. Worse, the top of the sack was folded over and cinched with a leather buckle-strap, which in turn was fastened with a padlock. Harry had taken pains to insure that I was securely locked in, so that the bag would appear no different from any of the others. His own bag, I assumed, could not have been so rigorously sealed, since he had no one on the outside to assist him.

Harry had helped me get in, but it appeared that I was going to have to get myself out. Twisting to get my hands into position, I tried to work my fingers through the top of the sack, but the folded canvas held fast like drying mortar—Harry had tightened the buckle-strap with his usual energy.

I cannot say how long I kept at it, or how many times I cursed my brother under my breath. The rough fabric became like dense brambles against my skin, and my fingers grew raw with the strain of trying to tunnel through the infernal fold at the top of the sack. At last I managed to get one hand free, like a chick hatching from an egg. Straining against my limited range of movement, I felt around for the padlock that held the strap in place. When I found it, I could not suppress a blue oath. My lock-picks would be useless—the lock had no keyhole. It was one of the modern rotary dial fasteners, which opened by a sequence of numbers dialed in combination, rather than a key.

For a moment I simply lay quiet, too exhausted by my efforts even to ponder my next move. Then, suddenly, I felt the entire sack lifted off the ground and placed on some elevated platform. An instant later the top opened and a welcome rush of light and cool air flooded over me.

"What were you waiting for, Dash?" came my brother's voice. "I realize that you are not the world's foremost self-liberator, but surely you must have learned a thing or two from me over the years! I thought you'd fallen asleep in there!"

"Harry?"

"Come on. It'll be light soon. We have less than an hour."

"I couldn't hear you. I thought—"

"I shouldn't wonder that you couldn't hear. You sounded as though you were throwing a calf! So much for stealth! What were you doing in there?"

I blinked in the light as I threw off the heavy sack. "Harry, those things are suffocating! You can't imagine how tortuous it is when that strap is properly fastened. It's like quicksand!"

"Really?" He looked at the discarded sack with sudden interest. "I wonder…"

A sudden noise interrupted the thought. We dove beneath the pile of mail sacks as a watchman's footsteps drew closer. We were aware of the beam of a bull's-eye lantern playing over the room, but then the footsteps receded.

"He's a bit ahead of schedule." said Harry, as we emerged once again. "We'd better hurry."

For the first time, I had leave to examine my surroundings. We were in the midst of a cavernous storage area, in which crates and sacks were haphazardly arranged amid a number of hand trolleys, loading straps and sorting tables. "This is where Le Roy's apparatus will be held until he collects it tomorrow," Harry explained. "He came ahead on an earlier train in order to make the theater arrangements. Look at all these crates!" He swept his hand through the air to indicate the vast storage area. "Finding Le Roy's apparatus among all this clutter will be difficult. Come on, Dash. We have a long search ahead of us. We must work quickly."

"Perhaps not, Harry."

"What do you mean?"

"Well, I may not be the world's foremost self-liberator, but if I were looking for the effects of a famous Belgian magician, I might start with those large crates marked 'Apparatus de Magie.'"

"Ah. Very good." Harry darted over to the crates I had indicated. Snatching up a metal crowbar from one of the work tables, he began prying open the lids of several of the containers.

"I still don't feel entirely at ease about this, Harry," I said, watching him paw through the packing straw inside one of the cases.

"Nor do I," he admitted. "We are spying on a brother magician. It is a violation of our code."

"Actually, I was referring to the fact that we're trespassing on government property."

"Oh, that," said Harry. "Honestly, Dash, you can be such a limp dish rag! We are investigating a murder! We are entitled to bend the law just a bit if we are able to achieve—"

"We're entitled to no such thing," I said with some heat. "We have a police department that investigates murders. You and I are just a pair of meddling amateurs."

"Perhaps so," Harry admitted, prying open the lid of another crate, "but your Lieutenant Murray doesn't know the first thing about illusions or sleight of hand or show business. He has admitted it himself. We are just giving him the benefit of our experience, as he requested."

"That may have been useful when he was interrogating Jim Collins," I said. "But I doubt if it extends to committing a robbery."

Harry murmured something under his breath.

"Pardon?" I asked.

"Nothing."

"You know I'm right, Harry. If we should happen to be arrested, Lieutenant Murray won't lift a finger to help us. And if you ever call me a 'moaning Minnie' again, I'll knock your teeth down your throat."

"You're always welcome to try, Dash, but I think you'll find—ah! Here we are!"

Harry had pushed aside a considerable amount of straw to reveal a slender pedestal, not unlike our own levitation banquette. "This must be it," he said. "Help me lift it out!"

I went around to the other end of the crate and grabbed the legs of the pedestal. It lifted out easily. "There must be more to it," I said. "You couldn't make anyone disappear with this thing. There are no traps of any kind, and no possible place of concealment."

"Perhaps Le Roy's Floating Lady doesn't need to disappear."

"What do you mean, Harry?"

"Well, we experimented with various methods of causing Princess Karnac to float using various harnesses and support devices. Perhaps Le Roy managed to perfect such a method."

I nudged the flimsy pedestal with my foot. "Even Bess couldn't possibly levitate off of this thing. No one could, no matter how small she happened to be. It's barely sturdy enough to support her weight. Even the most slender woman in the world would cause this thing to tip over before she ever managed to levitate. No leverage whatsoever. Far too top-heavy."

"Yes," Harry agreed, studying the pedestal with a critical eye. "There must be some other piece in one of these other trunks. Help me move this crate out of the way."

"All right, but—uh, Harry?"

"What is it, Dash?"

"Why does this empty crate weigh so much?"

Harry, straining to shove the wooden crate aside, suddenly let go and stepped back. "Excellent question," he said.

We pushed aside the rest of the straw packing at the bottom of the crate. "There's nothing in here except that scrap of packing cloth," Harry said. "Do you suppose the crate is constructed of some special—?"

"That's not packing cloth, Harry."

"No?"

"It's a round carpet. It must go underneath the pedestal."

"What of it?"

"Unless I'm very much mistaken, that carpet weighs upwards of three hundred pounds."

Harry reached in to grab the edge of the carpet, but couldn't budge it. "Brilliant," he said, with genuine wonder in his voice. "A three hundred pound carpet. Who would ever suspect it? The pedestal is too fragile and spindly to attract any suspicion, but underneath, the deceptively heavy rug provides all the leverage one could wish."

Together we lifted the rug from the crate and spread it on the floor. "Ingenious," Harry said. "With our method, the Floating Lady must be covered up at the beginning of the effect. Le Roy has made it possible for the audience to see her rising, without any covering at all! He must be quite gifted."

"Either that or he has some very inventive people working for him."

Harry did not appear to hear me. He was staring into the deep red and blue pattern of the rug. "Dash," he said. "This is a rather unfortunate development."

"I realize that, Harry."

"If Mr. Le Roy has developed his own completely unique and original method of performing the Floating Lady effect, then he would have no reason to try and steal the Kellar version."

"Exactly."

"Which means that he has no spies within the Kellar company."

"It seems unlikely."

"So we are no closer to discovering who is trying to put Mr. Kellar out of business. We have made no progress whatever in solving the murder of Francesca Moore." He sat down on the three hundred pound rug and let his head slump forward.

"Perhaps Mr. Collins is guilty after all. Could I have been so wrong about him?"

"This may not be the place to discuss the matter, Harry."

"Someone has gone to extraordinary lengths to thwart Mr. Kellar's plans for the Floating Lady. Extraordinary lengths. If not Mr. Le Roy, who could it be? Can it be that the intended victim was really not Miss Moore after all? Is it truly—"

"Harry," I said, shaking him by the shoulder, "the sun is coming up. We've broken into a locked warehouse in order to search the belongings of a rival magician. The guard will be coming back along in a few moments. Do you think we might put off this discussion until we're safely out of here?"

"All right, Dash," said Harry with a note of annoyance. "But you really are becoming a terrible fusspot."

As it happened, Harry's plan for getting out of the Grand Central storage facility was far simpler than the plan for getting in, though to this day I believe that he devised it on the spur of the moment. As daylight began to stream in through the high windows, we located a custodial closet near the wash rooms and picked the lock. Inside were a number of washermen's coverings, along with mops and wooden pails. Harry and I simply donned the appropriate clothing and spent half an hour or so mopping the floor of the main waiting room. We were joined shortly by members of the station's actual cleaning crew, none of whom found anything unusual in the presence of a pair of unfamiliar workers. After an appropriate interval, we stripped off the coverings, returned them to the custodial closet, and simply strolled out through the front gate of the station.

"What an utter waste of a night," Harry said, blinking in the morning light.

I stretched my sore limbs. "Let's discuss it later. Right now I need a bath and some sleep."

"We might as well admit defeat," he continued, as we began walking uptown. "Collins will die for this crime, whether he's guilty or not. And Mr. Kellar will carry the stigma with him until the end of his days."

"Please, Harry. I'm too tired to think about it right now."

"You care nothing for the fate of Jim Collins?"

"Of course I do. But unlike you, I can't keep going forever without food or sleep. I'm just a mortal, Harry. And right now I'm dog tired."

He fell silent for the rest of the walk home, having apparently added my fatigue to the lengthy catalog of my failings.

A walk of half an hour or so brought us to East 69th Street. For once the prospect of one of my mother's hearty breakfasts was a source of eager anticipation. I climbed the steps ahead of Harry, who was still absorbed in his reverie.

Bess met us at the kitchen door with a peculiar expression on her face.

"What is it?" I asked. "Is anything wrong?"

"You'd better brace yourselves," she said.

"What?" cried Harry, pushing forward. "Is Mama—?"

"She's fine." Bess swung the door open. "Don't say I didn't warn you."

Harry Kellar and another gentleman were sitting at our mother's breakfast table with white napkins tucked into their collars, eagerly attacking plates of food with their knives and forks. "Ah! Gentlemen! Good morning!" Kellar called cheerily as we came through the door. "I must say, Mrs. Weiss, this is the most delicious dish I have ever tasted! What did you call it?"

"*Kasheh*," said Mother.

"Wonderful!" Kellar exclaimed. He turned back to us, smiling at the stunned expressions on our faces. "Forgive me, I seem to have forgotten my manners. You are wondering who this gentleman is that I've brought with me." Kellar stood and pulled the napkin from under his chin.

"Allow me to present Mr. Servais Le Roy."

~ 13 ~

A LITTLE SOMETHING ON OUR STOMACHS

SERVAIS LE ROY WAS A SMALL, DAPPER MAN WITH SLICK BLACK hair and a waxed moustache, the tips of which extended a fair distance on either side of his face, in the manner of antennae. His black velvet suit featured buckled knee breeches and long stockings of the type once fashionable at court, making him quite the most singular-looking man I had ever seen. Certainly he was the most exotic visitor ever to grace my mother's breakfast table.

"I hope that you will forgive the intrusion," Le Roy said. His clear, pleasant voice was lightly accented with what I took to be Belgian rhythms. "Henry felt that it was imperative that we speak with you immediately. He was most insistent."

"Le Roy has had a brainstorm!" Kellar cried. "An absolute brainstorm!"

Harry and I exchanged a look, trying to appraise the situation. We were definitely not looking our best. We still wore our dark clothing from the previous night's escapade, and our labors at the Grand Central storage facility had left us a bit rough around the edges. The top of Harry's head looked like one of the mops we had used to make our escape, and I was covered with cuts and scrapes from my struggle with the mail bag.

"I, uh—you must pardon our appearance," Harry stammered.

"We—we've been helping a friend," I added, hoping that

this explanation would suffice.

"Tell them your idea, Le Roy!" said Kellar, too caught up in his excitement to notice. "I can't wait to hear what they think of it!"

Our dapper visitor, busy with a plate of my mother's pepper sausages, nodded enthusiastically. "Henry is being generous," he said, setting down his fork and dabbing at his lips. "The inspiration is not mine alone. It was he who suggested the hoop skirt."

Harry pulled back a chair and sat down. "I'm afraid you've left us completely in the dark," he said. "What hoop skirt?"

Kellar gave a barking laugh. "Sorry, Houdini," he said. "We must sound as if we're talking a lot of nonsense. We'll start from the beginning."

"I went to visit Henry at his hotel last night," Le Roy explained. "It seemed to be the only proper thing to do. Of course I had read all about the tragedy of the other night. It made our little rivalry seem quite absurd, and I wished to call in and pay my condolences."

"Very decent of him," Kellar said.

"Well, I also wished to explain my sudden appearance in New York—to present a Floating Lady, no less! The timing was terribly disagreeable, coming so close on the heels of the misfortune. It must have appeared"—he paused, searching for the proper word—"ghoulish, I suppose."

"No, no," said Harry, his face growing scarlet.

"Not at all," I hurried to add.

"But how could I have known? Yes, the timing was very disagreeable. I don't know what you must have thought of me. I had no idea that Mr. Kellar would be presenting a Floating Lady at this time, far less that there would be such a disaster on the opening night. After all, it is not as if Mr. Kellar and I are spying on one another."

"Of course not," Harry said, laughing nervously.

"What a ridiculous notion!" I added.

"Le Roy and I had never met before," Kellar said, taking up the story. "I suppose we were a bit wary of one another at first, but once the formalities were addressed, we warmed up rather quickly."

"Henry is quite generous with his bourbon," Le Roy observed.

"One thing led to another, and soon enough we had fallen into a debate over the Floating Lady. Very lively, it was. Le Roy has devised a rather crafty method of actually showing the lady rising above the levitation banquette. None of this covering her up with a cloak, either."

"You don't say?" asked Harry.

"Incredible, isn't it? You'll say it's impossible, but he's found a way to allow the lady to hover above the stage for a moment or so. And by his account, it will look sensational!"

"My levitation couch is quite delicate," Le Roy explained, "far more so than the one Henry has been using. The audience sees this fragile piece of furniture, and they are not at all suspicious of it. Intuitively they understand that it could not be part of some elaborate machinery, because it lacks the solid appearance of the usual run of magician's apparatus. You see what I'm suggesting?"

"The couch itself is not the mechanism of the levitation," Harry said. "You've found some other means of establishing the necessary leverage. A carpet, perhaps."

Le Roy drew back in surprise. "Why, yes! Exactly! How could you possibly have guessed that?"

I shot him a warning look. I suppose he couldn't help himself.

Keller gave another snort of laughter. "I told you these boys were clever! Don't get any ideas about stealing them away from me, Le Roy!"

Le Roy took another forkful of sausage, gazing at my brother with a wary expression.

"You can see how Le Roy's version offers a great advance over mine," Kellar resumed. "In our effect, we never actually saw the princess floating above the stage. She had to be covered with the cloth or it wouldn't work. It was fine for our purposes, but Le Roy's method is far more effective."

"So far as it goes," Le Roy added. "But with my version, the Floating Lady never left the stage. Your method of having her float out over the audience—it is an inspiration!"

Kellar nodded eagerly. "So naturally it occurred to us—"

"—If we were to combine the two effects—" Le Roy broke in.

"—Use bits of Le Roy's version and bits of mine—"

"—Then we would have the definitive version of the Floating Lady effect!"

Kellar turned to us with a happy expression on his features. "What do you think, boys?"

Harry and I were momentarily at a loss. A short time earlier, we had been plundering Le Roy's equipment. Now we were swapping secrets over a plate of mother's *kasheh*. My mind was racing to keep up.

"I think that Harry and Dash are a bit taken aback," Bess said, trying to cover our obvious discomposure. "For one thing, Mr. Kellar, we had understood that you never wished to perform this trick again. You even spoke of withdrawing from the stage forever. This morning you seem quite transformed."

A shadow passed across Kellar's face. "It's true," he said. "I imagine that my enthusiasm must seem misplaced in the circumstances, but I have had a chance to do a great deal of thinking since the tragedy. That lieutenant from the police department informs me that he is investigating this matter as a case of murder. Poor Collins has fallen under suspicion, it seems."

Harry spoke up. "We don't happen to believe that Collins is guilty," he said.

"Nor do I, Houdini. Nor do I. But that is a matter for the law." He paused, considering his words carefully. "I know that it may strike you as odd, and perhaps a bit unseemly, but the knowledge that Miss Moore was murdered has brought me a strange form of comfort. Though her death is no less terrible,

I am consoled to know that it was not caused by negligence on my part. A thing such as this is a great blow, and I have now seen it twice in my lifetime—first with the misfortune of my mentor, Mr. McGregor, and now with the events of Saturday night. In such circumstances, I may perhaps be forgiven if I allowed myself to grow morbid and fanciful. So long as I felt that Miss Moore had come to her end through some doing of mine, I could never have faced an audience again. As it is, her death will haunt me to my last breath, but I am encouraged to believe that there was nothing I might have done to prevent it. And who knows, perhaps the same might be said of Hermione McGregor as well. Perhaps this evening will afford me an opportunity to lay her spirit to rest once and for all."

"This evening?" Harry asked. "What is happening this evening?"

"This is why we have come to you this morning," Le Roy said. "Henry and I are anxious to test our combined method of performing the Floating Lady. My debut is not until tomorrow evening, and of course the Belasco is dark in honor of Miss Moore, so we thought we might have an opportunity to stage a dress rehearsal. We shall incorporate both techniques into a seamless presentation of the effect."

"What do you think, boys?" asked Kellar. "It would take a hard day's work to be ready in time, but I told Le Roy that the pair of you would be up to the challenge. Of course we'll have to build some new equipment in a terrible hurry, but we can get most of what we need from Le Roy. The rest of it we can knock together in the scene shop this afternoon." He glanced at me. "Hardeen? Are you listening?"

I gave a start. "Forgive me. I was thinking of—"

"The two of you want to perform the effect together?" Harry broke in.

"Certainly!" Kellar said. "Why not? Of course, there won't be an audience. We'll just do it for our own gratification, to see if we can agree on the staging. It's just this once, then we'll go back to business as usual, I'm afraid. Tomorrow Le Roy and I will be rivals once again. After all, a little competition is good for business."

"Indeed," said Le Roy. "I am a far better magician knowing that I must stay abreast of the great Harry Kellar."

"But what about the patent?" Harry asked. "What about all the money?"

Kellar and Le Roy looked at one another with raised eyebrows. "I suppose I'll have to let McAdow sort it out with your manager," Kellar said. "I can't wait to see the look on his face when I tell him I've handed over my best secret to Mr. Servais Le Roy!"

"Wherever will you find an aerialist by this evening?" Bess asked. "What happened to Miss Moore—"

"Ah, but there's the beauty of it!" said Kellar. "Le Roy has had a further inspiration that removes any remaining element of danger. We no longer require a trained wire-walker, simply because there is no longer any need of high-wire work."

Le Roy reached into his breast pocket and unfolded a piece of yellowed paper. "It is a notion I have had for some time," he said, spreading the illustration out on the breakfast table. "If the young lady were wearing the device I've envisioned here, it would offer far more safety than the conventional leather harness." Mr. Le Roy's drawing indicated a primitive type of gyroscope device that fastened about the assistant's knees and waist, keeping her level while supporting the back and legs. "I call it the 'Magic Corset.' "

"It's an exceptional idea," Harry said. "Quite remarkable. But how would it be possible to conceal such a device beneath the Princess Karnac robes?"

"We can't," said Kellar. "The Princess Karnac costume is useless to us now. We shall have to devise an entirely new story line—one that finds our Floating Lady wearing a hoop skirt."

"A hoop skirt," Harry said. "Yes, that might work."

"Mrs. Houdini," said Kellar, "would you honor us with your

assistance for the first-ever performance of the Kellar–Le Roy Floating Lady?"

Bess hesitated. "I—I'm not certain that I should, Mr. Kellar."

His face clouded. "I quite understand, my dear. After what happened on Saturday night, I can hardly blame you."

"No," said Bess. "It isn't that. I believe that Miss Wynn might be a more appropriate choice. She is taller, and perhaps better suited to the apparatus. Besides, I understand that she has her heart set on becoming your lead assistant."

"Miss Wynn will be a splendid choice, dear lady," said Kellar. "How gracious of you to—"

"This young lady," Le Roy broke in. "How tall is she?"

"Perhaps a head taller than I," said Bess. "Perhaps more."

Le Roy shook his head. "Too tall. The harness won't fit. I built it for my own assistant, who will not arrive until tomorrow. Marguerite is roughly your height, Mrs. Houdini."

"Won't you reconsider, Mrs. Houdini?" Kellar asked. "Just for this evening?"

Bess looked at Harry. He nodded. "I should be delighted, Mr. Kellar," she said.

Kellar rubbed his hands together. "Very good. Shall we repair to the theater? There is much work to be done." He pushed back his chair and set his napkin on the table. "Mrs. Weiss," he said, clasping Mother's hand, "I must compliment you once again on your wonderful cooking. This is the finest breakfast in all of New York."

"I quite agree," said Le Roy. "I've never had a finer in Paris or Brussels."

Mother beamed happily. "You both needed a little something on your stomachs."

"Dash?" Harry said, looking at me closely. "What is it? You've hardly said a word. You have the strangest look on your face."

"Do I?" I grinned weakly. "Just the excitement, I guess. Harry, may I see you in your office for a moment?"

"My office? I have no—"

"We'll return in a moment, gentlemen. Come along, Harry."

I led him down the center hall to the water closet. "Dash—what—?"

"Harry," I said, taking a seat on the edge of the tub, "you'll have to go ahead to the theater without me."

"What? You're not coming with us? You can sleep later, Dash!"

"I'm not going to bed, Harry, but I can't come to the theater right away, either."

"But what will I tell Mr. Kellar and Mr. Le Roy?"

"Tell them anything you like. Tell them I've had a sudden attack of gout. I don't want to face their questions just now."

"Dash, what's come over you? This is very strange behavior."

"Please. I'll join you at the Belasco in an hour or two. I just have to see a man about something. It shouldn't take long."

"See a man about—what are you going on about? What are you—" He stopped himself. "You've solved it," he said quietly. "You know who killed Francesca Moore."

"No. Not for certain."

"Who is it? Come now, Dash. Tell me!"

"Harry, I really don't know for certain. And if I'm wrong, I'll end up looking very foolish. In either case, I'm going to be sure that Lieutenant Murray attends our little demonstration this evening."

"Lieutenant Murray? You intend to unmask the murderer at the theater?" He nodded his approval. "Yes, that would be very dramatic."

"I don't intend to unmask anyone. But if I'm right, the murderer won't be able to resist seeing the Floating Lady one last time."

"But what about Bess? Will she be safe?"

I walked to the wash basin and splashed some water on my face. "Bess won't be in any danger," I said. "It's you I'm worried about."

Harry pressed me repeatedly for further details until I reminded him that the two most prominent magicians in the world were being kept waiting in the kitchen. Grudgingly, he returned to our guests and tendered my apologies, and after a moment the three of them set off for the Belasco, with Bess promising to join them later. I then spent the next half hour assuring my mother that I had not been felled by the sudden onset of leprosy, as Harry had led our visitors to believe, though I was required to eat another plate of pepper sausages to confirm that my health was uncompromised.

Leaving the flat a short time later, I went directly to one of my favorite haunts—the New York Public Library. The present building was still under construction at that time, but I knew that the book I wanted would be readily available at the temporary quarters on 40th Street. I presented myself at the front desk and headed straight for the theater arts section. I had the answer to my question within five minutes.

From the library I made my way further downtown to the offices of the *World*. Biggs was at his compositor's desk as usual, and I counted myself lucky that there were no horses running that day.

"Hardeen?" he asked, as I tapped him on the shoulder. "Didn't you get what you needed yesterday? I suppose you'll be wanting—say! What's the matter? You look terribly serious. And why are you dressed like a burglar?"

"Show me to the morgue, Biggs."

"Come on, Dash, what's—?"

"Do you want the story or not?"

He hopped down off his stool without another word. Moments later, he was putting up the lights in the dusty store room. "Which file do you need this time?" he asked.

I reached for a drawer.

"Ah!" he said. " 'K' for Kellar?"

"No," I answered. "Not exactly."

"Dash, would you mind telling me what—"

"Oh, lord," I said. "Good God in heaven."

"What is it? Dash? You look as if you've seen a ghost."

I looked up, my head spinning. "Are you interested in an exclusive, Biggs?"

"Of course I am. Let me get a—"

"Not now. Tonight. The Belasco Theater."

"But what—?"

"I'll tell you then. Oh, and one last thing…"

"Yes?"

"It's an opening of sorts. Dress appropriately."

"Hardeen—!"

I pushed past him and ran for the stairs.

∽∾ 14 ∽∾

ONCE MORE UNTO THE BREACH

IT WAS AN ODD, CURIOUSLY INTIMATE GATHERING IN THE FRONT rows of the Belasco theater that evening. The house lights had been lowered to half and the lobby and common areas were dark, imparting a hushed and shadowy ambiance to the proceedings. The faces were familiar, but we observed the formal proprieties of first-nighters.

Members of the Kellar company, including Malcolm Valletin and Silent Felsden, occupied the front row of seats, chatting happily before taking their places backstage. They were joined by a handful of visitors from Mr. Le Roy's troupe, chief among whom was a robust fellow who called himself Bosco.

"Not bad, Hardeen!" called Valletin, looking more like a cherub than ever with a brightly ornamented waistcoat under his dress coat. "The most exclusive show in New York!"

Behind him in the second row, Biggs and Frank Lyman sat side by side, both of them scribbling furiously in their note pads. Beside them sat Dudley McAdow with a scowl on his face, as though contemplating toilsome patent matters. Perhaps the greatest surprise was the appearance of Lieutenant Murray, who had arrived looking quite resplendent in a formal pigeon-breasted coat and black trousers. His opera pumps were shined to a high gloss.

"I must say, lieutenant," I said, as I showed him to a seat on the aisle, "this marks a change from your usual attire."

"You needn't look so surprised, Hardeen. My wife and I are quite fond of opera." He lowered his voice. "Are you sure I need to be there, Hardeen? You know I'm not keen on these theatrics from you and your brother."

"I think you will find it worth your time, lieutenant," I said.

"You think so, do you?"

"I'm sorry to be mysterious about it, Le Roy and Kellar were determined to go ahead with their presentation this evening, and that left us with very little time to prepare. I've barely had time to tell Harry—to give Harry his lines."

"Where is he, by the way?"

"Working behind the scenes."

The lieutenant sighed and lowered himself into his seat. I turned as Perdita Wynn motioned me to an empty seat beside her.

"How is your cousin Chester, Mr. Hardeen?" she asked as I sat down. "Is he fully recovered from whatever emergency tore you away last night? I've been so terribly worried."

"Well," I said, "his difficulties were not as urgent as I had been led to believe. Harry was simply looking for a pretext to draw me away."

"You don't say! I should never have guessed. Not with all that energetic winking and nudging. He is a master of subtlety, your brother."

"I—I—"

"Tell me, does he always appear just as you are about to make theater plans? You'll make a lady feel positively unwanted."

"You must accept my apologies," I said, finding my voice. "Harry and I were called away on a rather strange errand last night. I look forward to sharing the details at a later time, assuming I have not lost your favor."

She smiled beautifully. "We'll see," she said, squeezing my hand. "We'll see."

The house lights suddenly dimmed as Kellar and Le Roy walked onto the stage from opposite sides. The two men bowed to one another then turned to the footlights. "Friends," said Le Roy, "the effect that Mr. Kellar and I will attempt to present this evening truly represents a milestone in the magician's craft."

"We were all shocked by what occurred here on Saturday evening," said Kellar, taking up the theme. "Tonight, with your indulgence, we shall attempt to complete the effect that was cut so tragically short that evening. We offer this as a small tribute to the memory of Miss Francesca Moore." He nodded to the orchestra pit. "Gentlemen, if you would."

There were only about half of the normal complement of musicians in the pit that evening, which had the effect of making the music that normally accompanied the Princess Karnac effect sound even more ominous than usual. Mr. Le Roy gestured to the wings and my sister-in-law Bess emerged wearing the costume of a Southern Belle, complete with a rather ungainly hoop skirt. I turned to Perdita. "About the role—" I whispered.

She squeezed my hand a second time. "Mr. Kellar told me," she answered. "You were very gallant to commend me."

From the stage, Kellar bowed deeply as Bess stood beside the levitation couch. "Watch carefully as my colleague places Mrs. Houdini into a hypnotic trance," he said, as Le Roy waved his hands before Bess's eyes. "Now, as her eyes grow heavy, we shall place her upon this divan."

Le Roy moved to the front as Bess, her eyes closed, was laid out upon the sofa, leaning up on one elbow to face the audience. "I think that tonight we may safely dispense with the tale of the imperiled princess and the evil Pasha, ladies and gentlemen," Le Roy said with a wink. "We ask only that you keep your eyes trained upon the stage, so that you don't miss a single moment."

Kellar moved around to the front of the divan and the two men stood side by side with their backs to the audience, momentarily shielding Bess from view. Moving as one, they stretched their arms forward as if to urge the sleeping Bess to lift from her perch.

For a moment, nothing happened. As the music swelled,

a strange ruffling motion became apparent. Then, incredibly, the reclining figure of my sister-in-law could be seen rising horizontally into the air, slowly coming into full view above the heads of Le Roy and Kellar. There was no covering, no smoke, no wires or mirrors. It was quite the most amazing effect I have ever beheld. Our small audience erupted into spontaneous applause.

"Cast your eyes heavenward, ladies and gentlemen," Kellar intoned, "and watch as she rises…rises…rises…now she casts aside the high-flown theories of gravity and science like so much useless chaff. See how she floats, as though on a gentle zephyr, borne aloft by the hypnotic force of animal magnetism."

Just then, we saw Bess tilt to one side and vanish into shadow as the stage lights went low, as if swallowed by darkness. Le Roy and Kellar turned to face the audience, peering into the space above our heads. A smudge pot flashed suddenly, sending a billowing column of white smoke into the air. The ghostly image of Bess, flickering amid the curls of smoke, could plainly be seen floating high above the crowd, lost in the grip of Kellar's trance. For a moment she seemed to waver and undulate, then she vanished as the light dimmed.

Le Roy's voice came from the stage. "Now she is almost beyond our earthly grasp, ascending like Icarus himself toward the sky. Surely the gods themselves must watch in wonder as she floats up toward the vault of heaven."

A second geyser of flame burst forth. Once again the spectral image of Bess could be seen—more distant this time—nearing the high dome of the theater. "Can we believe our eyes?" came Kellar's voice. "Can we trust our senses when they behold that which is plainly impossible? Still she rises… higher and higher…borne aloft by a power we mortals cannot begin to comprehend."

I heard Lieutenant Murray twisting in his seat for a better view. "Not bad," he allowed. "Not bad at all."

"You haven't seen the half of it yet," I murmured.

From the stage, Kellar's voice sank to a lower register. "Now the lovely princess has neared the end of her strange journey. Soaring to the heavens, lifted by unseen hands, she completes her wondrous ascent. Behold!" Kellar thrust his hands up toward the dome.

We had reached the moment of crisis. Everyone in the theater recalled all too vividly what had happened two nights earlier as Kellar spoke these words—and most of us had been present to witness it. I heard a collective intake of breath as the lights were trained upon the majestic theater dome. The sight that greeted us was a welcome one. Bess, still under the 'hypnotic influence' of Mr. Kellar's spell, hovered gracefully in the empty space beneath the apex of the dome. It was a stunning sight, and the memory of it fills me with wonder even now.

"Bravo, Kellar!" shouted Dudley McAdow from his seat in the second row. "Bravo, Le Roy!"

The others joined in lusty cries of approval for several moments, falling away only as Kellar and Le Roy motioned for silence.

"Now we will bring our Floating Lady back to earth," Le Roy informed us. "As the mesmeric spell begins to lift, she will return safely to our stage."

I gripped the arm rests of my seat, bracing myself.

A shrill scream pierced the air. "My God!" I shouted. "It's Bess! What's wrong?"

"The lights!" cried Kellar. "All lights on full!"

For a moment the follow lights dipped and whirled before training upon the dome. We saw a flash of Bess's face contorted with terror as a second scream echoed through the dome. Then, as the lights danced across the darkened space, she flickered out of view.

I leapt from my seat. "She's falling!" I shouted. "Good God, no!" I sprinted up the center aisle as fast as my legs would take me, but she was already plummeting downward. I was aware of shouts and cries behind me as the falling figure struck the brass railing with a sickening thud.

I stood in a daze over the fallen figure as the others crowded around me.

"Hardeen, what—?"

"Is she—?"

"Not again—!"

"But how could—?"

I knelt down and gently stretched out my hand to roll the fallen body over. The face of Matilda the mannequin smiled happily back at me.

The cloud of voices rose in pitch, with Kellar's authoritative tones cutting through the discord. "Hardeen? What's the meaning of this?"

"One moment, sir." I rose and stepped to the aisle, craning my neck to see into the darkened dome.

"Harry?" I shouted.

"He's here, Dash!" came my brother's voice, drifting down from above. "You were right—he's—stop there! Come back here!"

"Get the lights up there!" I shouted. "Now!"

Another moment or two passed as the follow lights whirled into position. As the focusing lenses adjusted, a heart-stopping sight greeted us. Two men were grappling savagely with one another on the suspended platform high above the theater, the fragile surface undulating wildly beneath their shifting weight. The smaller of them, my brother Harry, appeared to be getting the upper hand, but the bigger fellow had the advantage of size and surprising agility.

As Harry stepped back to gain fighting room, moving perilously close to the edge of the platform, the follow light flashed upon the features of his opponent.

The face was that of Malcolm Valletin, and he no longer looked at all like a cherub.

～❧ 15 ❧～

KILLER ON THE HIGH WIRE

I BURST THROUGH THE LOBBY DOORS AND CHARGED THE STAIRS, with Lieutenant Murray and Silent Felsden at my heels.

"How did you know?" the lieutenant shouted after me, as I bolted through the office suite toward the upper staircase.

"Couldn't be certain," I returned, pushing through the second set of doors. "Knew he'd try to foil it—"

"But what—?"

Lieutenant Murray's question was cut short by a scream from Bess as we reached the top of the wooden steps. It sounded genuine this time. I yanked open the hatchway and ducked through to the catwalk.

Harry and Valletin were in a ferocious struggle on the suspended platform at the center of the dome, high above the half-lit theater. The narrow planking swayed wildly beneath their shifting weight as both men fought to maintain balance. As I came through the hatchway, Valletin managed to knock Harry onto one knee. He reared back to deliver a vicious kick that would send my brother over the edge of the platform. Bess, watching from the other side of the catwalk, let out another scream.

"Valletin!" I shouted. "You can't escape! Don't make it worse!"

He turned, his face crimson with fury, and saw Murray and Felsden coming through the hatch behind me.

He turned back to Harry. "Hope you can float, Houdini!" he snarled, delivering a brutal kick to Harry's ribs. I watched helplessly as the force of the blow knocked my brother over the side of the platform. Only Harry's extraordinary reflexes kept him from falling seventy-two feet to his death. Rolling with the kick, Harry managed to flip, head over heels, so as to grab hold of a support wire. The sudden shift of weight caused a violent lurching motion, knocking Valletin off his feet. He recovered with a speed I wouldn't have thought possible, scrambling across one of the support wires toward the opposite end of the catwalk.

"My God!" cried Lieutenant Murray. "He's like a cat on that wire!"

"Yes," I answered, edging cautiously out toward the platform to rescue Harry. "Exactly."

I did not have my brother's natural ease upon the high wire, and as the rope ladder was nowhere to be seen, my progress was damnably slow. I edged across the nearest support in a sitting position, grasping the braided wire firmly between my legs in order to reach my brother. I suppose only thirty seconds elapsed before I was able to pull him to safety, but it seemed like an eternity. Valletin, meanwhile, seeing that the dome hatchway was closed off as an avenue of escape, kicked his way through a ventilator covering and wriggled through the small opening.

"Where does that lead?" I called as Harry danced across one of the wires to reach the spot.

"The roof, I think," he answered. "Come on, lieutenant!"

I followed as quickly as I could across the gap between the platform and the catwalk, trying not to look down as I inched over the wire. Bess helped me onto the catwalk as I neared the edge, pointing to the ventilator opening through which the others had passed. I squeezed through, feeling a blast of frigid air on my face.

I found myself standing on the snow-covered roof of the theater, with a harsh wind whipping about me. Felsden and Murray stood near the ventilator opening, huddled on a narrow ledge of slate. Just beyond, the roof angled sharply downward toward a wide, low-pitched pediment topped by a lattice of ironwork. Harry and Valletin faced one another across the sharp downward pitch of the roof, their feet sliding perilously on the frost-covered slate. Beyond them, past the edge of the pediment, the roof fell away sharply, commanding a dizzying view of the street below.

"Can't you do anything?" I shouted to Lieutenant Murray, straining to be heard above the howling wind.

"Like what?" he answered.

"Don't you have a gun?"

"Haven't carried one in years!"

I drew a deep breath of cold air into my lungs and edged out onto the downward slope of the roof. Instantly I felt the grip of a powerful wind lashing about my legs, threatening to carry me over the side. Feeling my feet slipping out from under me, I fell hard with my hands splayed, making a sort of toboggan descent down the roof on my hind end. Valletin looked up at the sound of my noisy approach, allowing Harry to reel back and unload a powerful fist into his mid-section. The bigger man doubled over, then lashed out with the flat of his hand against Harry's knee, sending my brother skittering backward toward the angled pediment at the lower edge of the roof. Once again, Harry's reflexes prevented disaster. He wrapped a hand around the iron latticework as Valletin moved in for the kill, aiming a powerful kick that caught the bigger man in the kidney. Valletin let out a grunt and fell to his knees as Harry dove forward, wrapping his arms around his opponent's waist.

It proved to be a disastrous move. The combined weight of the two men sent them sprawling hard against the latticework, which shuddered and ripped loose from its supports. Harry managed to brace his feet against the pediment, stopping himself from going over the side, but Valletin was not so fortunate. He clawed at the ironwork as it toppled over the edge of the roof, slamming hard against a granite ledge some ten feet below. Harry and I peered over the side to see Valletin dangling head-down like a fish on a line. One foot was tangled in the remains of the iron railing, the other end of which was hooked precariously over a decorative cornice.

"That won't hold for long, Harry!" I cried, wiping the pelting snow from my eye.

"Valletin!" Harry shouted. "Don't move! You're hanging by a thread!"

Below us, Valletin stirred slightly, groggy from the fall. "What the hell—?" he began, but his movements caused his iron tether to shift, dropping him a good foot or so further below the ledge. "God! Houdini! Get me out of this!"

"Hold on!" Harry shouted. "I'm coming for you!" He edged out onto the pediment, with me holding onto one arm as he stretched the other downward.

"Harry, you can't climb down there!" I cried, my voice straining over the wind. "That railing won't hold both of you!"

Harry turned and shouted up to the dome, where Lieutenant Murray and Silent Felsden stood. "Silent! Bring me a rope!"

"How will we lower it to him, Harry? The ledge is in the way!"

"I'll have to think of a way to get further out, past the ledge." A thought struck him. "Felsden! Bring the corset!"

"Harry, you can't possibly be serious!"

"What choice do we have?" He peered over the edge. "Hold on, Valletin! I'll be right there!"

"I—I—can't—" the railing creaked in the wind, dropping Valletin another half a foot. He grabbed onto a decorative cornice with both hands. "For God's sake! Hurry!"

Felsden returned in an instant and sent a hank of rope skittering down the icy slope of the roof, followed by Le Roy's levitation harness.

"You're sure about this?" I asked, as Harry anchored the harness and rope to a stone buttress.

"Dash," he answered, "it's the only idea I have."

If anyone walking along Broadway at 37th Street that evening had chanced to look skyward, they would have beheld a most unusual scene. Just below the imposing pediment of the grand dome of the Belasco, Mr. Harry Houdini, the justly celebrated self-liberator, could be seen hovering in mid-air several stories above the busy thoroughfare. Though this might have struck the casual passer-by as remarkable enough in itself, the tableau was made even more curious by the fact that Mr. Houdini was wearing a ladies' hoop skirt as he floated through the night sky, the folds of which were lashing furiously against his legs.

It was a bold and audacious plan, and I doubt if even Le Roy himself could possibly have conceived of his device being put to such a use. While I stood bracing the rope against the edge of the buttress, Harry used the levitation harness to float down within five feet of the stricken man, though even now the jutting ledge prevented him from passing down the rope.

"I still can't quite reach you, Valletin!" Harry shouted, straining to be heard as the wind gathered force. "I can't get any closer! I'll have to swing the rope over to you! Grab hold!"

"I—I can't!" Valletin shouted. "I can't let go! I'm sure to fall!"

Harry strained to tilt himself further downwards. "I can't get any closer!"

"Careful, Harry!" I called. "That harness may not be able to take the strain!"

"You'll have to grab for the rope! I'll feed it to you nice and slow!"

"I can't!" he called, gripping the stone cornice even more tightly as the latticework creaked beneath his weight. "God! Help me!"

"We can't wait! The railing is slipping! Grab the rope and we'll pull you up! Nice and slow! Nice and—"

It should have worked. I think it would have if not for that infernal snowstorm. Sometimes when I close my eyes I can still see him letting go of the railing and clawing for the rope as it passed in front of his face. I can still see his cold-stiffened fingers batting the rope away in his panic, then snatching again a split second too late, as his foot pulled free of the railing and he began to spiral downward. I watched him fall as long as I could bear it, but I had to look away at the last instant.

Harry, still hovering in mid-air, closed his eyes and shuddered. "Get me out of this thing," he said. "There's nothing more we can do."

Moments later, after I reeled my brother to safety and we made the treacherous climb back up to the dome, I heard an unfamiliar noise at my side. Silent Felsden cleared his throat and spoke the first words I ever heard him say.

"It was bound to happen," he declared. "The man couldn't juggle to save his life."

16

MISS BECKER'S REVENGE

IT TOOK THE BETTER PART OF THREE HOURS BEFORE ANY SENSE of order was restored. In that time a series of police wagons converged upon the scene, and the laborious process of measuring, recording and interrogating began. Lieutenant Murray took command of the operation with his usual gruff authority, and when at last the body of Malcolm Valletin was loaded onto the back of an open cart, he dismissed the remaining officers.

"I don't suppose Dr. Peterson will find any water in the victim's lungs this time," I said as the wagon rolled away.

"No," he answered, "I think we can safely conclude that the fall killed him. Come on, Hardeen, let's get inside. You're frozen half to death."

No one had left the theater, and the buzz of excited voices as we came through the lobby doors told me that the shock of the evening's events had not yet begun to subside. Mr. Kellar had sent out to a nearby saloon for brandy and a crate of glasses, and the bottles were being passed from hand to hand in the front rows. Silent Felsden, having turned suddenly loquacious, sat at the center of a large knot of people, giving an animated account of what had occurred on the rooftop. Bess sat on the aisle with Harry crouched at her side, anxiously rubbing her hands.

"I'm all right, Harry," I heard her say. "Please stop fussing over me!"

"Bess?" I said as we came up to her. "You're not hurt? Valletin didn't try to—"

"I'm absolutely fine, Dash. Valletin never got within five feet of me. Not with Harry lying in wait on the catwalk."

Perdita Wynn, sitting behind Bess, nodded in agreement. "Your brother was right there."

"Are you all right, Perdita? Perhaps you'd better take a bit of this brandy."

"I'm fine." She smiled weakly, but her face was ashen. "It's been quite a shock. Thank heaven you're all right."

Lieutenant Murray put a hand on my shoulder. "Hardeen? If the ladies are finished with you, I'd like to ask a few more questions."

"Yes," said Biggs, leaping out of his seat. "How did you know Valletin was responsible? How could you have—"

"Indeed," Frank Lyman broke in, "how could you have known that—"

Lieutenant Murray held up his hand for silence. "Gentlemen, this is still a police investigation. With your indulgence, I'll ask the questions." He turned to me. "How'd you spot him, Hardeen? How did you know it was Valletin?"

"And how did he manage the murder of poor Francesca?" asked Kellar, handing me a glass with a generous measure of brandy in it. "Forgive me, lieutenant, but I feel we are all entitled to know."

"It was Harry's idea as much as mine," I began, after taking a sip of brandy. "He refused to believe that Collins could have killed Miss Moore."

"It was impossible!" Harry cried. "The man is utterly trustworthy! I knew it from the first!"

"Harry's conviction sort of rubbed off on me," I continued, "but we couldn't agree on why anyone would want to sabotage the Floating Lady. Harry was convinced that someone was trying to drive Mr. Kellar out of business and acquire the exclusive rights to the trick. Those rights would have become even more valuable with all the publicity in the wake of the tragedy. People would be flocking to see the so-called 'fatal illusion.' All of that seemed to point to a rival magician—Servais Le Roy."

"Preposterous!" cried Le Roy.

"I realize that now, sir. But you'll have to admit, if you were a less honorable sort of fellow, you'd have been able to turn this terrible business to your advantage."

He wrinkled his forehead. "What a devious mind you have, Hardeen."

"Actually, it was Harry's brainstorm, and you're quite right— he *does* have a devious mind."

"I had not had the pleasure of meeting Mr. Le Roy when the thought occurred to me," said Harry, blushing. "I know now that he is incapable of such a thing."

"Be that as it may," I continued, "I was approaching the problem from a different angle. I was convinced that Miss Moore was the intended victim. I couldn't believe that anyone would kill her just to get at Mr. Kellar. So I spent some time digging around in her background to see if there was anything to suggest a motive. I found nothing, absolutely nothing."

"But what about the lion?" asked Lieutenant Murray, cutting to the salient point, as always. "If Miss Moore was the intended target all along, why mess with the lion cage? There was no guarantee that the lion would attack Miss Moore."

"No," I said, "although she would have been the most likely victim. If Boris had escaped during the first performance in Albany, as seems to have been the intention, Miss Moore would have been the person standing closest to the cage. She was to play the part of the young bride threatened by the lion. As it happened, the mishap on stage meant that Boris got out quite a bit earlier than planned. Luckily, Harry was there to help capture him."

"So Miss Moore could have been Valletin's target in both cases," Murray said. "What did he have against her? Were they, uh"—he glanced at Bess and Perdita, struggling for a delicate euphemism—"were they, uh—"

"No, lieutenant. But I think Miss Moore learned something about Valletin that made her a risk to him, though she couldn't have realized its significance."

"What's that?"

"I'm afraid it has to do with the curse of Kalliffa. I believe—"

"Now look, Hardeen. If you expect the New York City Police Department to go chasing after some ghost, you're even crazier than your brother. No offense, Houdini."

"None taken," Harry answered.

I took another swig of brandy, feeling the warmth go to work on my frozen toes. "Tell me, lieutenant, do you believe in coincidence?"

He eyed me with suspicion. "Depends what you mean."

"Twenty-five years ago, a woman named Hermione McGregor fell to her death attempting to assist her husband with the Floating Lady effect. A quarter-century later, almost to the exact minute, Francesca Moore was murdered while performing the very same effect. I think that's quite a remarkable coincidence, don't you?"

"The Wizard of Kalliffa, right? What was his real name? Duncan McGregor?"

"That's right."

"I told you before, Hardeen. The murdered girl couldn't have had anything to do with that. She was far too young."

"That's true, but it's still the reason she was killed."

Biggs looked up suddenly from his frantic note-taking. " 'K' for Kalliffa," he said. "Not 'K' for Kellar, or 'K' for Kendall. You were looking for something on the background of the Wizard of Kalliffa."

"And I found it," I said. I reached into my pocket and pulled out a fading zinc-particle photograph. I passed it to Lieutenant

Murray. "The photograph shows Duncan McGregor with his arm around a small boy," I said for the benefit of Mr. Kellar. "The boy has the face of a cherub, and could only be—"

"Malcolm Valletin!" Lieutenant Murray cried. "Valletin was Duncan McGregor's son!"

"Exactly." I looked at Mr. Kellar, who had gone a terrible shade of white. "I'm sorry, sir, but Malcolm Valletin, the boy you once knew as Duncan McGregor, Jr., held you responsible for what happened to his father. He was determined to see you ruined, just as his father was."

"But—but there was nothing I could have done!" Kellar's hands were trembling. "McGregor insisted on performing the effect that night! I couldn't stop him! I tried, but he wouldn't listen!" His lips were quivering with emotion. "My God! McGregor's boy! If only I had known!"

Lieutenant Murray stared at the photograph, scrutinizing every detail. "It doesn't quite cover it, Hardeen," he said. "It doesn't explain how he was able to carry off the murder, or why."

"You saw how agile Valletin was on the high wire tonight," I said. "Obviously he had some training as an aerialist. I believe that his father must have spent some time sharing a bill with the Kendall Brothers during his long slide into obscurity. I think that Miss Moore must have realized that Malcolm Valletin had grown up around the Kendalls. Possibly she even discovered who he really was. In either case, she was dangerous to him. It's clear that Valletin knew all about Miss Moore's training with the Kendalls. He used it to manipulate her on the night of her death."

"The chalk?" Harry asked.

"Exactly. Valletin knew perfectly well that Miss Moore wouldn't go out on the wire without making two chalk marks to honor the Kendall tradition. All he had to do was remove the piece of chalk she was carrying in the Princess Karnac costume. Then, after she'd vanished from the levitation banquette at the start of the effect, she would be sure to return to the dressing room before she went up to the dome with Collins. Valletin must have been waiting in the dressing room."

"And he killed her," the lieutenant said. "Probably held her head down in the wash basin. That would account for her wet hair. But if Valletin was the killer, Collins must have been in on it with him. Collins said that he escorted Miss Moore up to the dome. He said she was alive when he left her there. If Valletin killed her down in the dressing room, Collins must be lying. The two of them must have worked it together."

"No," I said. "Valletin did it himself."

"But Collins said—"

"Collins was telling the truth. But you're right in a sense, lieutenant. Valletin had plenty of help." I took another gulp of brandy. "Why don't you tell us about it, Perdita?"

I have not had the stellar career of my brother, but there are a handful of performances of which I remain proud to this day. This was one of them. Everyone in the room was stunned into silence. One might have heard the sound of a mouse skittering across the grand dome. Only Perdita Wynn appeared unfazed. She simply stared at me with those enchanting eyes, the edges of her mouth curling upward as if amused by my audacity.

"I guess maybe Miss Becker taught me a little more than I realized," I said, meeting her gaze. "In any case, I double checked at the library this morning."

"Who's Miss Becker?" asked the lieutenant.

"An old school teacher of mine. Why don't you tell us the rest, Perdita?"

"You're insane, Mr. Hardeen," she said quietly. "It's a great shame."

"I'm afraid you tipped the gaffe," I continued. "You said that your father was mad for Shakespeare. It took me a while, but the penny finally dropped. *Macbeth*. They say that it's bad luck to say the name in a theater, but I think we've already had more than our fair share. In *Macbeth,* the character of Duncan has a son by the name of Malcolm. And in *The Winter's Tale*, Perdita is the daughter of—"

"Hermione!" Mr. Kellar staggered forward, stretching out his hands to Perdita Wynn. "Good God! You are Hermione's daughter! Mina McGregor! But you were just a child then! A mere baby!"

"Once I realized that you and Valletin were brother and sister, it all suddenly made sense," I said, ignoring Kellar's outburst. "You took Miss Moore's place, wearing an identical costume. Collins would never have known the difference, not with you all swathed in that Indian get-up. Only your eyes were showing, and they're every bit as striking as Miss Moore's were. Collins remarked that Miss Moore seemed pale, but that makes sense in the circumstances, since you're a good deal more fair than she was, even in make-up. You went up the stairs with Collins and walked calmly out onto the platform while he watched, just as Miss Moore would have done. You must have learned a lot from the Kendalls. Collins never suspected a thing. When he left, he must have passed your brother hiding in one of the offices with Miss Moore's body. With Collins out of the way, Valletin climbed up to the dome and threw the body over the edge of the catwalk. You simply hung onto the platform, and then ran back to the catwalk while everyone was watching the body fall." I kept staring straight into her eyes, watching the tears well up at the edges. "It was a hell of a plan," I said, "except for the water in Miss Moore's lungs."

Lieutenant Murray shook his head. "All that because you studied Shakespeare as a schoolboy? That's how you figured it out?"

Perdita's hands were trembling now, but her eyes never wavered, even as the tears began rolling down her cheeks. I passed her my pocket square. Her fingers brushed mine as she reached for it. "Always the gentleman, aren't you, Mr. Hardeen? Even now?"

I felt my mouth tighten as I pulled my hand away. "That's very kind of you," I said. "It's what Miss Becker would have wanted."

≈ 17 ≈

THE GREAT AND POWERFUL KELLAR

THERE WERE FIVE OF US STANDING ON THE ROOF OF THE BELASCO Theater at dawn, watching the sun come up over a snow-covered New York City. Le Roy, Kellar, Lyman, and I had passed most of the night working our way through a final bottle of brandy as we huddled on the slate ledge near the ventilator opening. Harry, abstemious even in these circumstances, was perched on the angled point of the pediment, gazing out over the city.

"For God's sake, be careful, Harry," I called down to him. "It's still slippery up here."

"But the view is beautiful," he called in reply. "Come and see, Dash!"

"I'm fine here," I said. "One broken neck ought to be enough in a single evening."

Kellar watched as Harry swung his legs over the edge of the roof, straining for a better view. "He's really not afraid of anything, is he?"

"No, sir, he's not. It can be a bit trying at times."

"Well, it was a godsend for me," he said. "Between your brains and his courage, the pair of you managed to save me from ruin."

"Hmm," said Lyman. "Brains. Courage." He made a note on his shirt cuff.

Kellar ignored him. "Even now I can't quite comprehend it. How could they have hated me so much? I didn't kill

Hermione. I didn't cause their father's deterioration. I tried to prevent it. Certainly I could have done more, but McGregor wouldn't accept my help. He was proud."

"I doubt if it would have made two cents' worth of difference," I said. "The pair of them lost their mother and then watched their father slide into dissolution. It takes a toll. They needed someone to blame—someone besides their father."

Kellar reached for the brandy bottle. "Eva said the same thing. She said there was no one to blame but McGregor himself—he just didn't have the heart to go on. I still feel I might have done more for him."

"Heart," said Lyman, making another note on his shirt cuff. "No heart."

"Lyman," said Kellar, "what are you doing? I already told you, our little collaboration is finished. I'll pay you, of course, but I've decided I must do this thing on my own."

"Collaboration?" I asked.

Kellar took a swallow and handed the brandy bottle to Le Roy. "It's a little embarrassing. I've reached the stage of my life where I feel it might be worthwhile to set down my memoirs. I am vain enough to suppose that they will be of interest to posterity. But my education was rather limited, having run away from home at the age of ten, and life on the road does not allow much time for the refinements of learning. I decided that I would hire Lyman to assist."

"A ghostwriter?"

"I preferred to think of it as a collaboration. In any case, I was embarrassed and didn't want the company to know about it. But I've thought better of it now. I shall try to set my memoirs down without any assistance from my learned friend. Again, Lyman, I apologize for wasting your time."

"Think nothing of it, sir," he answered cordially. "The time I've spent with you has been a wonderful education for me. I've been writing home to my wife about it, of course, and she says that our children are most eager to know more about Mr.

Kellar's adventures. I find myself inspired to try my hand at a children's tale of some sort. The idea came to me only yesterday. You'll be in it, Hardeen, and your brother, too. And even the poor unfortunate Mr. McGregor. But of course Mr. Kellar shall be the featured player. Every child's fable must have a great and powerful wizard."

"A child's tale," Kellar said. "I wish you every success, Lyman."

"As do I, Mr. Lyman."

"Please, dear boy, I tried to tell you earlier. Most of my friends call me by my middle name, Frank. Mr. Kellar is referring to me by my given name, Lyman. But my surname is Baum. Lyman Frank Baum. Never cared for the name Lyman, though. Can't quite see it on the spine of a book, either." He paused to consider the matter. "L. Frank Baum. That should do nicely." He made another note on his cuff.

Le Roy passed over the remains of the brandy bottle. "The tour will continue, Henry?"

"Of course, but I'm rather short-handed just now. Collins will be rejoining us, of course, but there are a pair of vacancies I may not be able to fill any time soon. Hardeen, may I count on you and your brother, and the charming Mrs. Houdini?"

Harry, who had been making his way up the angled slate roof, gave a vigorous assent. "We shall be very happy to remain with the troupe," he said. "Bess will be overjoyed at the prospect of travel."

"I hope that it may become something of a longer term arrangement," Kellar said, as Harry joined us on the ledge. "I may not be ready to retire just yet, but the day is not far off. I shall be looking for a successor, Houdini, and he would have to be a gifted young man. I had rather fancied Valletin for the job, but…" His voice trailed off.

I looked at Harry. This was the opportunity of which he had dreamed when we joined the company scarcely one week earlier. Now, strangely, he appeared unmoved. "I suppose that your successor would be stepping directly into your shoes," he said, "performing your act exactly as it has been done these many years."

"At first, certainly. It's a tried and true formula, Houdini. I have no doubt that you could learn to handle the illusions, and your sleight of hand is excellent. We might tour for a year or two together, to establish you in the role of my heir, and then I could hand over the entire show to you. Of course I would retain the rights to the illusions, and the show would be billed as the Kellar Show starring Harry Houdini. Dudley would work out an acceptable fee schedule, but a large share of the receipts would be yours. You'd be very comfortable, Houdini. Very comfortable, indeed."

"Comfortable," Harry said sadly. "I am not certain that I am ready to be comfortable. Your offer is exceptionally generous, Mr. Kellar. and I shall always be flattered that you considered me worthy of consideration as your successor. But the illusions are not for me. I have my own act—my own formula for success, if you will—and I still believe it is the only true path for me."

"The escapes?" Kellar shook his head. "You'd have to give those up, of course. They're all right as a novelty, but as an entire evening's entertainment? No, Houdini. It'll never work. The illusions are tried and tested. I urge you to reconsider."

"I'm afraid not," Harry said.

"I will let you do the escapes," said Le Roy. "Why not come and work for me?"

"See here, Le Roy—" Kellar began.

"It is a new day," Le Roy said, sweeping his hand toward the rising sun. "You and I are rivals once again, Henry. What do you say, Houdini? 'Servais Le Roy presents the escapologist Harry Houdini, exclusively with the Royal Illusionists.' It has a nice ring."

"This is really too much, Le Roy—" Kellar declared.

Harry held up his hands. "I must give you the same answer, Mr. Le Roy, though I do hope that one day I shall be fortunate enough to share a stage with you."

"Good for you, Houdini," said Mr. Baum. "Courage!"

"How about you, Hardeen?" asked Kellar. "You're a handsome chap. Skillful on stage. You could hold a big show together, I bet. Don't tell me you're set on becoming an escape artist, too."

"Not exactly, sir," I said, watching as my brother hopped over the ledge and began swarming up the exterior of the dome, clinging precariously to a copper vein. "But I'm afraid I can't accept either. Someone has to keep an eye on him."

"What did I say?" cried Baum. "The fellow has brains!"

"I think you're both making an enormous mistake," Kellar said. "But I'll respect your decision. If you ever need me, you may rely upon Harry Kellar." He looked out over the city, lying still under the new snow. "God. Was there ever anything more peaceful than New York on a snowy Tuesday morning?"

"It is beautiful," said Le Roy.

"It's better from up here," Harry shouted down to us. "I can see for miles in all directions."

"Harry—be careful!"

"But it's gorgeous! Come up, Dash!"

"Not me."

"I can see the Statue of Liberty from here! Come on, Dash. Don't be an old lady!"

Kellar lifted his brows, smiling. "As you said, someone has to keep an eye on him."

I shrugged. "All right, Harry. How do I get up there?"

"Simple! Right foot on the gargoyle, left on the drain-spout. Grab the copper seam and lift yourself up slowly. That's it. Slowly. Good! You see?"

"Harry, this is crazy."

"Small steps, Dash," he said, reaching down for my hand. "Everything in small steps."

THE HARRY HOUDINI MYSTERIES

THE HOUDINI SPECTER

DANIEL STASHOWER

TITAN BOOKS

~✺ 1 ✺~

THE MAN WITH THE CAST-IRON STOMACH

MONSTROUS.

The old man shifted on his walking stick and gazed sadly at the vast expanse of stone before him. It was not only vulgar but also profane, a bizarre collision of ego and some misplaced sense of piety. It offended every notion of taste and decency. The sheer ostentation might have brought a blush to the cheek of Croesus. Naturally, Harry had thought it was lovely.

Why couldn't he have allowed himself to be buried like a normal person? With a small, tasteful marker of some sort? No, not Harry. He had to go out with a flourish. A thousand tons of granite had been spoiled to create this eyesore, along with a considerable amount of Italian marble. What had they called it at the time? A Greek exedra? That presumably described the curved stone bench that invited silent contemplation. But how to explain the stone figure of the kneeling woman sobbing at the graveside? Over the years, the old man had given her the name Beulah. "Hello, Beulah," he would say, patting her fondly on the shoulder as he passed. "How are the pigeons treating you today?"

His feet were tired from the long walk, and the old man gave out a soft groan as he lowered himself onto the bench, gazing up at the solemn bust of his brother. Here was the crowning touch, he thought to himself. Harry in all his glory, stone-faced in death as he so often was in life, gazing magisterially over the other, presumably lesser, inhabitants of the Machpelah Cemetery. What would Rabbi Samuel Weiss have made of this display? Thou shalt not worship graven images.

With his eyes fixed on the marble bust, the old man reached into the pocket of his brown tick-weave jacket and withdrew a silver flask. *Well,* he thought, lifting the flask in a brisk salute, *another year gone, Harry. Here's to you, you pompous old goat.*

I miss you.

Mrs. Doggett was waiting on the porch when the old man returned to the house in Flatbush. "Those men are here," she said in a voice heavy with exasperation. "Again."

"Those men?" he asked.

"The reporters. From the city."

"Ah."

"It's the same two men," she continued. "One of them is a photographer. They're in the parlor, smoking like wet coal. I don't know why you speak to them every year. It only encourages them."

"You know why I speak to them," he answered, tugging at his French cuffs. "He would have wanted it that way."

"Him," she answered. "Always him."

Mrs. Doggett continued to give voice to her displeasure as she led him into the front room. Newspaper reporters ranked just below potted meat and Estes Kefauver in her esteem. Newspaper reporters who smoked were to be especially despised, more so if they also made slurping noises when they drank their tea.

The old man was no longer listening. He had come to expect this annual visitation from Matthews of the *Herald*, and he had passed a quiet hour at his brother's exedra preparing himself. This year, he had decided, he would try something different. At the start of the interview, he would allow Matthews to believe that he had gone senile. *What's a man to do, Mr. Matthews? You just can't get good fish paste any more. That's what's wrong with this country, my lad. And you can tell that to Mr. Estes Kefauver when you see him.*

Nothing more than a reverse bait and switch; a little something to keep himself entertained. He would wait until Matthews began stealing glances at his watch and then spring the trap. *What's that, Mr. Matthews? You need to be getting back to the city? What a shame. I was just about to tell you what happened to Lucius Craig. You remember him, do you? Yes, his disappearance was something of a scandal at the time. Left half the society matrons in New York brokenhearted, as I recall. I read an article just the other day speculating as to what might have become of him. Should have asked me. I've known for years.*

Interesting man, Mr. Craig. There were some who believed he could speak with the dead. I saw him do some amazing things myself. Spirit messages. Disembodied voices. That sort of thing. I always wondered if—pardon? You want to know what happened to him? Well, Mr. Matthews, I guess there's no easy way to say this.

And here the Great Hardeen would pause and gaze sadly into the distance. *You see, Mr. Matthews, I'm afraid my brother and I made him disappear.*

Permanently.

The old man smiled to himself, then pushed open the parlor door to face his interviewer.

What's that, Mr. Matthews? You'd like to hear the story? But I thought you and Mr. Parker had to be getting back—? No? Well, I can't blame you for wanting to know the truth of the matter. It was front page news at the time and one of the many secrets that the Great Houdini vowed to take to the grave. Me, I'll be content to go to my grave unburdened. Let me see if I can remember how it began. Ah, yes. Biggs. It all started with Biggs.

I seem to recall that the newspapers were filled with accounts of Commodore Dewey destroying the Spanish fleet, which I suppose places things in the late spring of 1898. Harry would have just turned twenty-four at the time; I was two years younger. As always, our finances were at a low ebb. We had recently been fortunate enough to pull a couple of months as touring assistants with Mr. Harry Kellar's illusion show, but at the close of the season we were once again at liberty. We came back to New York, where Harry had been forced to sign on as a platform magician at Huber's Fourteenth Street Museum. It was steady work but strictly small-time, and Harry considered it beneath him. I spent my days making the rounds with his leather-bound press book under my arm, trying to scare up suitable opportunities among the more reputable music halls and variety theaters. I was not wildly successful in this regard, and more than once I abandoned my duties in favor of Ganson's Billiards Hall on Houston.

My recollection is that it was raining heavily on that particular day. Bess was working the chorus at Ravelsen's Review on Thompson Street, and it was a source of some consternation for Harry that her position brought a slightly higher wage than he was earning at the dime museum. I caught up with him backstage at Huber's, where he was pulling a double shift in the Hall of Curiosities.

"Intolerable, Dash!" Harry cried as he came off between shows. He was wearing a feather headdress and a leather singlet for his role as the laconic Running Deer, Last of the Comanche Wizards. His skin was slathered with copperish paste, and there were heavy streaks of lip polish on his cheeks, meant to suggest war paint. "You will have to find something better!" he continued, tossing aside a wooden tomahawk. "I am required to do a degradingly simple rope trick and spout ridiculous noises! 'Hoonga-boonga!' Have you ever heard of an Indian saying 'Hoonga-boonga'?"

"I never heard of an Indian doing the Cut and Restored Rope, now that you mention it."

"At the very least they could have employed Bess as well. She could have played my squaw."

"Bess seems quite content," I answered. "She prefers a singing engagement to working as your assistant. She says she's tired of jumping in and out of boxes."

"She said that?" He leaned into a dressing table mirror to dab at his war paint. "I suppose she is trying to put a brave face on the situation. Yes, that must be it. But at heart I am quite certain that she finds these circumstances as unacceptable as I do. It simply won't do for the wife of the Great Houdini to be seen cavorting in some music hall chorus. I have my reputation to consider!"

"Reputation? Harry, you're lucky to be working back at Huber's. Albert only took you on because he needed someone who could double as a Fire-Proof Man."

"Fire-Proof Man! Of all the indignities! Clutching at a piece of hot coal to show that one is impervious to pain! Thrusting one's hand into a flaming brazier! Ludicrous! The Great Houdini is now reduced to a mere sideshow attraction!"

"How's the arm, by the way?"

"Fine," he answered, wincing slightly. "I just need a bit more practice, that's all." He pushed a feather out of his eyes and adjusted the headdress. "Dash, you must get me out of this booking. Find something where I can do the escape act. It is the only way I will ever break out of the small time. If you do not"—he paused and drew in a deep breath—"I shall be forced to seek other representation."

"Other representation?" I ran a hand through my hair. "Harry, you're welcome to seek other representation, but you'll find that there's a crucial difference between me and the other business managers you may run across."

"Such as?"

"The others expect to be paid."

Harry folded his arms, the very picture of a stoic Comanche. "I'm just asking you to show a bit more initiative, Dash."

"Harry, I'm doing all I can. I have an appointment with Hector Platt at the end of the afternoon."

"Hector Platt?"

"He runs a talent agency near Bleecker Street. He's about the only one in New York who hasn't turned me down flat in the past three weeks. You're welcome to tag along if you think I should be showing more initiative."

I regretted the words as soon as they were out of my mouth. For the rest of the afternoon, Harry could talk of nothing but his "rendezvous with destiny" in the offices of Hector Platt. On stage he appeared newly invigorated, and even the expression "Hoonga-boonga" was given an enthusiastic spin. Between performances he drew me aside to speak in hushed tones of the "celebrated and distinguished Mr. Platt," who would surely be the one to propel the Great Houdini into the front rank of vaudeville. "Mine is a talent that cannot easily be confined to a single venue," Harry told me after the final performance. "The celebrated and distinguished Mr. Platt may have some difficulty in choosing the proper method of highlighting my abilities." He whistled happily as he scrubbed away the last traces of copper body paint.

In truth, Hector Platt was neither celebrated nor distinguished. He was what used to be called a blue barnacle in the show business parlance of the day, a man who tenaciously attached himself to the lower edges of the scene while serving no clear purpose. Very occasionally he would throw a week or two of work my way with one of the lesser circus tours or carnival pitches, but on the whole I considered him a last resort in desperate circumstances. I tried to explain this to Harry as we made our way across town in a covered omnibus, but he would not hear of it.

"Mr. Platt has simply not had the opportunity to avail himself of a truly top-drawer performer," Harry insisted as we alighted on lower Broadway. "We shall both benefit from this fateful association." He rubbed his hands together. "Lead on, Dash! Destiny awaits!"

I shrugged and led Harry down a narrow, winding alley off Bleecker Street. Beneath a yellow boot-maker's lamp we came upon a door with the words "Platt Theatricals" etched on a pane of cracked glass. I pushed open the door and climbed a dark flight of stairs with Harry at my heels. At the first landing we found a door hanging open on broken hinges. I rapped twice. Hearing a gruff summons from inside, I entered the office.

Hector Platt sat in a high-backed wooden swivel chair, regarding us through the lenses of a brass pince-nez. He liked to think of himself as a country squire in the European fashion, and to that end he wore leather riding boots and silken cravats. An untidy scattering of papers littered the surface of his oblong desk, with a brown clay pipe smouldering in an ashtray within easy reach.

"Hardeen," said Platt in his booming bass drum of a voice. "Haven't seen you in a good four months. Where've you been? You can't possibly have been working all that time!"

"As a matter of fact, my brother and I have been touring with the company of Mr. Harry Kellar," I said primly. "We've only just returned and have elected to rejoin the New York season. You are undoubtedly familiar with the recent successes of my brother, Mr. Harry Houdini." I gestured to Harry, who stepped forward to shake Platt's hand. "Although the stresses of the recent tour have been considerable, my brother has decided that he is willing to entertain suitable offers at this time."

Platt's lips curled as he reached for his clay pipe. "I am gratified to hear it," he said, tamping the pipe bowl with the end of a letter opener. "However, I am obliged to report that news of your brother's triumphs has not yet reached our offices."

"Indeed?" I stroked my chin at this strange lapse. "Well, if you would care to examine our press book, you will find ample testimony to the drawing power of the Great Houdini. No less a journal than the *Milwaukee Sentinel* was inspired to remark that—"

Platt waved the book aside. "I've seen your cuttings more than once, Hardeen. It might be more profitable to learn of your recent attainments. Tell me, what was it that you and your brother were doing during your time with Mr. Kellar?"

It was a sore point, as Platt undoubtedly realized. At that time Harry Kellar was the most celebrated conjurer in the entire world. He did not require the services of additional magicians in his company, so Harry and I had served as minor assistants in some of the larger production numbers. I had quite enjoyed my role in the background, but Harry had chafed at his small handful of assignments. Chief among these was a novelty number that required him to don a leopard-pattern loincloth and heft large weights as Brakko the Strongman.

"Our duties were varied," I said, examining my fingernails with a careless air, "and I may say in all modesty that Mr. Kellar was most reluctant to see us depart."

"Was he, indeed?" Platt's smile broadened as he sent up a cloud of noxious black smoke. "I do hope that he will be able to carry on. Now, Mr. Hardeen, I seem to recall that you and your brother have some experience performing a magical act of your own devising. I regret to say that at present I have no need of a magical act."

"It is not simply a magical act," I said. "My brother has devised an entirely new form of entertainment, one that is certain to place his name in the very fore-front of popular entertainment."

Platt unclipped the pince-nez and rubbed the bridge of his nose. "Not the escape act," he said wearily, closing his eyes. "I told you last time, there is simply no audience for such a thing."

Harry, who had showed uncharacteristic restraint during this exchange, now stepped forward and grasped the edge of Platt's desk. "I would be very pleased to offer a demonstration of my abilities," he said. "I guarantee that you will find it worth your attention."

Platt waved the back of his hand. "Please, Mr. Houdini. I do not allow every passing entertainer to audition here in my office. I should have no end of singers warbling the latest tunes and Shakespeareans declaiming from *Hamlet*. It wouldn't do to encourage such behavior."

Harry smiled as if Platt had made a delightful witticism.

"Singers are a penny to the dozen," he said. "Actors can be found on every street corner. The Great Houdini, as my brother has said, is entirely unique. I fear that mere words cannot convey the power of what I am able to achieve upon the stage. Only a demonstration will suffice. Have you a pair of regulation handcuffs?"

"Handcuffs?" Platt leaned back in his swivel chair. "No, Mr. Houdini. I do not happen to have a pair of handcuffs lying about."

"You're certain? Perhaps a good set of Palmer manacles or a nice solid pair of Lilly bar irons? I would also settle for leg restraints or thumbscrews."

"Mr. Houdini, I do not keep such things about my person. What sort of establishment do you suppose I am running?"

Harry's face fell. "It will be difficult to demonstrate my facility with handcuffs if no handcuffs are forthcoming," he allowed.

"I shouldn't be surprised," said Platt, squaring a pile of documents on his desk. "Now, gentlemen, if you would be so good as to excuse me, I have some rather pressing—"

"Mr. Platt," I said, struggling to regain some purchase on his attention, "I beg that you give my brother some chance to demonstrate his value as an entertainer. I offer my assurance that he is the most exceptional performer in New York today."

"I must find a solution," Harry was saying, musing aloud over the strange absence of restraining devices in Platt's office. "I suppose that I could provide my own handcuffs in these situations, but people would naturally assume that they were gaffed in some way. What to do?"

Platt ignored him. "Hardeen, I've already told you that I don't place any stock in the entertainment value of a man who escapes from things. It's a silly notion. I know that you and your brother are fair magicians, but I don't have any need of magicians just now." He paused as a new thought struck him. "Is Mr. Houdini's wife seeking opportunities at present? I might have something coming open in the chorus at the Blair."

"She is fully booked at the moment," I said. "My brother and I—"

"Yes, yes," said Platt heavily. "I know all about you and your brother."

"I suppose it is a question of advertising my intentions in advance," Harry murmured to himself. "I could post a notice or handbill to the effect that the Great Houdini intends to accept any and all challenges to escape from regulation handcuffs. Then people would be forewarned to provide their own restraints. That might resolve the difficulty."

"Are there any other opportunities that might be suitable?" I asked Platt. "Anything at all?"

Platt reached across the desk for a folded sheet of paper. "I shouldn't think so," he said. "But don't despair, Hardeen. If your brother truly is the most exceptional performer in New York, the other agencies are undoubtedly clamoring for his services." He unfolded the paper and ran the pince-nez over the print.

"Perhaps there could be a trained locksmith on hand as I took the stage," Harry was saying. "He could confirm that the handcuffs had not been tampered with or altered in any way. It would lend an official touch to the proceedings. The Houdini Handcuff Challenge. That would look well in print." He glanced at me. "Don't you agree, Dash?"

"Harry, perhaps we might confine our attention to the matter at hand. Mr. Platt is consulting his books to see if—"

"I'm afraid there's nothing," said Platt, tossing the folded sheet onto the desk. "Unless, of course, your remarkable brother happens to have a cast-iron stomach."

"Pardon?"

"A cast-iron stomach. The Portain Circus has an opening in two weeks' time. I'm looking to send a man with a cast-iron stomach."

"I don't quite follow you," I said.

"A stone-eater," Harry said impatiently. "An omnivore." He made an exaggerated chewing motion. "Someone who will eat whatever the audience throws at him."

"Precisely," said Platt. "I have the honor to represent Mr. Bradley Wareham, who earns a fine living in this manner. At present, however, he is indisposed."

My hand went to my mid-section. "A stomach complaint, by any chance?"

"Not at all. A gouty foot, as it happens." Platt snatched a handbill from amid the clutter on his desk. "Mr. Wareham is proving to be a difficult man to replace. Listen to this: 'For the amusement of all present the Man with the Cast-Iron Stomach will ingest all manner of small objects presented to him by the audience, including rocks and gravel, potsherds, flints, bits of glass, and other savories. Upon conclusion of the display, this Gustatory Marvel will allow onlookers to strike his stomach to hear the rattling of the strange objects within." Platt lowered his pince-nez and regarded us with a bemused expression. "I don't suppose this is an act you might be willing to undertake."

"Certainly not," I said. "The talents of the Brothers Houdini lie in an entirely different sphere of—"

"Would I be able to take my wife?" Harry asked.

"Harry!" I cried. "What are you thinking? You're not a—"

"The Portain Circus is a very reputable organization," my brother said evenly. "If I could establish myself in the company, I might be able to win a spot more in keeping with the usual run of my talents. Moreover, I would be able to rescue Bess from her servitude in the chorus line at Ravelsen's Review."

"Your reasoning is flawless," I said with considerable asperity, "except for the part which requires you to eat rocks and glass. How do you propose to overcome that little difficulty?"

Harry turned to Platt, who had been pulling contentedly at his clay pipe during this exchange.

"You say that I would have two weeks to prepare?" Harry asked.

Platt folded his hands. "Yes, Mr. Houdini. Two weeks. But

I warn you, this act is no place for an amateur. Do you really think you're up to it?"

By way of an answer, Harry reached across Platt's desk and plucked the clay pipe from his fingers.

"Harry!" I cried, as he placed the smoldering bowl into his mouth. "Don't—"

But he had already bitten off the bowl of the pipe at its stem and was now happily chewing on the glowing contents.

"What did he say?" Platt asked, as Harry tried to speak through a mouthful of clay and burning embers.

"I can't be certain," I said, "but I believe it was 'Hoonga-boonga.'"

ABOUT THE AUTHOR

DANIEL STASHOWER IS A NOVELIST AND MAGICIAN. HIS WORKS include: *Elephants in the Distance*, *The Beautiful Cigar Girl*, the Sherlock Holmes novel, *The Ectoplasmic Man* and the Edgar-Award-winning Sir Arthur Conan Doyle biography, *Teller of Tales*. He is also the co-editor of two Sherlock Holmes anthologies, *The Ghosts of Baker Street* and *Sherlock Holmes in America,* and the annotated collection *Arthur Conan Doyle: A Life in Letters.*

WWW.TITANBOOKS.COM